Against All Odds

For Caroline
Best Wishes
Margaret Shebbeare

Also by Margaret Sherlock

NON-FICTION
Seven Sisters Down Under

A humorous account of how seven sisters, with
seven very different personalities, struggled
through a three-week trip to Australia.

Margaret Sherlock

Against All Odds

Shorelines  Publishing

First published in 2011 by

Shorelines Publishing
3 St. Mark's Drive, Meadfoot, Torquay, Devon. TQ1 2EJ

Copyright © 2011 Margaret Sherlock
ISBN: 978-0-9559710-2-0

Cover artwork tracey.turner@blueyonder.co.uk
Typesetter elainesharples@btinternet.com
Printed by Short Run Press Limited, Exeter

Dedicated to Barry

For so many things

Providence set by the Gods

Who am I, to play the odds?

Chapter 1

Wednesday Morning

Lyn Porter wasn't used to the corrosive effects of fear and worry. At forty-six, she had to admit that life so far had been no picnic, but never before had she felt so desperate, so helpless and so alone.

Squally showers spat viciously from all directions making it almost impossible to gain any shelter from the umbrella that Lyn was struggling to hold onto. Twice it had blown inside out, damaging two of the spokes, and as the next unpredictable gust almost wrenched the damn thing from her grasp, she gave up the struggle. Gran had given her the umbrella for her forty-fourth birthday, *this'll last you for donkey's years Lynda, it's a really good one.* Gran had died fourteen months later. Now, with a twinge of sadness and guilt, Lyn watched as the mangled contraption disappeared into the cavernous depths of a commercial rubbish bin, instantly regretting that she hadn't tried to repair it. She'd been brought up to make do and mend; God knew her circumstances wouldn't allow for any unnecessary spending but she was quickly losing all impetus to try and make things better.

Pulling up the hood of her dampened coat she continued to drag her weary body up the steep incline of road that led away from the harbour. Eventually she reached the gap, a place she would always stop, no matter what the weather. Lingering here to absorb the scene below – dozens of tiny fishing boats rocking on the ruffled water – was a simple pleasure that she'd enjoyed for years, confirming the gratitude she felt at living in such a beautiful part of England. But lately, appreciation of her surroundings had disappeared along with everything else that had seemed good in her life. In its place, was a tight, fist-sized knot that lodged in the pit of her stomach; a constant reminder of her stupid mistakes and her naive gullibility. Two seagulls glided expertly above her head, defying the erratic bluster of wind which carried their mocking cries. Suddenly the wind died. For a few seconds there was an eerie silence before the dark-clouded heavens opened with a deluge of rain so heavy that Lyn was sent scurrying for shelter.

The sharp hissing sound of the percolating coffee brought James Fairbank's attention back to what he was supposed to be doing. He'd been sitting at his large walnut desk deliberating about who he should phone next, when his eyes were drawn to a lone figure standing in his line of vision, seemingly unperturbed by the atrocious weather.

Clara, his secretary, was on six months maternity leave and although three weeks had passed since she'd left – assuring him that she had at least two, good temping-secretaries who were more than happy to fill in – he still hadn't done anything about employing one. The truth of the matter was that business was so bad, he honestly didn't feel that he needed a secretary and he certainly couldn't afford to pay a good salary to someone who would be no more than a glorified filing clerk cum coffee maker.

On his forty-ninth birthday, just a few months ago, James, had celebrated his status as a successful, independent solicitor. Today he wasn't as convinced. True, his personal life wasn't wonderful, but his chosen profession, after the long years of training and two decades of working all hours, had paid off. He had been told on numerous occasions that he was the best conveyancing solicitor for miles and during the last ten years he'd concentrated exclusively on the speedy transition of property, both residential and commercial. He'd had plenty of offers over the years, from would be partners to large legal conglomerates, eager for him to become affiliated, but he had remained true to his belief that remaining small meant keeping control.

No one could have foreseen the seriousness of the current property crash, at least that's what James repeatedly told himself, and the repercussions of it were being felt right around the globe. But he had to make something happen soon; otherwise the bank would carry out their threat of calling in his substantial loans, or worse still, repossession of his properties. Against his better judgement, Clara had talked him into edging his way into the Debt Management market. Even the title made him cringe with embarrassment. She meant well, and he was well aware of her guilt at having to take time out during such a worrying time. She'd printed his posters, had arranged for some pretty good free publicity and even pointed two of her acquaintances in his direction; acquaintances who were more than happy to share his coffee, pour out their money troubles, then draw on all his hard earned knowledge to better their situation; but when it came to making an appointment with charges, they became as elusive as the property sales.

"Enough of these negative thoughts James, coffee and chocolate biscuit first, phone calls later," he announced to his empty office as he rose to tend to his refreshments.

As he left his office to walk the few yards to the small kitchen, which was situated at the back of the building, a slight commotion in the vicinity of his vestibule stopped James dead in his tracks. "It is not a prospective client, it is a women sheltering from the rain," he said in a lowered voice, aware now that another human being was in earshot. She had caught his attention earlier whilst she was being buffeted by strong winds at the Harbour View Gap. He had no objection to her taking shelter; she had no other means of keeping the sudden deluge of rain from soaking her to the bone.

Lyn almost tumbled into the open porch of the smart Georgian building, just as a white-shirted man walked across the inner hall. "Damn this shoe lace" she cursed through clenched teeth as she bent to fasten it for the umpteenth time. She hadn't worn these particular shoes for ages and she'd completely forgotten about the annoying idiosyncrasy of the left shoe. Half expecting him to frog march her back into the pouring rain she started to read the poster that had been neatly placed on the inside, corner of his window. She followed the words with her index finger, just in case he thought she was only using his porch for shelter.

DEBT MANAGEMENT, proclaimed the notice in large fancy print. Lyn's eyes scrolled quickly to the bottom where the same large fancy print announced FREE CONSULTATION. Amongst the smaller print of Lyn's hurried reading, the only words that grabbed her attention were: mortgage arrears and house repossession. A deep-seated, cold fear clambered up her spine, shattering the relief she'd felt at being sheltered from the rain and blustering wind.

If only she'd stuck to her usual routine, she moaned inwardly, she would be home now cleaning through the place and clearing out the cupboards, again. Checking out the job centre on a Wednesday had proved to be a bad idea anyway. She'd gone regularly every Monday for the past five weeks, full of hope and expectation, and when nothing had been forthcoming, she'd started to suspect Andrea, her allocated job centre helper, of favouritism and passing on the word of new positions to friends and acquaintances.

Andrea had been exasperated to see her again after only two days. She'd launched into a tirade of reasons for the current lack of jobs and spouted off about recession and businesses going broke and redundancies, as if she'd been talking to a little kid who didn't know what was happening in the world. Just because Lyn guarded her privacy, didn't mean that her life was all hunky dory. In fact Lyn was quickly reaching the stage where even a cleaning job would be welcome, it wouldn't cover her outgoings, but it would help to stop her going mad with worry.

A movement in the inner hall caught her attention. I can't just stand here like a spare part she thought, gripping the highly polished brass knob of the half-glazed, inner porch door. The slight push, which was halted when the gap became two inches wide, released a stream of warm air mingled with the aroma of fresh coffee and furniture polish. Lyn stood hesitating, catching sight of her bedraggled reflection, mirrored in the upper door. No! I can't do it, she thought, pulling the door to close it; but before it clicked home, a strong male voice carried on the warm scented air.

"I promise not to bite."

Lyn stared at the tall white-shirted figure holding a tray. He wasn't well defined, behind the obscured glass of the door and several yards of hallway, but the broad smile on his face was clear enough. Still hesitating, she caught sight of the polished brass plate, just inches from her hand. This revealed the name JAMES FAIRBANK SOLICITOR. Lots of letters followed which didn't mean anything to Lyn, but one thing was certain, she had no intention of being sucked into anything involving a solicitor. *Whatever you do Lynda, never get in the hands of solicitors, they're slippery buggers the lot of em.*

"I... I'm sorry to disturb you, I just wanted to make an appointment to see the debt councillor." Her voice sounded confident enough, but her hand remained clamped to the door knob to maintain the two inch gap, whilst an unseen hand gripped the knot in her stomach.

"Please do come in, you're soaked to the skin. Here let me put your coat over the boiler in my kitchen; go into the office there's a chair over by the radiator."

Lyn sat in the comfortably upholstered chair by the radiator wondering how she could get herself out of this embarrassing situation. He'd taken her coat so she couldn't just make a run for it, besides so long as she remembered not to sign anything, well, what harm could be done? Steam rose gently from the stainless steel coffee pot filling the beautifully proportioned room with its irresistible aroma. Several chocolate digestive biscuits were placed in neat formation on a square-shaped, white, china plate and two matching cups with square saucers were placed alongside. For some reason, It was the two cups that alarmed her most.

"Sorry to desert you like that, I needed to alter the settings on the boiler and I'm embarrassed to admit that my secretary usually deals with it; I needed to refer to the manual. How do you like your coffee?"

"Where is your secretary?" Lyn asked, relieved that she wasn't the only other person in this large Georgian building and wondering if the second cup was really meant for her.

"She's taking six months maternity leave so I'm coping alone at present."

"Look, like I said earlier, I only wanted to make an appointment to see your debt councillor, I really don't want to waste anybody's time."

"*I am* the debt councillor, let's have coffee and biscuits to help thaw you out then we can talk shop." With a cautious "thank you, Lyn accepted the cup of steaming black coffee and two chocolate biscuits that rested on a double piece of white kitchen towel. Settling back in her chair, she made a silent promise to the spirit of her dead Gran that this bribe would not lead her to signing any documents or parting with any money.

The phone rang, making Lyn jump and almost spilling her coffee whilst taking the first sip. James Fairbank apologised with a sigh and a broad smile. The broad smile continued for a while as he spoke to the caller named George who, by the sound of it, was a good friend or colleague. Then the conversation became more business-like and revolved around completed refurbishments and contracts ready to be signed. Lyn studied his face whilst listening, realizing that all was not going to plan for James Fairbank when his face crumpled into concern.

"Look I have a client with me at the moment George, I'll call you later, no don't apologise, it's not your fault, we'll speak later, bye for now."

James Fairbank replaced the receiver very slowly and very carefully with a faraway look on his face.

"Bad news?" enquired Lyn, feeling less uncomfortable but not fully understanding why.

"Not really bad news but certainly disappointing news" offered the solicitor. He then went on to explain how a prospective tenant had just pulled out from signing contracts at the eleventh hour. Apparently, James Fairbank also owned the next door property; which was a carbon copy of this one, except for the complete refurbishment.

"Oh I'm sure you'll find another tenant soon enough", cut in Lyn impatiently.

"I do apologise. Let's get back to your debt problems." His voice was surprisingly amicable, considering the disappointing phone call, and as he lifted a pad from his desk drawer and looked enquiringly into Lyn's eyes, it took her several seconds to respond.

"I never said that it was *me* with the debt problems! What I mean is it could be my daughter or a friend that needs help!" Lyn felt foolish. She lowered her eyes knowing that the intense green of his were still locked on her face, reading the stupidity that showed.

The solicitor leaned forward and lowered his voice."Times are very hard and lots of people are in difficulties that are making them feel desperate, there is nothing wrong in seeking help and advice."

A second cup of coffee was poured and during the sipping of it, Lyn revealed the extent of her debt and some of her concerns; keeping all personal details, such as name and address out of the conversation. Throughout her selective disclosure, James Fairbank's silent attention remained focussed on her face. She'd expected him to take notes on his pad, but the room remained silent save for her lowered voice and the soft ticking of an expensive-looking clock.

There was no doubt about it the telephone call from George had unnerved James. This was the second time in three months that he'd proceeded, almost to exchange of contract, on the adjoining property. He was trying hard to remain composed whilst dealing with Lynda… whatever her name, but inside he was an extremely worried man. Getting to grips with someone else's problems usually helped, but this woman was making it very difficult for him to advise her. After a lengthy pause, during which each of them drank their remaining coffee, he tried again: this time from a different angle in the hope of drawing her out a little more.

"Lynda, who do you think is responsible, for the difficult situation you find yourself in?"

"I am," she replied without any hesitation. "I borrowed the money."

"Yes, but you couldn't have foreseen your redundancy could you? I feel sure that you would be entitled to a whole raft of government benefits whilst you're seeking out suitable employment; but I will need more details from you."

"I've got no intention of going on benefits I just thought you could send maybe a character reference to my bank to keep them off my back until I find a position that pays a reasonable salary."

"If I carry out any work on your behalf Lynda, there will be charges; but these charges can be recouped through benefits."

Told ya Lynda, slippery buggers the lot of em. Heeding Gran's warning Lyn rose from the chair and carefully placed her empty cup and saucer on the tray.

"Thank you for the coffee, I have to go."

"Think about what I've said, Lynda, I would like to help if I can." Frustrated, James left the office to retrieve the woman's coat.

A rectangular Persian rug almost covered the natural wood flooring of the solicitor's hallway. Lyn stepped gingerly onto it and peered into the empty room across the hallway from his office. The door had been left open, either in a bid to capture some of the warmth from the hallway or to help dissipate the smell of new paint. Two large windows, free from the restriction of blinds or curtains, captured two stupendous views, which in Lyn's opinion, were the best in town. Without realizing what she was doing, she walked across to the windows and became absorbed in the beautiful vistas. A movement from behind – too close for comfort – broke the spell and brought forth a mumbling apology for being nosey.

The solicitor slipped the warm, dry coat over her shoulders and with a charming smile said "Believe me I pray constantly for nosey people to come looking over the property; maybe one of them will decide to rent the place before I lose it to the bank."

"But I thought you said you owned it"

"I bought it eight years ago, with two sitting tenants paying very low rents; eventually the place became vacant, allowing me, at last, to fully restore it. Two things went against me by this time; building costs had soared, forcing me to borrow more than expected, and rentals had become much more competitive. I could have cut back on the quality of the refurbishment but that's not my way. The sad thing is I've borrowed too much, and if I don't find a tenant soon, my bank will call in the loan!

"Surely, you could sell it; it must be worth a fortune."

"Nothing is selling because the banks aren't lending. These are very worrying times Lynda, for everyone!"

Lyn left the comfortable confines of the smart Georgian building, clutching the umbrella that James Fairbank had insisted she borrow. She'd tried her best to dissuade him by explaining what had happened to hers. His smile, like the trust in her honesty to return it, hadn't wavered even when she told him that his services wouldn't be needed.

James Fairbank closed the door and retreated back to his warm office. He knew deep down what he ought to be doing, but the chance encounter with someone who was going through similar worries as himself had somehow lightened his burden and encouraged him into a speculative train of thinking.

Although the size of this woman's debt was meagre compared to his; in her present situation, she had more chance of winning the lottery than paying off her bank loan; especially with the rise in unemployment in her line of work. And yet, she seemed so self-contained and independent about sorting out her problems. She had been badly let down, that much was obvious; and the refusal to share any details only enlarged his respect for her. Most of the women from his network of friends were selfish through and through. They blamed everyone but themselves when life didn't go according to their plan, including his ex-wife, who remained with him just long enough to realise there was more money to be had from his wealthy university chum, Charles. After the fourteen months marriage, divorce was almost welcome. Thankfully there were no children to consider, otherwise he might still have been saddled with her and even greater debt.

The heavy rain had retreated to a steady drizzle and this side of the road was definitely more sheltered from the wind. When the solicitor had mentioned this climatic phenomenon, after voicing her worry of inverting his brolly, she'd only half believed him; after all, she'd walked this road hundreds of times over the years. But now as she thought about it, the opposite side with the sea view had always been her preferred choice – the downside to enjoying the view, meant having to put up with the prevailing wind. Maybe she should have taken on board more of his advice; slippery bugger or not, he was such an easy bloke to talk to.

A slapping sound in the vicinity of her feet caused Lyn to curse mildly under her breath. The damn shoelace had worked loose again and was whipping her ankle with sodden regularity. With brolly handle tucked under her chin she hunched down to retie the wet lace. Barely ten inches from the attended shoe Lyn caught a glimpse of bright metal. A £1 coin standing on its edge between the high kerbstone and the rough surface of the road was just visible in this crouched position. With a reverence that was out of all proportion to its value, Lyn placed the wet, chubby disc in the centre of her left palm and straightened her back. Her fingers closed around the chilled metal bringing it warmth; and the warmth increased as Lyn's attention became completely absorbed by it. An elderly man passed by, raising his cap in greeting, thinking that the smile on Lyn's face was for him alone.

Chapter 2

Wednesday Evening

Two small logs were placed on the dying embers of the multi-fuel stove. Warmth emanated through its open doors and the hiss and crackle of the hungry flames intruded on the hitherto silent room. All lights were turned off except for one small desk lamp which cast a soft warm glow over the four framed photographs on top of Lyn's antique, china cabinet – an heirloom from Gran which was in danger of being sold – *this will be yours one day Lynda and it's worth a bob or two so don't let some Tom, Dick or Harry rob you blind.* It was 2.35am but Lyn didn't feel the slightest bit tired as she sat waiting for the freshly made pot of tea to brew. Normally, a warm drink and half an hours reading, were the only things necessary to pull her down into sleep; but too many thoughts and emotions were vying for her attention tonight.

Three minutes later, cradling a steaming mug of tea, Lyn relaxed into her old, comfortable sofa and gazed at the largest and the most recent, (seven months exactly), of the framed photographs. Her twenty-four year old daughter Sarah – pressed into the protective arms of her husband

Fergus, smiled back. This image of Sarah in her extravagant wedding dress, Fergus in top hat and tails, standing in the foyer of one of Dublin's finest hotels had been a constant reminder of her daughter's selfishness and Lyn's misplaced guilt – guilt that had led to Lyn's financial problems.

Funny how the lifting of a heavy burden can alter one's perspective; what Lyn saw now, was a beautiful, intelligent, young woman who had abandoned her university education to marry an Irish farmer nearly twice her age. Insecurity was the bane of Sarah's life and this insecurity had intensified with the sudden death of her father nine years ago. Unease registered at the thought of Martin's death and Lyn closed her eyes.

There was a cardboard box stuffed full of photographs on top of Lyn's wardrobe. Like most family snaps, they were only looked at once in a while; but this framed photograph of Lyn and Martin was not of this ilk. The soft glow from the lamp fell directly on their faces and the dancing flames from the stove projected movement into this soft glow, adding a life-like animation which momentarily burdened Lyn's heart. The photograph was taken by a friend on her twenty-first birthday, the day she became engaged to Martin. They were very much in love and it showed. She remembered well the spontaneity of that day; how she'd used part of her birthday money from Gran to have her hair cut and set into the latest 1980's style. Gran didn't like it. *You wasted all that money Lynda just to make your head look twice as big.* Martin liked it, proof of that was when he'd handed Lyn the small leather box containing his 'surprise' – a diamond, solitaire ring.

Six months later and already two and a half months

pregnant with Sarah, Lyn and Martin were married at the local Registry Office. The small album of photographs that recorded this celebratory day lay in the cardboard box with the other family snaps.

Money was borrowed from Martin's parents for the deposit on a modest house (this house) and every evening and every weekend was spent making it a home before the baby arrived.

Gran had wanted them to move in with her until after the birth but Martin wouldn't hear of it; a final compromise, after many heated discussions, was to buy a house in Gran's neighbourhood, but not in the same road. *I know I'm not getting any younger Lynda but you'll need a baby sitter, especially when you go back to work.* Time passed, and the more Gran helped the more Martin wanted to move away.

One day he arrived home with a sheaf of papers tucked under his arm and a broad grin on his face. "Lyn I've got the chance of landing a really good job in Australia," she remembered him saying as he laid out the brightly coloured brochures on the kitchen table. After a terrible row, nothing more was ever discussed about Martin's strong desire to move abroad; however his engineering skills were in great demand and Lyn soon found that Martin took every opportunity to work away from home. Oil rigs in the North Sea, Saudi Arabia, or Scandinavia he was always happy to oblige his bosses. Money was plentiful and life seemed good except for the fact that Martin was barely home. He was allowed plenty of time off in between his working schedule, but his favourite hobby – rock-climbing – swallowed up most of his free time.

There was no doubting that he loved Lyn and Sarah, (his princess), letters, phone calls and arms filled with presents was proof of this; as were the short but wonderful holidays shared as a family. Lyn gently replaced the photograph on the cabinet as her thoughts lurched forward to the day of Martin's tragic accident.

It was Saturday April 23rd and the day was warm and sunny. Martin was leaving for Snowdonia in the early afternoon and he'd spent the morning checking his equipment and packing for the four day trip with two of his climbing buddies. Lyn, loaded down with shopping, had arrived home at midday to find the under-stairs cupboard door wide open and the hallway stacked with camping gear and all manner of climbing paraphernalia blocking her entrance to the kitchen. No one had answered her frustrated calls, so two bags were shoved, by foot, to just inside the cupboard, allowing her just enough room to squeeze through the gap.

When Martin arrived home ten minutes later, rushed and panicked about keeping his friends waiting because his lunch wasn't ready, Lyn had hit the roof. His excuse, of needing to give Sarah and her two friends a lift before he could load the car, only added fuel to the heated argument that followed. As Lyn had marched out of the open front door, leaving Martin to prepare his own lunch as well as packing the car, she heard him say.

"That's right, bugger off to Gran's, she means more to you than I ever have!" These were the last words that ever passed between them! But everything that happened during the next twenty-four hours was etched deeply in Lyn's memory.

Gran had recently had one of her "funny turns" and like Lyn had remained at home for most of the afternoon; after the usual carping about Sarah being allowed to do exactly as she pleased because her father was never around to control her. Lyn had spent the last few hours of daylight clearing weeds from her back garden – in preparation for the new spring planting. A chicken salad supper, an hour's television, followed by a long warm bath, was all that was needed to send her into a deep restorative sleep. She knew Martin wouldn't ring until Sunday evening when Sarah was home, and Sarah had arranged to stay over at Helen's so that the two of them could get an early, Sunday morning start. Helen's parents managed a nearby livestock farm which included two horses. Helen wasn't one of Sarah's best friends; but horse riding was Sarah's favourite pastime.

The heavy dew of Sunday morning, a leftover from the chilly night, was burned off by 10am; and Lyn clearly remembered leaving early to drive the short distance to the local garden centre clutching her long list of plants and seeds. She loved her back garden, and had complete charge over it. Martin and Sarah were happy enough to share its fragrant confines while enjoying an alfresco meal; or linger on the sun bed during a hot summer's afternoon; but neither were prepared to invest any time in its layout or maintenance.

At 2.14pm the telephone had rung. Feeling put out, Lyn brushed the soil from her knees and kicked off her gardening clogs before dashing into the kitchen to answer it. It was Greg, Martin's climbing friend. At first Greg seemed unable to say anything apart from sorry... and... tragic accident. He was in shock, but between his bouts of

18

stuttered nonsensical words, and the periods of silence except for his loud ragged breathing, Lyn learned the awful truth that Martin had lost his footing and fallen to his death. Once Greg had unburdened this salient point, Lyn was unable to focus on anything more that was said, but it seemed necessary for Greg to describe in more detail what had happened and how the rescue services had been so wonderful and done everything in their power to save him. Lyn had gently replaced the receiver and returned to her planting.

The next few weeks had melted into a grey haze of shock and grief interspersed with the mundane attendance to death certificates, coroner's meetings and funeral arrangements – all virgin territory for Lyn – but Gran, ever dependable, lent her strong guiding hand. Sarah, naturally, had taken her father's death very badly; and even her strong dependable Nan couldn't break through to the once bubbly, confident fifteen-year old.

On the evening after Martin's funeral, Lyn carried a tray of hot soup and bread to Sarah's room. She knocked lightly and was surprised to be given entry immediately.

"Sarah we *will* come through this sweetheart", she said earnestly to her pale daughter.

"Oh sure Mum, you're a florist's assistant, how is that going to produce enough money to keep us both and to put me through college. Dad was gonna…"at this point she had broken down and Lyn held her tight until the sobbing subsided. "He'd promised to buy me my very own pony next birthday; we're gonna be poor for the rest of our lives, aren't we?"

"Dad had life insurance baby, it'll take time to go

through the paperwork but now the funeral is over I'll get it sorted and we'll be fine; but please, you must try and eat a little something."

Within the next few days, after countless phone calls, several visits to the bank, building society and insurance company, Lyn had unearthed the true extent of their financial situation. The Life Insurance Policy that Martin had taken out – signed in Lyn's presence when Sarah was a babe in her arms – no longer existed. In his wisdom, Martin had cancelled this policy fourteen months later and replaced it with a much cheaper, Mortgage Protection Policy. Another sobering discovery came to light after an appointment at Martins bank; apparently, he was several thousand pounds in debt from credit cards and personal loans – "but", the bank manager had said with a sickly grin on his pink, fat face, "you're not to worry your pretty head about that; I feel sure the bank will be covered against such losses."

Feeling unable to share this devastating news with anyone – especially Sarah, who at this point, was making it quite clear that the wrong parent had died and Lyn had been the cause of all her Daddy's problems – she was forced into a false sense of security that all would eventually work out fine. But as well as the lack of money, other issues were burdening Lyn's mind at this time.

Two days earlier, Lyn had been having one of her "full-blown" house cleans – usually done in an effort to banish stress rather than the need to remove household dirt – but on this occasion it was in preparation for the mourners to return to the house after the funeral. Whilst pushing the long vacuum-cleaner nozzle into the corner of the carpeted under-stairs cupboard, a soft, bulky mass had barred her way. Fifteen minutes passed without notice as Lyn crouched within the confines of the cupboard, completely unaware that her feet were numb from lack of circulation.

Two sports bags – the two that Lyn had pushed by foot out of her way on the morning of Martin's departure to Snowdonia – lay unzipped before her. The bare light bulb of the cupboard illuminated the contents of the first, as they were spilled onto the floor. Several tee-shirts, boxer shorts and paired-up socks were gathered lovingly into Lyn's arms; each item held against her face as she'd sniffed greedily in the hope of capturing some lingering scent of Martin. At the bottom of this same bag, lay two very explicit 'For Men Only' magazines. Shock mingled with hurt raced through Lyn's taught body. On emptying the second bag, panic and guilt froze out all previous emotions.

The sound of a key turning in the lock and the front door being kicked open then closed with a loud thud, had snapped Lyn's attention back to the pre-funeral cleaning. She'd scrambled out of the cupboard just in time to catch Sarah's cold glare – a silent challenge to the house rule of, no door banging. Sarah marched up to her room and closed the door with a booted slam. Lyn pushed the guilt producing bag – complete with contents – back into the darkest corner of the cupboard and closed the door. The embarrassing magazines were placed between several newspapers then buried deep inside the weed filled dustbin and Martin's laundered clothes were carefully carried upstairs.

The day of the funeral had been cold and damp and it seemed to go on forever. Sarah spoke barely two words to anyone. When the mourners began to disperse from the house, Lyn retrieved the sports bag from the under stairs cupboard and handed it to Greg.

"I'm sure Martin would have wanted you to have these." As Greg had peered into the bag, his forced smile folded into a confused frown. "I don't understand; Martin should have had these with him on the climb!" Lyn remained silent as his fingers probed amongst the thick ropes and steel pulleys.

"Why, is that important?" she'd asked without a second thought; her first thought being, to be rid of the bag and the guilt it produced. He'd looked briefly at the telephone then shook his head. After hugging her awkwardly and promising to help in any way he could, he left, carrying the sports bag.

The sudden noise of something shifting, jerked Lyn from a doze. The room felt colder and the almost empty mug of tea, still lightly gripped between both hands, had also lost its comforting warmth. She looked over to the fireplace and saw at once the cause of her abrupt wakefulness. The entire core of the two logs had been consumed, leaving only the fragile outer form which inevitably collapsed into a cascade of spitting, red and grey ash. The log-basket was empty and Lyn made a mental note to fill it at daylight; for now, she felt too emotionally drained to even climb the stairs to her unheated bedroom; and as this room still held some residue of heat, she pulled the nearby knitted throw over her body and closed her eyes.

Chapter 3

Thursday morning

Lyn woke feeling surprisingly refreshed, apart from a slight ache in her left shoulder – a remnant of sawing large logs into smaller ones two days ago. She'd had barely three hours sleep but felt more than capable of tackling the long list of must-do tasks that were hurriedly written down, in order of importance, the evening before. Two phone numbers, in bold, red ink, were at the top of the list alongside the underlined word, <u>confirmation;</u> but these couldn't be dealt with yet, it was only just gone seven o'clock. Before showering, she decided to attend to the grubbiest but most satisfying of the tasks – filling the log basket.

The rain had stopped but the early November air was cold and damp and the flagstone path that led to the bottom of the garden was slippery with moss; but Lyn's tread was light and sure and although it took only a minute or so to fill the large, wicker basket, she chose to linger a while under the open-ended log store.

Her eyes swept over the lower third of her ninety-metre garden and shame momentarily eclipsed her positive mood.

Even allowing for the time of year, which had at least kept the upper grassed section of the garden from growing, the area looked tired and neglected. Years ago, a large Ash tree had stood on the lower boundary of this property, where a wide variety of birds built their nests – adding to the dawn chorus that rang out throughout the spring months. For Sarah's fifth birthday, Martin had built a summer house within its larger branches with a rope swing ladder for access; for years, school holidays were more manageable thanks to that tree-house, no matter how many of her friends visited. It was their Den, a place where arguments and confidences could be aired and won over, without interference from the adult world. The tree also provided very welcome shade during hot afternoons; and the semi-circular, wooden bench, built and positioned around its sturdy trunk, was Gran's favourite place for thinking, so she had said on numerous occasions. Then, without warning, the tree came to the end of its life during a relatively light storm. Lyn and Martin had woken one February morning to find it lying diagonally across the lower left-hand corner of the garden. There was no apparent damage to the tree and the only damage caused by this strange act of nature was the dislodging of several large chunks from the neighbour's thick, stone wall, as the tree came to rest.

Within ten days the neighbour's wall was restored and the tree was stacked neatly inside the old bike shed. Everyone, including Gran, thought Lyn was mad to insist on keeping several tons of logs especially as the house had full central heating and a fire was only lit once in a blue moon *Lynda what on earth are you thinking of? Open fires are filthy and give nothing but bad chests.* But Lyn had insisted, reasoning that the logs weren't taking up any useful space and they could come in handy in the future. Also, after seeing the flower growing potential, now that the bottom of the garden would be bathed in full sun, she felt less guilty by holding on to the tree, albeit in altered form.

The young tree surgeon they'd hired had advised them not to burn the wood straight away. He'd said jovially; "leave it for at least a year to dry, after that, it'll burn as sweet as a nut". No one took much notice of this strange remark; but, in the last few weeks Lyn had come to understand its meaning. Since mid-September, the heating of her modest house, was provided solely from burning ash logs. Dire financial straits had forced her to make cut backs wherever she could and every evening as the kindling passed on its flames to the eager acceptance of the sacrificial, wooden limbs, Lyn would say with a satisfied smile, "sweet as a nut".

Looking now over the dwindling pile of creamy-white wood, she figured that there was still more than enough to carry her through the remaining cold months. And even though changes might give her the option to return to a less primitive way of keeping warm; she knew in her heart which she would choose. The tree had given so much of itself in life, the least she could do, was to enjoy its comforting bounty until every single appreciated section had been cremated.

Sitting at the window-table of the little café, opposite the florist where Lyn used to work, provided the perfect opportunity to see how the shop was doing and also to rationalise about what choices her future held. All her domestic chores on the list were done, including the two telephone calls, so the rest of her afternoon was free. Enjoying a light lunch whilst chatting to Pauline would be invaluable to Lyn's developing plans.

The freshly toasted sandwich was every bit as tasty as she'd remembered them to be; but a major ingredient was missing – service with a smile. Jim and Pauline, who had run this little café for donkey's years, had suddenly decided to take early retirement and move to Spain. Lyn knew full well that they were well on in their sixties and didn't for one minute begrudge them their last few years relaxing in sunnier climes; what she did resent, was having to virtually wring this information from the haughty, middle-aged, female who had bought the café and was beginning to take exception to Lyn's questions. The table for four where Lyn had chosen to sit – the only table that could serve her purpose today – had always been a favourite for customers; and as the café began to steadily fill, the café owner's displeasure increased.

Looking around the once friendly meeting place, Lyn couldn't find one familiar face amongst the dozen or so customers; who were mainly suited business men, scanning the Financial Times whilst sipping on large mugs of coffee. The décor and all the furnishings had also changed; which admittedly, was a vast improvement on the dull mushroom-coloured walls and faded yellow, Formica tables. These, might possibly have been fashionable in the late seventies when Jim and Pauline set up business; but over thirty years of constant use had left them scrubbed out and covered with lots of dirt-collecting chips, around the edges – unnoticed or forgiven by regulars, especially when those regulars understood the lean times that were facing all small businesses – but it was short-sighted if you needed to attract new business.

No sooner had Lyn swallowed her last mouthful of food, the toffee-nosed mare, cleared and wiped down the steel and glass-topped table, slapping down the bill on its still-wet surface. Refusing to be intimidated Lyn ordered another coffee; then sipped it slowly as her eyes remained fixed on the opposite side of the road.

One of the four photographs positioned on Gran's china cabinet was taken in front of the shop that was holding Lyn's full attention. She smiled as she recalled the excitement of that day; her sense of achievement at having won first prize for the best designed bouquet from the dozens of participating florists. She still had the newspaper cutting at home; showing a full page spread, titled: Lynda's Rosy Future. Beryl was so proud, and the extra business that was generated from the publicity, put the shop on a whole new footing.

Beryl's Florist was well positioned, being just a hop, skip and a jump from the town cemetery and crematorium. It had been there even longer than the café she was sitting in – according to Beryl – and she'd never known Beryl to lie. It was Lyn's first job after leaving school at eighteen. She had hoped to attend a three year art and design course with her best friend Jill. She had passed all the necessary entrance exams with a guaranteed place waiting but Gran had talked her out of it. *Lynda, I can't believe you want to waste three years at an arty-farty college without earning a penny and have no guarantee of a job at the end of it.* And, as Gran's heart was giving her problems at the time, Lyn gave way and took her advice.

Jill travels down from London to visit her parents every now and then, when her highly successful Interior-Design business allows; but apart from a yearly Christmas card, Lyn hasn't been in touch since leaving school. She now makes a mental note to add Jill, to her very recently compiled list of, Contacts from the Past.

Taking the locally-advertised Florist's Assistant job was meant to be a stop gap. Lyn stayed for over twenty five years and had no doubt that she'd still have been there today if Beryl was still alive and kicking. But her kicking was halted by a massive stroke, brought on according to her doctor, by the unhealthy life-style that everybody rabbits on about these days. According to Beryl, it was predetermined that's how she would go because that was how both her parents and her elder brother had passed over. They were all heavy smokers and grossly overweight, but in Beryl's mind this small factor, played no part in their relatively early demise. Lyn loved the woman; and there was no one else she missed more in the entire world – including Martin and Gran. Beryl had been the Mother she'd never had, and the best friend she'd waved off to London. Behind Beryl's day to day jollity and energy, in running the small retail outlet, lay the mind of a sensitive, extremely caring woman; a woman who had eagerly passed on to Lyn everything she knew about the floristry business; as well as opening a door on the exotic, sweet smelling, colourful world of flowers; giving Lyn the opportunity to satisfy a deep creative need.

The short ding-dong-sound, of the florist shop door opposite, pulled Lyn's attention back to the purpose of her being here. She was one hundred percent sure that no one had entered the shop in the last forty minutes; and from where she sat, she could clearly see that no one had already been in the shop, waiting to be served. Two men, dressed in suits, emerged from the fully-glazed door and stood with their backs to Lyn as if to admire the frontage of the, more recently renamed, Floral Occasions, although everyone still referred to it as Beryl's Florist. She had no doubt identifying the shorter man, in spite of the suit – which was probably the same one he'd worn to Beryl's funeral, and the only other time Lyn had seen him wearing one. The extremely short hair, emphasizing the broad, muscular neck and shoulders, the overly-confident way he stood with hands on hips and chest pushed out, left her in no doubt that it was Vince Conway, to whom she now refers, as "Vinny the Con."

"How the hell?" uttered Lyn, louder than intended, as she stood to wipe a circle of clarity in the misted window, jogging the table and spilling her coffee as she did so. She watched as the two men briefly faced each other and after a cursory hand shake the taller man walked away, leaving Lyn completely baffled. What could James Fairbank possibly need from Vinny the Con?

The disappointment of losing the latest potential tenant had been short lived. James Fairbank walked with a spring in his step and a cheerful tune whistled from his lips, as he headed back to his office. He loved his work and there was nothing more satisfying than being completely involved in it. He knew deep down that the debt-counselling wouldn't be successful; his heart wasn't in it because he never believed for one minute that *he* could solve another person's debt problems because only *they* could learn to live within their means and control their outgoings. But Clara had meant well, and after all her efforts, it would have been sheer bad manners, not to try.

A long-standing client of his was in the final stages of buying the little florist shop down by the cemetery; the conveyancing seemed straight forward enough, but James had used the excuse of the sale, as an opportunity to meet the shop's current owner.

She seemed pleasant enough, but not at all as he had imagined. He prided himself on being a good judge of character and could have sworn that the person who was doing most of the talking was indeed the owner; but he was soon to learn that Victor Connor was Ms Dais' accountant. The solicitor apologised and aimed his further questions at her. Her demeanour changed. The confident smile disappeared and was replaced by what James could only describe as near-panic. Victor Connor came to her rescue, explaining that Ms Dais was a shy and retiring person and that was why he was there by her side, all the time. James accepted the explanation and continued the conversation with Mr Connor, but he had to admit, he was a little baffled, and disappointed.

He'd heard from several sources that the florist shop was doing well, his long-standing client wouldn't be inclined to purchase otherwise; but Ms Dais seemed so young and inexperienced and because this lady, according to her accountant, was very interested in taking on the solicitor's next-door property, he was anxious to find out as much as possible about her situation.

Lyn shouted once again as she tried to capture James Fairbank's attention. Good God he was marching like a soldier on parade. He'd gained quite a distance on her because of the snooty mare taking her time. In her haste to catch hold of the solicitor, Lyn had almost left the café without paying, but eagle-eyes, followed by grasping hands on her arms had forced Lyn to return to the slopped on table and wait for a fresh bill to be issued. She had tried to pay at the counter but sour face, sensing Lyn's hurry to be off, wouldn't hear of it. Still, the power walk had calmed her mind. She needed information from this guy; no point in rushing in and burning her boats before she knew what the hell was going on.

Out of breath and just a couple of paces behind, Lyn could clearly hear him whistling Waltzing Matilda. She reached into her plastic carrier-bag and pulled out the umbrella that belonged to the chap she now prodded. "Hi, I was on my way to returning this," she gasped, between heavy pants.

"Oh! Hello, Lynda," he said smiling and completely relaxed at being spiked from behind by an almost total stranger. "Thought any more about your financial situation," he ventured, completely ignoring the proffered umbrella.

"Please call me Lyn, everyone else does except for Gran and she's dead now."

"Lyn it is, and you can call me James, and you may hold onto that until you have replaced your own."

His smile and his eyes remained on her face, disturbing the self confidence that had started to emerge. Well, she thought, holding onto his umbrella would give her another chance to confront him about Vinny; she couldn't very well start giving him the third degree right here on the street. "Thanks for the offer, I'll return it tomorrow, I do have another one." Lyn slipped it back into her bag and turned to go.

"And what do you intend to do about your financial situation Lyn?" he asked again, determined this time to get a response.

"Pay them off." See you tomorrow" and off she went in the opposite direction before he could delve any further.

Chapter 4

Thursday Evening

Lyn replaced the telephone receiver and returned to the warmth of her sitting room. It had been freezing in the hallway, and not for the first time, she regretted giving Gran her wireless, rechargeable phone. She had never really wanted it and had never used it. When Lyn had asked for it back, she'd been told that it had been passed on to someone more in need of it. *I'm not taking a telephone to bed with me Lynda; my heart will give out one day, no point in announcing it to the world while it's happening.*

After all the years of concern about Gran's heart, it had been pneumonia that had finally ended her life – after slipping on the front doorstep and shattering her right hip. She'd wanted to die in her own bed – dragged several promises to that effect from Lyn – but when the accident happened and she was whisked into the local hospital, a part of Gran knew she would never return home, and the eighty-two year old, who Lyn had regarded as the strongest woman in the world, just gave up and died. Lyn had found the wireless phone tucked at the back of Gran's underwear drawer; but just like the old lady, something catastrophic had happened to it and it never worked again.

The evening news had finished and American voices filled the room, changing its usual ambience. Lyn pressed the off button impatiently and sat back on her sofa determined to try and get her head around how she needed to proceed.

She committed herself to two things and was determined to follow them through. James Fairbank didn't know it yet, but she had no intention of leaving his office tomorrow until she'd found out his connection to Vinny the Con. Her second commitment, involved staying in London for several days – the prospect of this had filled her with dread – but after plucking up the courage to phone Jill, and spending almost an hour dissolving the twenty-eight years of non-communication between each other, Lyn felt relieved and excited about their planned reunion.

Sitting now with only the soft crackle of the burning logs for company, she reached out and lifted the oldest of the framed photographs from its resting place, holding it close to her chest. She could remember every detail of this sixty-three year old sepia image because it had been prominently on view at Gran's for as long as she could remember. The photograph, showed a nineteen year old Ethel on the arm of her beloved, twenty-four year old Edward. It was the day they got married, and the stern look on both of their faces, belied the fact that they were very much in love – although Gran had reiterated this every time she'd lifted the frame to tenderly remove the dust.

It was 1943 when this loving union was formalised

between Ethel and Edward Cartwright, during a short leave from the Second World War and the horrendous hostilities that were sweeping across Europe. Edward was in the RAF and his smart uniform confirmed it; but Gran was always coy about exactly what he did; preferring others to conclude that he was a pilot. However, when he'd died, just a few months before the war ended and three weeks after Ethel gave birth to their daughter, she learned by telegraph, he'd been shot whilst on routine ground-patrol in France.

From that day forth, as far as Ethel was concerned, anyone who wasn't born and bred within the shores of the British Isles, was a treacherous foreigner. But the most treacherous foreigner of all was Almighty God, for allowing it to happen. *When I read the telegram Lynda, I made up my mind there and then that my God-bothering days were over, and I haven't set foot in a church since.*

There was no doubting the hardship that Gran had faced in those post-war years. Times were lean enough, what with food on ration and money in short supply, without having to bring up a child single-handedly. She was a good looking woman in spite of the fact that she looked much older than her years; but she'd never married again, choosing instead to devote her life solely to the seed of Edward's loins.

God's treachery hadn't ended there. After sacrificing the best years of her life struggling to make ends meet, the Almighty God, in his infinite wisdom, saw fit to not only rob Ethel of her only daughter, but to saddle her with more responsibility. Lyn's parents had been killed in a tragic road accident whilst moving their few possessions to a small flat in nearby Bethnel Green; leaving Gran little choice but to adopt the eighteen-month-old child that had been left in her care whilst the move was underway.

A three-inch-square, Polaroid photograph, was the only image that Lyn possessed of her mother; it showed a strikingly beautiful woman, in a powder blue suit, smiling down into the face of her recently born daughter. The background – which Lyn took to be the frontage of Gran's house – typified thousands of the back to back terraced houses in the poorest parts of London; but the obvious delight on the woman's face, seemed to nullify the degradation. On the back of the photograph, in faded black ink, was one short line of neat handwriting which read: *spring 1962 my beautiful flower.* Mindful of the emotions that always surfaced after Lyn's pondering over the photograph, she tucked it back into the bottom left-hand corner of Gran and Grandfather's silver frame and returned it to its designated place.

It had been fourteen months ago, whilst Lyn was clearing Gran's flat after her death, that the photograph had come to light, along with two very disturbing letters. A large, heavy chest of drawers – riddled with woodworm, according to the shifty looking bloke who was doing the clearance with her – needed to be dismantled before loading it into his van, and Lyn had just extracted the fifth and final drawer with an almighty effort of will and exasperation. Sitting back on her heels to recover from the exertion, she noticed at once what had caused the binding problem; a linen handkerchief had slipped down from an upper drawer, and lodged on the runner of the bottom one. Over the years, several other items had found their way to the lower corners of the inside framework and amongst the faded receipts, hair grips and safety-pins, Lyn found two envelopes tied together with baby-pink ribbon.

Gran had moved down to the West Country in 1963, obviously wanting to bring up her new charge in a healthier environment and to escape from a place that was riddled with bad memories. All this was relayed to Lyn whenever she asked about her past. As to the absence of any pictures of her parents and herself as a baby; she was told that all personal documents, including photographs, were destroyed in the burnt-out wreckage of the fated car. When Lyn reached her early teens, she went through a stage where she hounded Gran for information about her parents; and it was about this time that Gran announced that she had a bad heart and how it could give out without warning if she was under too much stress. *What's done is done Lynda haven't I suffered enough for you?* Not wanting to be left completely alone in the world, Lyn held back her questions and buried the curiosity deep into her subconscious.

Forcing all thoughts of the past from her mind, Lyn decided to have a luxuriously warm bath; instead of the quick, barely-tepid shower she'd become accustomed to. She knew that she'd have to switch on the wall-mounted fan blower in the bathroom, otherwise any body-parts that weren't beneath the water would freeze. "Sod the expense!" she said aloud, as she mounted the stairs two at a time.

Standing before the full length mirror of her wardrobe, Lyn's earlier dread of the London trip returned. She was searching hard for the bodily attributes of years ago when she and Jill would candidly point them out for each other. Apart from a good figure – which everyone seemed to have in those days because obesity was almost unknown in young people – Lyn's best feature was her hair. The thick chestnut locks – highlighted during the summer months with natural, sun-kissed, golden streaks – were always worn long, (until the day she got engaged to Martin). Jill was always envious of Lyn's best feature, probably because her hair happened to be her weakest. Although Jill was a natural blonde, the hair itself was thin and lacking in body and no matter how many times Lyn tried to help her friend, by rolling it in curlers or back-combing it into a greater mass, within an hour it would be back to lank, flat and straight. Lyn advised her on several occasions to have it cut short and layered, insisting that it would create more volume, but Jill wouldn't have it.

The pony-tail clip that had become part of Lyn's everyday dress for several weeks was removed and the chestnut, silken mass fell onto her shoulders. Lack of sunshine had meant the loss of golden streaks – replaced, in part, by fine streaks of silver – and lack of money had forced Lyn to abandon the regular visits to Caz, who had kept her hair in good shape whilst working in the public eye.

Dashing into the bathroom to turn off the taps, Lyn made the snap decision to visit her hairdresser before Monday; and after turning off the fan-blower and opening the bathroom door to barely a two inch gap, she slid beneath the warmth of the lavender-scented water.

"Shit!" the telephone started to ring and Lyn gripped the side of the bath in automatic response to someone else's demand for attention; then relaxed again acknowledging the true benefit of having an answering machine. Sarah's cheerful voice found its way through the two-inch gap by Lyn's right ear.

"Hi Mum, it's too early for you to be in bed so hope you're out on a hot date. I know its weeks away, but we wondered if you'd like to visit for Christmas? There's lots of room here and Fergi reckons you're the best Mammy-in law he could wish for. Give us a bell during the week-end, love you, bye."

Of all the emotions that had surfaced over the last few days, Lyn's resentment toward her daughter was the most disturbing. Her mounting debts to the bank; to pay for Sarah's education, driving lessons and buying her first car and then helping to finance the elaborate wedding, was not really her daughter's fault. She had simply accepted what her father had always told her; that he would provide for all his princess's material needs until another man walked her down the isle. Sarah, unaware of the lack of funds from her father's insurance, and denied the truth of this by her mother, had merrily spent what *she* thought was rightfully hers. The financial cost to Lyn had been huge, but the cost, in terms of the fractured relationship between mother and daughter was beyond measure. As the hot tears flowed free and the bath water began to chill, Lyn's resolve to right the wrongs was increased.

Chapter 5

Friday Morning

Friday morning was grey with drizzle, adding to Lyn's sense of foreboding. The nine hours of uninterrupted sleep should have had her bouncing around and feeling on top form; but she felt tired and had to push hard to get her sluggish body to do anything. Falling into sleep with too many imponderables swirling around inside her head had been to blame; they'd mixed and tumbled into a maze of nonsensical dreams – none of which she could remember. Out of habit she aimed for the kitchen; a mug of black coffee should help get her grounded into the real world and drill home the fact that if she was to achieve her goals for the morning she'd better get her backside into gear.

After dressing and undressing several times, a smart rust-coloured trouser suit and cream silk shirt were decided on. Lyn's concern now was how to keep her outfit dry after handing back the umbrella to the solicitor. The smart dress-code was for Caz – pride wouldn't allow her long-acquainted hairdresser to see the depths to which she had sunk – but the fair amount of walking, between solicitors, hairdresser and booking a rail ticket to London, also required protection from the elements.

Lyn caught sight of the clock and frustration mounted as the strong resolve of the previous evening began to waver. Reaching for the small, white envelope, which she'd left propped against the photo of her proudest achievement, she held it against her lips. Her resolve stabilised. Concealed within the envelopes flimsy protection was the prospect of restitution; but it had to remain a secret. A secret which Lyn had no intention of disclosing to anyone; not her own daughter, her best friend and especially not to a privileged, public-schooled solicitor who was probably as crooked as Vinny the Con!

The sitting room curtains remained closed whilst Lyn removed the small bundle of twenty-pound notes from the body of the Art-Deco tea pot. In its place, she stowed the small, white envelope. No point in taking any risks, she thought, hurriedly flicking the curtains back to the open position before setting out with only the borrowed umbrella for protection from the elements.

A flicker of movement at the back of the small hair-salon induced Lyn to hammer with both fists on the locked front door. She'd been peering through the narrow gap of glass around a large yellow poster which read:

Due to unforeseen circumstances CURL UP AND DYE will no longer be operating from these premises. Carol will be more than happy to offer her services in the comfort of your own home.

A sigh of relief misted the shop window when Caz's heart-shaped face came into view and then disappeared for several seconds, before she reappeared holding a large bunch of keys.

"Ayah, honey, 'aven't seen you in ages, 'ow's things? The warm, friendly response from Caz, after she'd finally managed to unlock both of the complicated mechanisms, raised Lyn's hopes.

"I've been over in Ireland," Lyn lied, "helping Sarah settle into her new home; what's all this about home visits only?"

"A little bird told me that Sarah 'ad a real fancy wedding, must 'av cost a bomb."

"A legacy from her father covered everything. Tell me what's happening here."

Lyn was in no mood for Caz's usual game of extracting information about anyone and anything; and which little bird – she would dearly like to ask – had been free and easy with *her* private affairs. With less than ten inches between them, Lyn stood her ground determined not to say another word until Caz answered her question

"My lease runs out Monday, can't afford to renew, I was just clearing out a few things. Anyway, most of my ladies are keen on home visits, and I've got a couple of contracts with nursing homes, so I'll probably be quid's in, 'ow's the flower trade?"

"Caz can you do me a really big favour and sort my hair before Monday? I wouldn't pressure like this but…"

"I can do it now or come to your house on Sunday, your choice," interrupted Caz, giving Lyn no choice but to accept the first option as Sunday was already fully allotted.

She set to work clearing a space in the far corner where heaped up boxes covered every available surface.

"It's good of you to do this Caz; I haven't been much of a customer lately."

"No problem, Lyn, but I would appreciate cash; the robbing bastards have had enough tax off me over the years. I'm sick of seeing my hard-earned money squandered on illegal bloody foreigners."

"You sound like my old Gran, what time is your next appointment?" Lyn asked conversationally, giving herself a legitimate reason to keep checking her watch.

It took Caz several minutes to answer, during which, she gathered together the necessary containers of hair products – including hair-dye – and two large black towels. Lyn knew it was pointless to argue; in the past Caz had always been given carte blanche to do anything that was necessary for making her hair look good; and to be fair, apart from the veiled interrogations, she was good-hearted and always saw the funny side of things. But above all, she was the best hairdresser for miles. Caz's own hair changed colour regularly, and at this time, three differing shades of purple sprouted from the main body of a carefully arranged heap of ash-blonde spikes, all of which suited the hairdresser's features, perfectly.

Swaddled in the black towels and facing Caz's reflection, Lyn was eventually informed that her next customer – the only one for today – couldn't remember her own name, so she wouldn't be concerned about what time Caz arrived.

"I was sorry to hear about your new shop closing down Lyn, how's the old one doing?"

The sudden change of subject caught Lyn off-guard and

feeling panicked rambled on about visiting her old school friend in London. She then quickly changed the subject to highlights and doing something different with the tired looking locks that Caz was at present separating into sections. Both women knew that it was just a delaying tactic, and both women knew it would have to be answered sooner or later. Caz made it sooner and easier for Lyn.

"You got nothing to be ashamed of Lyn; you set up a lovely shop in Seaward Parade; and when all the shops in that parade started going down like dominoes, well it's only a matter of time honey before you follow. Besides, you got the other shop, that'll never run short of custom."

"Like I said Caz, I've been in Ireland a lot lately; when your only child gets married you find yourself at a crossroads in life, Martin left me financially secure so I *have* got choices." Lyn had no intention of discussing any such choices, so she rapidly changed the subject. "So this customer of yours with Alzheimer's, it must be difficult holding a conversation, and you're not the silent type!"

"Polly Pemberton's her name and I've been doing her hair for years. She's a retired school teacher, was real brainy before she got, you know. When anybody telephones, she picks up and says in her real posh voice, "Polly Parrot speaking." Drives her daughter mad, but she can't help it."

Caz continued to enlighten Lyn about conversations held between herself and Polly; where every item, person or place was thing, thingummy or thingamajig. At one point, tears of laughter rolled down Lyn's face as she sadly realised how long it had been since she'd had a good laugh and how it had taken another person's misfortune to produce it.

Two and a half hours later Lyn peeled two notes from her bundle and gave Caz a long heart-felt hug. The forty pounds was way below the current charge but Caz wouldn't accept a penny more. Before leaving, Lyn asked for the name of Polly Pemberton's daughter, thinking that she might know her, but Caz's reply sent them both into another fit of the giggles.

"I once asked her what her daughter's name was and Polly said; "How would I know? You'll, have to ask *her*."

Fortunately, the drizzle had stopped during Lyn's 'make-over'. It was almost lunchtime so sorting out the train to London would have to wait; other things were much more pressing. As she strode purposefully up the steep gradient to James Fairbank's office, a gentle breeze lifted and inspected the forty-pound hair-do. Lyn marched on, preoccupied.

James Fairbank whistled the tune that had followed the nine o'clock news; and which had stubbornly insisted on breaking forth at every opportunity since then. It was now ten minutes to one and he was happily preparing to head off in the direction of the harbour to enjoy a midday meal at his favourite restaurant. This used to be a regular Friday lunch-time treat for James and Clara; but since his secretary's absence, he hadn't fancied eating there alone, or, spending money he couldn't really afford. But after the morning's developments, the latter of these reasons, could now, hopefully, be disregarded.

For the second time, in as many days, he had spoken with Victor Connor and Ms Charlene Dais, although, like the previous day, Mr Connor had done all the talking. He had telephoned James at nine-thirty, asking if they might come straight away to view his property, as it sounded as though it was just what they were looking for. James obliged by giving them an eleven o'clock appointment; easily rearranging his other scheduled work.

On first arriving, it was hard to establish their reaction to the place because all communication between the pair was carried out in tight little whispers and mainly out of James's earshot. He had respected their privacy and allowed them to look over the place without breathing down their necks; but found their whispering, both discourteous and unnecessary. Nevertheless, all this was forgiven after they knocked on his office door half an hour later and announced that they, (although again, it was Victor who was doing the talking) were very interested and would like to, 'talk terms', but not until contracts were exchanged on the shop. James had felt both relief and bewilderment; but had smiled at the thought that his fortunes were at last taking a turn for the better.

A light tap on his sitting room door, followed by Sadie's voice, halted his whistling in mid-bar.

"I've finished downstairs Mr Fairbank, would you like me to clean up here?"

"I'm having lunch out today, Sadie, leave it till next time; but it won't affect your pay."

"That's very good of you sir, by the way, there's a young woman in the front room of the empty house; she says she arranged to see you this morning and wanted to do some measuring; was it alright to let her in?"

"Is she alone Sadie?" James asked, feeling perplexed – a perplexity that deepened when Sadie confirmed that she was. Now is the time to find out a little more about my future tenant, he thought, as he descended the stairs two at a time.

It was three minutes to one, when Lyn arrived at the solicitor's front door – out of breath and bursting for the loo. She knew his lunch hour started at one and her determination to arrive before that, had forced her to hold onto the contents of her bladder even though she'd passed two public conveniences. Her heart sank when she peered into the office through the half-glazed, locked door; and regretted – not for the first time – that she no longer possessed a car. An elderly cleaner was vacuuming the carpeted stairs that led from the hall and the poor woman almost jumped out of her skin when Lyn accosted her from behind.

"I've come to see Mr Fairbank", gasped Lyn, expecting the cleaner to turn off the deafening noise from her ancient vacuum cleaner; but instead stated quite calmly that he was at lunch. "Shit!" Lyn blurted out, loud enough, to be heard by the cleaner who cast an old fashioned look in her direction before saying.

"Can I give him a message?"

"I said I'd pop in and… I've been looking over Mr Fairbank's property and… I'd like to take some measurements, starting in the toilet." Lyn followed the direction of the cleaner's pointing finger.

Relieved at last from her discomfort and resigned to at least an hours wait, Lyn wandered appreciatively around the spacious areas of the Georgian property. But it was the room at the front-elevation that captivated her most. Lyn was aware of the negative aspects of her character and jealousy wasn't one of them; but as she stood, like two days previous, in front of the two large windows, captivated by the view; she felt more than a little envious of James Fairbank's first, prospective tenant.

James stood watching the back of the lone figure for several seconds. Unfortunately it wasn't Ms Charlene Dais; this woman was taller and held herself erect and confident and the hair was completely different to the ultra-straight style that Ms Dais and most young woman seemed to prefer these days.

"Can I help you?" he eventually asked causing the woman to turn and reveal who she was. "Oh! It's you!" James heard his own disappointment register on the woman's changed expression. Her response was fiery.

"I'm so sorry to interrupt your lunch break, I was only returning this," Lyn waved his umbrella in the air, "and I didn't want to just leave it without saying thank you."

"You can say thank you by joining me for lunch, I love your new hair-do, Lyn, and does this herald a positive change in your circumstances?" Lyn's first instinct was to tell him to mind his own business and to stick his lunch where the sun didn't shine; but instead, she returned his smile which held the hidden premise that in spite of the morning's setbacks, here was the perfect opportunity for gaining the information she needed.

The light drizzle barely registered as James strode purposefully back to his office. He'd insisted that Lyn should use his umbrella again, pointing out the importance of protecting her fabulous new hair style rather than worry about a drop of rain on his jacket that was years old. What was, concerning him however, was this chap Vince or Victor whatever his name. If James was honest, he'd never really taken to the man, and it wasn't just the limp, clammy hand-shake – although James had always instinctively trusted his first impressions – it was the total lack of respect for Ms Dais, who was after all, his client, and the way he inferred that James had to "play ball".

He'd tried hard not to let it spoil their lunch; which for him was the perfect opportunity for getting to know Lyn better; although he had to confess it was proving to be very difficult. But, her secretiveness fascinated him and the more she struggled to hang onto her private life, the more fascinated he became. They hadn't parted on the best of terms, but, she still had his umbrella; and he knew her well enough to know that she would return it soon.

The day was ending as it had begun, except the sense of foreboding seemed deeper and darker – a mental black tunnel without a glimmer of light at the end. Lyn was nursing a mug of cocoa in front of the fire, although it wasn't yet seven o'clock, hoping that this simple, end of the day ritual, would unleash its usual magic and still her frenzied thoughts. She reached for the pocket-sized address book and tapped it nervously, uncertain about which of the two calls she should make.

The invitation to lunch had been accepted eagerly; the need to satisfy her rumbling stomach a welcome by product of the main goal, and all was going well until she learned the reason behind Vinny the Con's meeting with the solicitor.

James had escorted her into R.C. Food – a small, select, sea-food restaurant positioned on the harbour. Lyn had walked by this restaurant many times but after glancing over the prices on the outside menu had never been enticed inside; although, she had wondered about its unusual name. With boyish delight, James had satisfied her wonderings. The restaurant was owned by two brothers, Rick and Chris. Rick was a Master Chef and Chris was a very accomplished fisherman, so they came up with a name that would announce to the inhabitants and visitors of Torbay that the "fruits of the sea" were caught daily and cooked fresh by the Master Chef.

Bowing to James's greater knowledge of the place, she had followed his recommendation of Today's Special's by ordering: Monkfish Tail with orange and Saffron Sauce, served with Sauté Potatoes, Julienne Carrots and Fine Green Beans, washed down with a single glass of sparkling, white wine. This was followed by a light Champagne Mousse and a whole deluge of compliments about Lyn's new hairstyle; which softened her up for his next few personal questions. He'd started off by pointing to Lyn's adorned wedding finger and asked how long she'd been married. After bristling slightly Lyn had answered with the question of how long he'd been divorced.

"Tell you what," he'd responded, smiling comfortably, "we'll take turns in asking each other questions – "ladies first".

By playing this little game of his, Lyn had learnt of his short marriage – exited via a painless divorce; of working-class parents who had struggled to enable James and his sister, Helen, qualify in professions of their choosing

(Helen, apparently, was an architect and worked in Exeter) and that he felt happy and fulfilled, but sometimes a little lonely.In return, he had discovered about Martin's death, Sarah's marriage and new homeland, and how she was brought up by Gran – who died fourteen months ago. It was at this point in their hide and seek game of questioning that James had laid his warm hand over hers; and she, keeping her voice amicable, had asked the only question that really interested her.

"How long have you been associated with Vince Conway?" She'd scrutinised his face for any marked change of expression. There *had* been a change, but not what she'd expected. He'd softly mouthed the name under his breath, followed by a slight shake of head.

"Can't place him Lyn, how far back are we going?"

Don't tell this slippery bugger anything else Lynda, I warned ya, they're all the same. But even Gran's powerful warning couldn't halt what had been started.

"We are going back to yesterday. *I* saw you shaking his hand outside Beryl's Florist." Lyn's voice had taken on a hard edge and she could see this registering in his eyes; he'd removed his warm hand and his smile had melted into confusion. Then suddenly he'd brightened – bringing back the captivating smile and grasping both her hands.

"Ah, you silly goose, you're confused over the guy's name, its Victor Connor not Vince Conway, and the shop in question is Floral Celebrations. My mother makes these kinds of mistakes all the time, blames it on old age, but in your case…"

Lyn interrupted, "I think I'd know the name of the low-life who'd conned me out of over forty grand, wouldn't you agree? And, I'd still like to know about you're involvement with him." James had cast a nervous eye to the next occupied table and indicated – by hand signal – that Lyn ought to lower her rising voice. She'd continued her interrogation through clenched teeth and in an accusing, hissing whisper had asked what the hell he was doing in the shop anyway.

"My job", he'd responded simply, leaving Lyn frustrated and waiting for more. "I am a conveyancing solicitor Lyn and I'm in the final stages of transferring the shop to a valued client of mine; the sale should be completed within days, and I needed to verify one or two things."

This devastating news stopped Lyn in her verbal tracks. James had continued talking and Lyn had ceased to listen until he had mentioned that he was actually more interested in the present owner, Ms Dais. After shaking her head in silent disbelief, Lyn had asked pointedly who was buying the shop; and James – just as pointedly – refused to tell her, spouting all manner of client-confidentiality as an excuse for denying her the information that was hers by right. At this point, she'd thrown down her napkin, looked at her watch and said that she had to go!

Chapter 6

Victor Connor was trying very hard to get used to his new name which he'd adopted for one purpose only and which, if all went according to plan, he'd be able to ditch very soon and return to his old self – high-flying, go-getter – Vinny Conway.

At forty-two, he felt that he'd done really well for himself, considering the lack of any further education. The local comprehensive school he'd attended had failed to teach him anything useful, so why would he want to waste more of his life listening to the same old clap-trap, when he could be out there in the real world ducking and diving and earning good money.

Aunt Beryl's death had put Vinny squarely on the road to better things. He was her only living relative and as such, inherited her long-established florist business which included the mortgage-free, premises. His first instinct had been to sell it – where's the street-cred in telling your mates you own a flower shop? But Aunt Beryl had insisted before she died, that her long-time assistant and friend – Lyn Porter – should remain running the shop, 'or else'. He'd never really found out what the 'or else' meant, but Aunt Beryl was a tough old bird who had frightened him on several occasions so he'd gone along with her dying wish.

The shop, although profitable, was old-fashioned; and the two bedroomed flat above, was downright archaic – far too embarrassing to bring home any birds that he'd met at the gym. What he'd needed, was a good chunk of dough to give the place a complete makeover without putting himself or his newly acquired property in the hands of the rip-off banks. Lyn Porter had fulfilled this need perfectly. In fact at one point he'd tried to bed her, to further his plans even more and make what he had in mind easier, but the frigid bitch wouldn't play ball. Still, he had snared her into accepting his brilliant plan, and everything would still be hunky-dory, if only…

"It's ready Vinny". The sound of Charlene's high pitched voice cut his thoughts off in mid stream. The swift movement, which belied his heavy, muscular frame, brought him to Charlene's side in two seconds flat. Seeing and smelling the cheap, ready-prepared meal that she'd just taken from the microwave added fire to his barely suppressed anger.

"You stupid bitch, how many times have I told you, my name is now Victor, V.I.C.T.O.R." He'd pulled Charlene backwards by her hair in order to blast this message in her ear loud and clear; and as her arms flailed around in surprise and panic, the steaming food was sent crashing to the floor.

"Get that slop cleaned up then run down to the chippy for some proper food, and I mean run, I need to be away in forty minutes!" Vinny forced himself to sit down and take several deep-breaths – an exercise that helped control his anger. The clip-clop of Charlene's high heels as she descended the stairs was as irritating as her whining voice; but it was the sound of the cash register being opened then closed that brought his simmering anger back to the surface. As soon as this deal is wrapped up, he thought, *she* is gone! He abandoned the deep breathing and headed for the bathroom to shave his head and face, wondering, not for the first time, why he had been so attracted to Charlene in the first place. She was useless in the shop; how hard can it be to stick a few flowers together in a pretty pattern? She'd had three months of coaching, before Lyn, had been moved to the town-centre shop; and still the takings dwindled – everybody wanted Lyn bloody Porter to do their wreath – what difference could it possibly make to the poor sod being cremated?

Charlene had been working on reception at the Gym where Vinny spent most of his evenings; she also worked as personal trainer to several wimps who came to unload their day-time stresses from banks or offices within the town's catchment area. She had quite a following, which to Vinny's mind, meant she was relieving their stresses in more ways than one. Fortunately for him, she wasn't as squeaky clean as she smelt. After flipping her fingers across the keyboard of the Gym's computer, she managed to wangle a whole year's free membership for him, repeating the same for his good pal Carl, three weeks later. Charlene performed this act of true devotion after Vinny promised to rescue her from the demands of the stressed out wimps and offer her the position of running his thriving floristry business. He thought now about her great body and how uninhibited she was about using it. His mind probed into the memory bank of steamy pleasure that was his, just for the taking. His manhood swelled as he planned what he would do to her at the end of the day; tweaking one of his most desirable and oldest fantasies.

His anger was well under control by the time Charlene returned with his favourite food – chicken, chips and two sausages – and after wolfing it down, he too headed for the cash till to supply his expenses for the evening. Looking around the shop, which was overflowing with flowers of every size and colour, reminded him of Friday evenings years ago; when Aunt Beryl and Lyn Porter would still have been working right up to nine o'clock, preparing wreaths and bouquets to fulfil the weekend orders. The cash till, back in those days, was always bulging with money The cash till, back in those days, was always bulging with money but the two of them still lived like peasants. Aunt Beryl who, by her own admission was well and truly married to the job had slowly but surely conditioned Lyn Porter to be just the same. But not Vinny, no way, he wanted the good things in life, and nothing was going to stop him from getting them. This amount of stock had been ordered for one purpose only – to fool that poser of a solicitor. He couldn't allow the new owner to think that business was crap!

Charlene gave an audible sigh of relief as the shop door closed and the five-lever lock gave its comforting clunking sound, of being locked. She'd made up her mind to bring her planned escape forward, possibly as early as next weekend. And having made this decision she celebrated by relaxing full length on the sofa whilst sipping on a chilled glass of Chardonnay

Since giving up her expensive flat and moving in with Vinny; not only had she paid off her credit cards, she'd accrued a nice little bundle of cash which should see her through to starting her new position in January. Her salary at the Gym – a salary that was diminishing week by week because of lack of new clients, could never have given her this opportunity of a fresh start in so short a time. As well as the free board and lodging, she had made him pay for every single time he had forced himself upon her; and the more brutally he'd behaved, the more it had cost him. Of course Vinny wasn't aware of these payments. He'd been so impressed by the little fiddle of altering his membership status on the Gym's computer; it had never crossed his tiny mind that Charlene could do the same on his computerised cash till. His downfall, apart from being a bully who was as thick as two short planks, was wanting all the latest gadgets without knowing the first thing about how to use them.

God only knows why he decided to open the town-centre shop and allow Lyn Porter– the best asset his business possessed – to moulder away there, while this place was left neglected and vulnerable; making it easy for Charlene to drain its life blood under the guise of diminishing custom because of the 'credit crunch'. Another mistake, was deciding to close on Sundays – the day most people visit the cemetery to tidy up their loved-one's plots and lay fresh flowers.

The shop telephone rang for the third time. Vinny wasn't around and it was out of shop hours so Charlene had no intention of answering it, even though an extension had been installed barely three feet away from where she lay relaxing. The first two calls had been from the same bloke – who'd sounded quite distressed and put out that no one was available to discuss his need of a suitable wreath for his recently, dearly departed wife. She gave a heavy sigh during the next interval of the film and stretched out to delete the messages, completely ignoring the bloke's plea to phone him back. The third call had cut off at the first sign of the answer phone being activated, so hopefully he'd now allow her some peace; but when Charlene's mobile rang out its cheerful melody, she sat up and took notice.

Her mind reeled around who it could be. Vinny didn't know of its existence even though she'd had it for two years and she only ever remembered giving her number to one or two trusted friends. She kept it for furthering her plan, far too risky having the London numbers show up on the itemised shop bill. Vinny was almost illiterate but his animal-like cunning enabled him to root out a scam at the first hint of something dodgy. The ringing continued as Charlene upended her large shoulder bag, spilling its contents onto the sofa. A zipped section, cleverly concealed in the inner base of the expensive bag, held all her most private belongings, including money and passport; and it was from this compartment that the neat, little phone continued to ring.

"Hi Lyn, sorry I took so long, haven't used this phone for ages." Charlene was flummoxed trying to remember when she'd given Lyn Porter her number although she'd obviously stored Lyn's landline on *her* phone.

"So why keep it switched on?"

It was obvious by Lyn's tone that she was still smarting from the shop closure that put her out of a job. She was after information, which meant Charlene needed to be very careful and very discreet. "Vinny's not here Lyn, you know how he likes to keep toned at the Gym."

"I've got no intention of speaking to that scum bag ever again Charlene; I'd just like you to tell me, who is buying the shop? And this phone call will remain between *us.*" Total silence followed as Charlene mentally sifted through all the possible ramifications of handing over information that Vinny had specifically asked to be kept secret at all costs, until the final signings were over.

"As God is my witness Lyn, I haven't a clue; you know Vinny, always plays things close to his chest, until things are signed and sealed. I just sell the flowers and do as I'm told; you know how…" Suddenly, the phone went dead! Charlene's fingers and eyes remained fixed on the small block of plastic; worry lines creasing and spoiling her formally relaxed, lovely face as thoughts raced around her head. How the hell did Lyn Porter get to know that the shop had been sold? Was she aware that Charlene had taken over, temporarily, as the owner? Oh my God! What if the nosey bitch phones again on this private number and Vinny's in earshot! For three days, Charlene had been waiting for a promised phone call from the agency, to confirm acceptance for the position she'd applied for. Now, thanks to Lyn (bloody) Porter, she'd have to rethink how the agency could make contact.

Within seconds of putting the receiver down on Charlene, Lyn had found what she wanted in the directory and was punching in the telephone number of James Fairbank. How on earth could she prevent the sale of the shop, when she didn't even know who was buying it? In her ignorance, she'd assumed that acquiring the necessary funds was all that was required to reversing her present predicament; but the mountain of deception that was unfolding before her, left her floundering about who she could trust.

After five rings, a clicking sound and a shift in tone led Lyn to believe that an answer phone would pick up the message she'd already mentally prepared to leave; so it was both surprising, and a little unnerving, when the solicitor's cheerful voice, cut a swathe of warmth through the chilly hallway.

"James Fairbank, my office is closed until Monday morning but, if it's important, I'm happy to speak with you now."

Lyn felt torn between humility and hostility, and struck a balance between the two. "Hi James, its Lyn, I just wanted to thank you for lunch and explain why I felt so uptight when I heard about Beryl's being sold."

"You mean, Floral Celebrations," he corrected, in a playful manner that tipped the scales toward hostility.

"Yeah whatever" she responded in a tired voice which changed James Fairbank's to audible concern.

"Lyn, please share your problems with me, that alone will make you feel better. I'll leave the first hour free on Monday morning if you like?"

"I'm going up to London on Monday morning and I'll be gone for several days, maybe even a week and if the shop is sold by then, well… my problems won't be solvable anyway." Lyn hadn't wanted to sound so desolate, but it was too late in the day for keeping up the pretence. "James, I know you don't work Saturdays; but could you allow me that hour tomorrow morning? She crossed the fingers on her right hand and bit down on her lower lip during the few seconds of silence that followed.

"How far away are you from my office?" His question restored some of her hope.

"Fifteen minutes walk, and I promise not to keep you long, I only…" Uncharacteristically, James cut her off in mid-sentence, telling her that Saturday was his young nephew's birthday and part of James's present, was a day spent hunting fossils at Lyme Regis; and it would be unthinkable to renege on the, already given promise.

What he proposed instead, was to take the few minutes drive to her home, where they could hopefully resolve some of her anxieties over a civilised cup of tea. Without giving any thought to the consequences of her actions, Lyn verbally handed over her address while Gran beat a warning tattoo over and over again *Mark my words Lynda, you'll live to regret this.*

Chapter 7

Early Hours of Saturday Morning

Strobe lighting flashed and darted through the gossamer curtains of Lyn's bedroom. One minute she seemed to be sleeping deeply, the next found her standing by the window, disorientated by what she thought was the 'Blitz' her Gran had often talked about. Not a single drop of rain accompanied the storm that raged directly above her home. She stood spellbound for several minutes, captivated by this dramatic release of energy. As the next blast of light lit up the harbour two miles away, she could clearly make out the clock tower, and was surprised to see that it was only 1-45am.

The chill of the bedroom began to seep into her lower limbs; and knowing that she wouldn't sleep until the storm passed over, reached for her dressing gown and headed downstairs. On reaching the bottom stair another throbbing light caught her attention. The tiny point of flashing red on the answering machine sent waves of panic and guilt as Lyn remembered reading about the dangers of leaving such things connected during overhead storms. Panic disappeared along with the red light as the plugs were pulled from their sockets; guilt remained because she hadn't yet responded to Sarah's message.

Entering the lounge lifted her spirit. A soft glow of red ash from the grate both lit and warmed the room. Captured within the warmth, was a distinct remnant of James Fairbank's after-shave. She also noticed, and this, for some unknown reason brought a smile to her face, the large red cushion on the fireside chair that had supported his body, was still indented with his shape. She sat within this shape and closed her eyes.

He'd arrived within half an hour of her phone call, looking very relaxed in blue denim jeans and cable-knit, navy sweater – which was later removed to reveal a flawless white tee shirt. During the half hour wait, Lyn had dashed around her home like a woman possessed, checking that each of her already tidy rooms had nothing out of place, the stove was stacked with logs and that *she* was presentable. After placing a CD of classical guitar music in the player she'd sat straight-backed, taken several deep breaths and focussed on relaxing. On hearing the slam of a car door, she'd jumped up nervously, turned it off and stood waiting for the ring of the doorbell.

Relief washed over her when he'd refused the offer of a glass of wine; she only had the one bottle – a leftover from the previous Christmas and of dubious origin. Then anger had erupted from nowhere when his decline continued in a matter-of-fact casual way.

"I'm here to help you Lyn, to share a pot of tea while we talk will be fine."

Lyn had blurted out that the only way he could help her was to prevent the sale going through on the florist shop.

His only response was to relax more into the cushion behind him and wait for further information. Feeling tired and vulnerable, Lyn had unburdened the whole sorry story.

She'd told him, that after working at the same shop for over twenty years she was given the opportunity of buying into a partnership with Vince Conway. Vince had inherited the business but didn't have a clue about running it; she, on the other hand, could run the business single-handed but didn't have any capital. Anyway, to cut a long story short, she'd said, taking extra care as she poured the brewed tea, afraid that her hand would shake and indicate the rising emotion within; we opened a second shop in the newly developed Seaward Parade; which I agreed to manage for one year to allow it to get established. During this time, the newly trained florist's assistant and Vince were left to run the main shop. However, more than two years passed before a combination of: excessively high overheads, a down turn in the economy, and Vince taking more of the cash till than the business could stand, forced us to close the Seaward Parade shop.

It was at this point in the one-sided conversation that James had asked if he might remove his wool sweater; the two burning logs were at their optimum of heat production and his face was turning red. Lyn had foolishly apologised for the heat from the fire and both of them had smiled; easing the next stage of the conversation which seemed to Lyn more like a confessional.

Naturally, she'd expected to return to managing the main shop, she'd continued when James, looking more comfortable, indicated that she go on with the story. She'd known things would be tight for a while but was confident that they could ride out the recession. What she hadn't been expecting, and still couldn't quite believe, was the financial straits that the main shop was suffering. Vince told her he had no choice but to file for bankruptcy. At the mention of this, James's composed face creased into a frown and for several seconds it was obvious that his mind was elsewhere. A slight shake of the head had brought his attention back.

"I do sympathise Lyn, but this sort of thing is happening to hundreds of businesses every week."

Again his words had seemed too matter-of-fact. "I don't want your sympathy; I need your help in preventing the shop being sold over my head. Over forty thousand pounds of *my* money went into modernising the place and that bastard's filed for bankruptcy *after* transferring it into his girlfriend's name." Lyn's hot rebuke had completely altered the atmosphere Tension had increased further when he'd nonchalantly asked if she and Vince had been lovers.

"I was led to believe that you were here to help, not pry into my private life". She'd been amazed at how controlled she'd sounded in spite of the turmoil taking place within. He'd stood and walked over to look at the four framed photographs, an obvious prelude to his departure. Each one was picked up, studied and treated to a positive remark, including Gran, whose stern expression was interpreted as, a strong-looking character. Captivated by his curiosity, Lyn had watched from behind as his eyes probed into the snatched moments of her personal life. After what seemed to her like a long time, he'd turned and apologised for upsetting her, returned to his seat and topped up both of their teacups.

The tension abated in the near silence that followed, as each of them drank from the replenished cups and watched as the gyrating, hissing flames fed greedily on the disintegrating logs.

James had spoken first; explaining to her, in plain language, that there were no financial charges against the business or the shop premises. In fact, he'd continued, the business, according to the latest accounts, is very profitable considering the economic climate; that's why John Haydon is anxious to purchase. She hadn't been sure if he'd noticed the split-second of triumph that surely must have shown on her face; because, as always, his eyes were locked there whenever they communicated. Lyn had placed the name carefully in her memory bank, and feeling a whole lot better, decided to enlighten him a little more.

"Vinny has a friend who is referred to as his 'creative accountant'. This friend, who I believe is employed by one of the four major banks, is as crooked as a dog's hind leg and will do anything provided there's a big enough bung in it. In hindsight, I would have gone down the route of a business development loan in place of the mortgage charged against my home; but, this 'creative accountant' was very convincing with the repayment figures – which incidentally, were covered easily by my increased manager's salary. Lyn had ended this imparted knowledge with a brief flurry, informing James that as well as financing the improvements to the shop, she'd needed a lump sum for personal reasons. This guy's argument, of keeping everything within the one loan, sounded cheaper and easier all round.

Unburdened, Lyn lay back in her chair to mimic his

good hand found purchase down his heaving, sweating chest.

"You Bitch!" He snarled, looking down at the four bleeding lines that ended just above his right nipple. His knees pressed hard on either side of her armpits, squeezing her naked breasts together, causing her to gasp. A manic grin, the perfect accompaniment to the psychotic eyes, was the last thing Charlene saw before she was flipped over onto her stomach and imprisoned between his heavy, muscular thighs. She gave up the struggle, knowing that by doing so, the nightmare would soon be over. His plate-sized hands lifted the hips of her yielding body as he entered her from behind. Less than a minute of brutal thrusting, accompanied by animal-like grunts and groans, and it was over. But the damage done and its lingering pain would last for a long time.

Chapter 8

Saturday Morning

Within a few seconds of reconnecting the phone and answering machine, its loud trilling sound filled the narrow space of the hallway causing Lyn to jump in fright. Wondering who could be phoning her at eight-thirty in the morning? She tentatively lifted the receiver.

"Mum... Mum are you there?"

"Yes I'm here Sarah, what's happened?" Lyn heard relief in her daughter's voice as she relayed to her husband that she'd managed, at last, to get through to her mother.

"Did you get my message about Christmas Mum, please say you'll come?"

"Of course I will sweetheart. Sorry I haven't had a chance to get back to you, I've been really busy at work and..."

"I haven't been able to reach you at work; what's going on there?"

Sarah's questions had always been straight to the point and Lyn had always prided herself on answering in a similar way. It was with dented pride that Lyn felt compelled to say. "I'll be late for work if I don't leave now sweetheart; and by the way I'm going to London first thing Monday, for five days, promise I'll phone next weekend and tell you all about it."

Feeling ashamed, she marched through to the lounge and plumped up the dented cushions, despising the weakness she'd wallowed in just a few short hours before. *You* were very quiet, she thought, looking accusingly at the photo of her stern Gran, charmed by him were you? The demanding ring of the phone cut into Lyn's thoughts and she bolted through her lounge to answer it, eager now to formulate her plan and set aside all other distractions.

The call had been from Jill; a short friendly reminder that she was happy to meet Lyn at Paddington station on Monday provided it wasn't before 11-30 in the morning. As it turned out the reminder had been gratefully received and 'Ticket Office' was added to the morning's list.

As Lyn turned up her collar against the chill of the clear morning air the phone rang yet again; but as the front door was already slammed shut and her mind focused on one thing only, she left whoever it was to the service of the answer phone.

A strong feeling of déjà vu descended as Lyn thumped on the locked door of Floral Occasions. Was it only twenty-four hours ago that she was doing the self same thing outside the salon? At least Caz had had the decency to let her clients know what was happening, Lyn thought, as her impatience mounted. She was still smarting from the fierce run-in she'd had at the railway ticket office; the open return ticket to London had seriously dented her only available cash; no need now to scour the shops for a couple of bargain-priced tops to enhance her denuded wardrobe. Her bank balance would soon be much healthier, but not one to count her chickens, Lyn continued with her strict budgeting.

An elderly woman, whose face brightened on seeing and recognising Lyn lent her frail, age-spotted-fists to the tirade of loud knocking; which produced nothing but a slight twitch from an upstairs curtain. Lyn was in no mood to be messed around by the likes of Vinny. She hammered even harder.

"Nice to have you back Lyn, the place has gone to the dogs and no mistake about it; our Mabel locked herself out last week, had police out and everything, keys were in her bag all the time, slipped down a hole in the lining."

Elsie Wilson hadn't stopped talking from the minute she'd arrived at the shop; but, for the sake of her sanity, Lyn had stopped listening. However, something contained in Elsie's last few words, penetrated through Lyn's agitated defence barrier. Tipping the contents of her bag onto the pavement, Lyn snatched up a set of keys that had lain forgotten and unused for ages. Silently praying to all the Gods of the world, that the locks hadn't been changed, she slipped the larger of the two keys into the strong mechanism and let herself in – instinctively waiting at the threshold for the alarm to kick-in. Silence reined. On turning to relock the door, Elsie Wilson pushed passed and marched up to the counter to be served. Harnessing her impatience and resigned to the fact that it was down to Elsie that she was in the shop at all, Lyn relented.

"You off to have a nice chat with Albert, what colour do you fancy today?" Lyn smiled at the old lady, remembering her weekly visits to the cemetery where Albert – her long-dead husband – would be brought up to date on everything, including why she had chosen a certain colour theme of flowers.

"I think yellow and orange; cheer him up a bit, the place is very grim this time of year and lots of folks can't afford the flowers now, and Albert always loved his flowers, used to grow his own." Elsie rambled on whilst Lyn set to work satisfying her request, from the shady room that was stuffed with flowers of every colour and hue. Several bunches were expertly arranged into one massive bouquet, and for the fist time in ten minutes Elsie fell silent wondering if she'd brought enough money. After finishing off with a sunshine-yellow ribbon, Lyn handed the impressive piece of work to Elsie; with a peck on the cheek, and a whisper in her ear that this one was on Floral Occasions. Before Lyn had a chance to shoo Elsie out of the door, a shy, young teenager slipped through wanting a bunch of roses as a present for his Mum's birthday. Grabbing two bunches of the soft-pink variety they were hurriedly wrapped and pushed into the youth's arms as he was frog-marched out of the door, which was locked behind him. Sighing heavily from relief, Lyn turned and was startled to find Charlene standing at the back of the shop.

"What the hell are you doing?" asked Charlene, in a rough guttural voice that was loaded with accusation.

"Your job, Charlene, you should have been open over an hour ago; I've been serving long-standing clients that have paid your wages and allowed your boss to sell a business that's apparently worth over £300,000."

"Two customers have walked out with goods and the cash till hasn't been used; I suppose the money went straight into your pocket, so don't criticize me, Lyn high and mighty Porter."

Lyn resisted a strong urge to slap her face and brought the temptation of a scathing rebuke under control, knowing that this kind of tit for tat would lead nowhere.

"I've come to talk with my ex-business partner about relinquishing, my input of funds, *before* the business is sold on." Charlene gave a loud scoff and turned to climb the stairs to the upper floor; doing her best to disguise the limp from Lyn, who followed close behind.

In a voice that was obviously constrained by a sore throat, Lyn was informed that Vinny wouldn't be back until lunchtime at the very earliest. "Besides", Charlene continued huskily, "you haven't got a cat-in hells-chance of getting a penny because, as you obviously already know, Vinny is not the current owner and the sale will be completed by Tuesday, no matter what you do."

Disappointment deflated Lyn's strong resolve but she was determined not to let it show. She was intrigued, not only by what Charlene had just said – regarding the sudden change of time frame for the sale – but by the state of her body. In the light of the upstairs kitchen, Lyn could see that it wasn't just a sore throat that was responsible for Charlene's absence in the shop. Her face had taken a hefty blow down the right side; swelling and discolouration was already present, but within twenty-four hours it would be black and blue. Her ankle had no signs of injury but it was obviously painful each time her weight bore down on that side. And curiosity got the better of her as Charlene kept her right hand concealed in her dressing gown pocket. Trying her best to sound friendly, Lyn said

"What've you been up to? You look like you've done three rounds with a heavy-weight. I'm waiting for Vinny anyway so we might as well have a cuppa; you want one?" No answer. Lyn decided it was time to pull out all the stops and dip into her own pot of wily cunning, which out of necessity, had deepened over the last few days.

After making tea for them both; Lyn studied Charlene through the fragrant steam of the brew.

"Show me your hand Charlene." Lyn's directness left her no alternative and as the bruised and badly swollen hand was placed between them Lyn felt her anger boil over. A packet of frozen peas was draped over the wrist whilst Lyn went in search of a crepe bandage. The careful administering of help paid off. Charlene answered all but one of Lyn's veiled questions. She also agreed to follow Lyn's advice (which contained a financial incentive) to disappear out of Vinny's life forever.

Sitting behind the counter of the reopened shop Lyn mulled over the latest revelations; whilst Charlene's offset-footsteps could be heard moving from room to room as she gathered her possessions. Charlene's injuries were superficial but the damage inflicted on her pride ran deep; and sensing the strong desire for revenge, Lyn coaxed her in the direction where it would hurt Vinny the most.

At least she now knew the connecting link between Vinny and James Fairbank. Charlene hadn't needed to give the name or the address of the solicitor, who was to be drawn unwittingly into parting with a beautiful Georgian property, (at way below market value). Lyn couldn't decide which bothered her most; James Fairbank being ripped off, although he deserved it for not trusting Lyn with the identity of his expected new tenant, or, a slob like Vinny, taking possession of the room with the beautiful view.

At the sound of the shop door opening, Lyn greeted the second customer in half an hour who, in stark contrast to Elsie Wilson, asked for the cheapest bunch of flowers available.

"It's only for the cemetery, shame really to waste good money on the dead," had been intimated from both of the young women. Was this a diminishing lack of respect for the dead, or an increased absence of income in these recessionary times? Whatever the reason, Lyn hoped with all her heart that she wouldn't have too long to wait for the inevitable confrontation with Vinny.

Charlene smiled as she wandered from room to room gathering her belongings which she knew would fit comfortably into the one suitcase. She'd moved many times since her sixteenth birthday and staying with her cousin in Bristol would serve her purpose perfectly. The long awaited text message had signalled her acceptance to a position she'd dreamed of for months. By mid-January, when everyone else – including Vinny the brute and Lynda the stuck-up cow – were freezing to death in this God-forsaken country, Charlene would be part of an elite team on a luxury cruise liner – employed as personal trainer to the rich and famous.

Going along with Lyn Porter's little scheme was an added bonus which would place a further £5,000 into savings that were growing by the day; in spite of the miniscule amount of interest that building societies were paying these days. The stupid woman mistook Charlene's condition to be entirely down to Vinny; unenlightened of the fall in the shower that had caused the painful ankle and bruising to her face. Vinny's little escapade the night before was nothing compared to the abuse her step-father had meted out. There was no doubting that Vinny would return, full of apologies and loaded down with cheap gifts. Visualising the look on his face when confronted by Lyn Porter instead, made her want to break out laughing; but Charlene found safety in resisting this natural urge.

Vinny was in a good mood as he walked back to the shop carrying a plastic bag concealing a box of milk chocolates and a bottle of white wine – both had been on special offer and both could be enjoyed that evening as he cuddled up to Charlene on the sofa and watched a saucy film.

He'd woken early that morning feeling famished and finding Charlene still fast asleep in her own bed, decided on the mile and a half walk to the harbour café for a man-sized fry-up. Carl wouldn't be about for a couple of hours yet, so Vinny had bought a newspaper, something he'd taken to doing more and more lately. A serious businessman had to keep his eye on the ball; and he could tell that Carl was impressed when he saw him with a newspaper tucked under his arm. Plus, a paper was a handy tool for keeping chatterboxes away.

The paper had been filled with negative stories about the sorry state of the economy, the rising unemployed and the devastating amount of repossessions. Several old farts had the cheek to interrupt Vinny, adding their unwanted opinions as to what they thought the government ought to do to the out-of-control financiers. Vinny had nodded just to shut 'em up. Secretly he didn't give a damn about the collapse of the banking system; for the first time in his life *he* would have the wherewithal to put himself firmly on the road to making lots of money, and he had the credit-crunch and his best mate Carl to thank for it.

He'd hung around the Gym for over half an hour before catching sight of Carl's lean, muscular body when he'd peered through the port holes of the 'aqua room'. Not wanting to be coaxed into joining him in the swimming pool, Vinny had hung about a little longer until his friend had emerged fresh and rosy-faced through the double swinging doors, bringing with him the smell of chlorinated air.

"Vinny, my man, thanks for last night what can I do you for?" Vinny envied Carl's relaxed easy confidence and was happy to be seen in the company of this popular banker who had taught him so much about the easy way to make money; provided you had a commanding address and the right-sounding company name. But he was starting to feel impatient and bored with the waiting.

"You sure that letter went out to Fairbank yesterday, I mean he should be feeling his balls being squeezed as we speak, has he been in touch with the bank this morning?"

"Hey, cool it man don't be such a prole, it's Saturday, the professional class think before they act; like I explained last night, ring him Monday morning, tell him you got someone else interested in the shop and you want to complete by close of business on Tuesday. By the time you've got the money, Fairbank will have had his repossession notice, and will be more than grateful to accept your offer and save his reputation. By this time next week, I'll have finished drawing up the paperwork for V.C. Enterprises, and you will be deciding on the colour scheme of your new home."

Reassured by Carl's confidence, Vinny whistled the rest of the way home whilst toying with the idea of keeping Charlene on board for a while longer.

Chapter 9

Saturday Afternoon

Boredom and frustration ejected Lyn once again from her seat behind the counter.

Charlene had left over an hour ago. Strict instructions were given, as to how and when Lyn would be in touch, and the dire consequences she'd suffer if she went back on her word and contacted Vinny,

Since serving the two hard up women, Lyn had had only one customer. A mealy-mouthed, well-spoken, middle-aged man, had spent ten minutes advising Lyn on the state of the economy, how unfortunate it was that his parent's 'ruby' wedding-anniversary should fall at such a time and how he thought that flowers, on the whole, were such a waste of money

"Let's get to the point shall we", Lyn had cut in, fed up with his moaning and groaning. "How much do you want to spend on flowers for your parent's big day?"

"I'd like to spend £10 but I'll run to £15 if I must."

Exasperated, Lyn had handed him two bunches of appropriately-coloured dahlias, three sprigs of fern and a strip of burgundy, satin ribbon; then told him that £15 wouldn't cover the cost of arranging them. He'd silently walked out of her sight, cradling his £15 worth as though it were a new-born babe.

Looking through the order book for the third time added nothing to the information already gleaned. The flower-room was well stocked but orders were almost non-existent; unless the computer held a new spread sheet that she couldn't access. She'd tried the obvious routes, but gave up when her head had begun to throb.

Her boredom came to an abrupt end when the flower shop door opened and Vinny stood on the threshold looking totally confused. His responses to the unusual had never been that quick but after several seconds of total silence Lyn felt compelled to break his shocked silence.

"Business has been very quiet for a Saturday morning Vinny; or should I call you Victor? And I can't understand your reasoning behind holding all this stock, unless it's to impress the prospective new owner – should he happen by."

Vinny's mouth clamped shut and then opened in a snarl as he hollered for Charlene, brushing Lyn aside as he headed for the back staircase. She heard his heavy frame moving between the few upper rooms calling her name over and over again and when it was made clear to him that Charlene and her belongings had vanished he returned, panting with rage.

"Where is she, what the fuck have you done with her?" He spat the words into Lyn's face as she involuntarily took a step back, realising too late that this very act would only add to his inflated sense of power over her. Remembering him as a spotty-faced, weak-bodied youth, gave her the courage to retake that all important ground. Particularly, as her knee was positioned in such a way, that if necessary, she could send it with great force to his most vulnerable area.

"She's in a safe house and the address, as you know, is kept secret from the partners and spouses of battered women." Any threat to Lyn subsided for a minute as Vinny took in her words, then, moving deftly out of range from Lyn's knee, he grabbed her by the wrist and demanded again Charlene's whereabouts.

"Is breaking women's wrists a favourite hobby of yours Vinny? I have to say it was a bit short-sighted of you to disable the very hand that you need to sign over the shop to John Haydon." She could see that at last the penny was very slowly beginning to clang home. She wriggled easily from his sweaty grasp. "I know everything there is to know about you and your banker friend's scam; I'm here to retrieve what's rightfully mine, Vinny, and you're in deep shit if I don't get it."

Grabbing the two large bunches of yellow roses that she'd put together whilst waiting for Vinny's return, Lyn left him to calm down, saying she'd be back in an hour to discuss retrieving her money in a businesslike manner. His loud, aggressive voice stopped her as she opened the shop door.

"How the fuck did you get in here?"

"Like I said, see you within the hour, changing the locks is not an option Vinny, if *you* want this sale to go ahead, *I* want what's due to me."

Her own keys were tucked back inside her purse; and Charlene's, the distinguished bunch she held up to him with a provocative little wave, were then concealed in her jacket pocket. Lyn remembered the verbal struggle she'd gone through to get Charlene to part with them. Even though she'd seemed eager to go and never return, Lyn never quite trusted her. But the threat, of laying all Lyn's gained information, at Charlene's door was enough, she felt sure, to keep her off the scene until she returned from London.

The cloak of bravado fell from Lyn's shoulders as she entered the peaceful confines of the cemetery and headed for Gran's memorial stone. There was a time when Lyn would visit 'Gran's Spot' on a weekly basis, keeping it weed-free and supplied with fresh flowers. That was before she found the two mysterious letters. If the first house clearance firm hadn't let her down, she would never have found them. Desperation, due to a greedy landlord threatening to charge Lyn full rent if she didn't clear 'the junk', drove her to hiring a van and a man, neither of which were efficient. Since then, she'd found it difficult to continue the one-way discussions that so many of her customers had advised as a way to ease bereavement. With a hint of shame, Lyn realised that it was nearly three months since her last visit and all thoughts were put on hold whilst she worked hard, returning the small patch of consecrated ground to respectability.

Vinny felt compelled to lock-up. How the hell could he be expected to serve whining old biddies with bunches of cheap flowers during a crisis like this. Twice he'd picked up the phone, only to replace it as he dashed to the loo, the worry of what Carl would say, loosening the contents of his bowels. Deciding to play it cool and wait to see what the frigid cow could actually do to upset their plans; he turned on the telly and poured himself a chilled beer, knowing that Saturday afternoon football, would take his mind off everything.

Returning 'Gran's Spot' to respectability hadn't taken Lyn as long as she'd expected; but the emotional link that had once allowed her to communicate her thoughts to Gran was still broken. Maybe after next week she would know the answers to several questions, or maybe, there'll be no answers just more questions. Her head began to hurt from the pressure of all the imminent problems to be dealt with. Reading a few epitaphs on her way over to the far side of the cemetery sobered her thoughts.

Martin's resting place always looked neat. The last time it was visited, was four days before Sarah's wedding. The two of them had planted a three inch high, heather in the far right-hand corner of the granite chippings which filled the enclosed, marked grave. Sarah had wanted to offer her father something that would last longer than the cut flowers, which usually died within hours of arranging. Lyn had suggested the heather, knowing that it was the only plant to survive the harsh elements of this particular plot. Sarah had agreed enthusiastically, remembering the tales her father had told her of heather-carpeted hills in places he loved to visit and climb.

The chippings were weed-free and the heather was triple in size with clusters of tiny mauve flowers smothering its surface. Martin hated clutter, and it was more from luck than judgement, that this spot, one of the highest and most exposed in the cemetery, had turned out to be so perfectly suited.

Knowing they wouldn't last long but doing it anyway, Lyn arranged the sunshine-coloured roses in a curving spray across the cold, grey granite; pressing the last one to her lips before carefully laying it in place. Resting back on her heels, she read the simple epitaph, and wondered if by the next anniversary, she could finally confront the guilt.

Martin Porter
1959 – 1999
Loved By All Who Knew Him

With time to spare and a stomach that needed satisfying Lyn decided to grab a bite to eat in the only place where she could keep a watchful eye on the comings and goings of Vinny. Sitting at the same table that she'd occupied two days earlier, Lyn ordered a tuna salad. In stark contrast to her previous visit, the young, Polish waitress, who took the order, was cheerful and courteous. From where Lyn sat, the florist opposite looked dowdy and desolate. Pangs of nostalgia infiltrated her memories as she recalled Beryl's words while setting up the outside trestle table and filling it to capacity with the most colourful and sweetest-smelling flowers.

"They won't be able to resist 'em, Lyn. When women's lives are filled with boredom and drudgery, one whiff of a lovely, sweet-smelling flower, and they're transported to a better place. If only men realised – and to be fair, some do – women would be like putty in their hands if they were kept supplied with flowers – and of course a bit of the other."

The tuna salad arrived and Lyn ate it absentmindedly whilst concentrating on the florist. The 'Open' sign was clearly visible, although two people had pushed on the door then walked away confused at not being able to enter, Lyn had long ago given up on the workings of Vinny's business acumen. But even if only for the sake of appearances and the saving of the perishable stock, he'd be wise to make some effort at keeping things turning over; especially as he'd been offered such a good price for a business that was, after all, in a secondary position.

Confident with the stranglehold she held on Vinny's imminent plans and convinced he wasn't going to enlighten her any further for the time being, Lyn hammered one more time on the locked and bolted shop door, knowing that he was still skulking somewhere inside.

Part of the money she'd invested in this business was supposed to have been spent on installing a separate entrance to the above apartment. The extra outlay involved, would easily be recouped in the added value to the property, by allowing the above space to be rented out separately. But that, along with finance for incorporating chilling facilities for the summer months when cut flowers died prematurely, had never happened. Beryl would have turned in her grave, (had she not been cremated and scattered on the ocean; a very moving though unusual final request from a soul who had derived such pleasure from nature's solid earth).

Earlier, whilst rooting around under the shop counter, Lyn had found the framed picture of her and Beryl that used to hang in the shop. It had been shoved carelessly at the back of a drawer. Vinny had insisted on removing it when Beryl died and Lyn had presumed he wanted it in the apartment; a reminder of his wonderful aunt and her generous bequest. This was the only photograph she'd ever seen of Beryl; and it saddened her now, thinking of the lost opportunity of slipping it into her bag.

Sadness continued as Lyn wandered around the town centre area, worryingly counting off several more businesses that had folded in the last month. The atmosphere in every shop she wandered through was impregnated with fear and anxiety at the thought that they too could be next in line. It was after all, the middle of Saturday afternoon; peak spending time for most town centre shops; but glancing around, you could see that people weren't parting with their money. Rain started to fall and grateful that she still carried the solicitor's umbrella, Lyn headed up the steep incline away from the town.

Just like Floral Occasions, James Fairbank's premises was closed; the rain making it seem less welcoming with the front door locked, barring the way to the sheltering porch behind. She pictured his green penetrating eyes, brightened with laughter as he enjoyed the celebratory day with his nephew and remembered that he too was a victim of the credit crunch – and soon to be an unsuspecting victim of V.C. Enterprises.

The match had been crap. Both teams had played like a bunch of girls – whining and calling 'foul' at the slightest knock – and not a single goal was scored between them. Vinny pressed the 'off' button with more force than was necessary then turned his mind back to the dilemma of finding out the whereabouts of Charlene.

He'd never been completely comfortable with handing

over his business to her, even though it was in name only, but Carl had assured him that this was the only way to safeguard maximum funds from the sale. Christ, Carl would think he was a right twat if he couldn't sort out his own domestic problems. He had until Tuesday to find Charlene and persuade her, by whatever means, to sign on the dotted line. This would be far less costly, and more satisfying than pandering to the likes of Lyn Porter.

After making sure that the alarm was set, Vinny set out to the one place where he could focus all his attention – pumping iron at the gym – hoping that he wouldn't run into Carl or Lyn Porter before he'd had a chance to plan his next move.

Chapter 10

Saturday Evening

The telephone rang three times before it was picked up with a heavy sigh from Matt. Conversation halted and all eyes turned in the direction from where the intruding noise originated. Minutes passed in silence whilst Matt, listening attentively, did nothing more than slightly shake his head, before confirming to the caller that he'd be there in ten minutes.

"Darling, this is the third time in a week that you've been called out, I'm sure there's more than one anaesthetist in the whole hospital." Helen knew she sounded peevish, but the hope of an uninterrupted evening in the company of the three most important males in her life, had been dashed. "Remember Jack's birthday tomorrow! Surely they'll take you 'off call' for that, won't they?"

"Helen, there's been a nasty accident on the A38 involving a coach. There are children involved; and who knows, some of them may never reach their next birthday. All available doctors are being called in and I don't know how long I'll be away." Before disappearing out of his comfortable, sitting room Matt kissed his wife, brushing aside her humbled apology. James stood to receive the firm, warm handshake of his brother-in-law, who thanked him once again, for giving his son a day to remember. Relieved that Jack was safely at home, Matt wrapped his arms around his son's slight frame, and promised he'd see him sometime during the next day.

On hearing the front door close, Helen glanced at her brother with a resigned look and disappeared into the kitchen; closely followed by James with offers of help to clear and clean the remnants of the wonderful meal they'd all just enjoyed.

"Jack looks exhausted, he was awake with excitement hours before you arrived, would you mind doing the honours while I fill the dishwasher?"

"I hope you realise dear sister that I've got the best end of the deal, Jack will be asleep before I'm two lines into a story, but I have to warn you, I won't be down until all clattering has ceased and my glass of wine has been topped up."

Jack wasn't the slightest bit interested in a story of make-believe, nor did it seem, he was exhausted. When James entered his bedroom, he was already in pyjamas and swore on his honour that his teeth had been brushed. The wide awake concentration on his rosy-cheeked face, as he scanned the pages of 'Fossils of the Jurassic Coast' – an early birthday gift from James which accompanied a small geological hammer was a delight to see. The day, though tiring had been a great success, and the proceeds from their joint efforts lay lovingly on a piece of white kitchen tissue on Jack's duvet-covered knees.

"I've already found a picture of this ammonite Uncle

James, look!" And James kicked off his shoes and climbed aboard the soft raft, recollecting with joy the day's adventure.

It was forty minutes later, after promising a further trip during his next school holiday that James succeeded in persuaded his nephew to close the book and lie down. Within two minutes Jack was fast asleep.

Helen smiled knowingly as she handed James a freshly-poured glass of chilled Australian Chardonnay. "Thank you for today James, he's been so looking forward to it, I hope tomorrow won't be an anti-climax for him."

"Helen, Matt has his job to do; it doesn't mean he'd rather be there than here with you and Jack. I know Father wasn't around sometimes for our birthdays, which cut deep with you, but at the end of the day he loved us and *his* hard work provided *our* education."

The silence that followed was misinterpreted by each sibling. Helen was feverishly wondering if she could reschedule the next day's plans; but given the amount of people involved, gave up on the idea. James's thoughts were of a much more serious nature. Before leaving that morning, he'd made the mistake of opening the one letter that his postman, John, had thrust into his hand, accompanied with his jovial, "have a nice weekend." He knew the sender, there was a pile of similar envelopes concealed in his desk drawer; he also knew what the letter was bound to contain – the threat of it was made plain in the same pile of letters, concealed in his desk drawer. How simple life would be, if, by hiding what was unpleasant and unwanted we could just walk away and forget they ever existed. James had been reared to face up to whatever life offered and as he still held total respect for both of his parents, although his father had died years ago, he'd calmly slit the top of the envelope and proceeded to read the few lines of neatly typed words.

Dear Mr Fairbank,
After repeated requests to set an appointment, in order to discuss a way forward in meeting the large debts incurred against the above property; we have no alternative but to serve a repossession order which will take effect ten days from the above date.

There had been more; a few lines to soften and render the severity of the content down to more friendly terms, but unlike the above, James hadn't committed them to memory. A gentle squeeze on the shoulder from Helen lifted James from the unpleasant recollection.

"I've got the spare room ready; you will stay over won't you?" Helen knew James would never drink and drive; he'd already agreed to stay the night whilst drinking wine with dinner, but she wanted to talk, she needed to talk and James seemed so preoccupied since her childish show of insecurity.

"How's your love-life Helen?" They both smiled. Since they'd been teenagers – James, the oldest by two years – they had always confided in each other and this closeness had remained, helping to balance each others weaknesses, and learn from each others strengths.

"Matt wants me to think again about sending Jack off to a school, where his chances of gaining a good education increase by tenfold; what do you think of that?" Helen returned to her seat opposite James; and in the glow of the nearby table-lamp, he noticed for the first time how tired she looked and how that tiredness added several years to a face that once seemed immune from the rigours of life.

"Seems an understandable request given that the schools in this area are pretty good, and by your own admission, work isn't easy to come by thanks to 'the credit crunch'. At the light-hearted mention of the last three words and James's two index fingers wriggling up above his head, Helen's returned smile wiped away some of those added years and lifted the atmosphere to a more harmonious level.

"With Jack away at school, I'd be free to work full time without any of the annoying late-starts and early-finishes that I know the rest of my colleagues resent. It's not easy being the only woman with a young child in a male-dominated firm. I've worked long and hard to get to where I am James, if I'm ousted at the next inevitable shake-up, we'll be left surviving on Matt's salary." She reached for her glass needing a few moments respite from James's searching eyes. "Like most professions," she continued without looking at him directly, "there are too many architects chasing ever diminishing assignments."

The worry lines returned and James realised how much of a bone of contention this must be between his sister and her husband. Matt, fortunately would never be without work and his salary alone, would be more than enough to keep a family of three; but this wasn't the time to voice this simple truth. Helen needed to fathom her own insecurities and realise what an enviable position she was in.

"And how is this awful recession affecting *you* James; has

your new tenant moved in yet?" Eager to move out of the limelight and take her turn as cross-examiner, Helen nestled comfortably into the cushion behind her and looked directly into her brother's vivid green eyes; prepared for: light-hearted banter, colour schemes, furniture style and all the latest information on the fortunate new tenant who would reside in his lovely place. After emitting a heavy sigh, James enlightened his sister and recounted the developments of the past few days.

"What will you do?" she asked in a small voice, feeling ashamed and close to tears.

"I'll arrange a meeting with my bank manager; tell him there's still the chance of a tenant, and try to secure more time. That's all I can do." James hoped that her question was fully answered and they could now move on to more pleasant subjects.

"How is Mother? I haven't seen her since last month, shall *I* drive over and pick her up tomorrow."

"Oh that would be a great help James. You know, *she's* got money tucked away, and she wouldn't want to see you in such a tight..." She was cut off in mid-sentence.

"No Helen! Promise me that what I've told you won't be mentioned or hinted at to anyone, except Matt of course. Mother may need every penny she's got, including the proceeds from her house, if her illness deteriorates further."

The telephone rang and Helen leapt up to answer it knowing that at this late hour it could only be Matt. Her face was turned away from James but her stance portrayed the tension as she silently listened. Suddenly her body visibly relaxed.

"Darling that's wonderful news, see you about midnight, of course I don't mind waiting up, James and I have a lot of catching up to do." She relayed Matt's side of the conversation to her brother, happy with relief that no one was too seriously injured in the coach crash. Several people, including two children were being admitted, but none of their injuries were life-threatening. "Who is Lyn? You mentioned her three times in your sorry tale, how does she fit into it all?" Helen knew she'd caught him off-guard, she also knew he was compelled to answer – an unwritten rule stemming from their teenage confidences.

"She worked in the shop that John Haydon's buying; the florist down by the cemetery." James had forgotten how tenacious his sister became at the mention of a female's name. After his divorce; he was subjected to dozens of match-making dinner-invitation, until on the last occasion he made a point of standing to announce that he'd finally found the courage to admit that he wasn't interested in women any more. He had to bear the discomfort of Helen, Matt and the latest prospective match – a woman whose name he couldn't recall – but his claim did have the desired effect; no more invitations to make up a foursome were issued.

"Ah, that Lyn! The Lyn you had a crush on for ages until the fat lady who owned the shop put a flea in your ear." Helen couldn't stop herself from laughing at the memory of her brother in his mid-twenties, finding any excuse to buy flowers just so that he could ogle a woman who was already spoken for. James found his face growing hot and colouring at the memories that Helen had a knack of retaining. He had spent weeks plucking up the courage to ask the pretty florist's assistant out, but before he got the chance, 'Big Beryl' – affectionately named for miles around – confronted him on his final visit.

"Don't think that your custom isn't appreciated son, but I think it only fair to warn you that my assistant is happily married with a child on the way." James remembered colouring bright red on that occasion too.

"Is she still married or are you in with a chance, mind you, her prospects can't be good if the shop's being sold, speaking of which, why would John Haydon be interested in such a grotty place?" James gave up, knowing full well that he'd be badgered into answering, in detail, every point to her question; although he had to admit he didn't know all the answers.

"The most curious thing about Lyn, who incidentally, has been widowed for nine years;" at this point James heard Helen's sharp intake of breath; "the first time we met, and this was only a few days ago, she was beside herself with worry over her mounting debts and no prospects of settling them. Twenty-four hours later, her whole demeanour had changed; although her circumstances, as far as I could tell, remained just as dire."

"You sound like two of a kind to me; invite her over I'll find out all you need to know. I'm a past master at winkling out harboured secrets."

Helen left James to his own thoughts whilst she prepared a coffee tray in the adjoining, spacious kitchen – a kitchen which she had designed along with the rest of the conversions. She loved this house; fell in love with it the moment she'd stepped over the threshold fifteen years ago, although it now bore no resemblance to the typical Devon farmhouse it was back then. She remembered clearly breezing from room to room, visualising the potential of each given space. The location was perfect – close enough for both her and Matt to drive to their work in Exeter, but quiet enough, with two acres of lush greenery surrounding the house, to give the illusion that you were living in the deepest heart of lush, Devon countryside.

Coupled with working full-time, the conversions had taken nearly seven years, and a whole stack of money, to complete. After which, both Matt and Helen, mindful of her ticking, biological clock, began in earnest to produce the family they'd hitherto dreamed of. Jack was conceived easily; but the obvious joy that this news brought to the wider family was tainted seven months into Helen's pregnancy by the sudden massive heart-attack that struck down their father.

Her grieving, compounded with guilt that her father would never hold the grandchild he'd longed for, affected her for a long time. Well-meaning friends and family insisted that once the child was born, the joy of a new life would heal the devastation of her loss.

Even with paid assistance, Helen found the first eighteen months of motherhood very hard to cope with. The sleepless nights, the loss of one's own personality to satisfy every need and whim of another human being day on day, nearly drove her mad. The worst thing of all, at this point in her sad reminiscences, she looked about her with a sigh of relief, the very worst thing was coping with all the extra paraphernalia that one small baby needed. Sterilizing units, hoards of plastic bottles, teats and cups cluttered up her kitchen; great bundles of disposable nappies threatened to take over and spilled out from the nursery and the hallway seemed to be constantly choked with, buggy, car seat or push-along toys. As Jack grew she had to impose more and more rules on keeping toys out of the lounge and passing on items to allow space for new ones.

Their original plan was to have a second child within two to three years of the first – before reaching her fortieth birthday – but the few tentative discussions on the subject had always been scuppered by Helen. There had seemed no point in time where she was ready to face that ordeal again and at forty-seven, it was now, thankfully, too late.

James relaxed back into the plush, black leather armchair. Tensions had subsided and Helen's plans were back on track; the father of the 'birthday-boy 'could resume his rightful role as co-organiser to the twenty-eight expected guests. A large marquee had been set up in the garden, complete with every convenience including free-standing heaters – heaven forbid that a hoard of ten year olds should be given free reign to run wild over Helen's show-case to her talent – and she is very talented, James thought fondly, remembering her tenacious, up-hill struggle to prove it. Her innovative ideas on the positive use of space, had gained her several prestigious awards over the years; her greatest, in James's opinion, was what he called her 'under-floor' office.

Determined to keep her head, and fingers, firmly on the pulse in her progressive field whilst rearing a family, Helen had created a fold-away-drawing-office at home by using the space beneath the split level flooring of their large open-plan, ground-floor space. With well-honed foresight and flawless planning, the lowering of the whole floor area was done right at the beginning of the conversions, before she and Matt had moved in. The time and the cost of the necessary excavations for this were immense; putting a strain on their joint funding (and, as James recalled, their relationship.) But throughout the very turbulent months, Helen had remained calm and focussed. Matt had held a surprise party on its completion; and it was at this party, that one of the senior partners of a rival Design Group, nominated her for an award of the highest endorsement. Six months later, with this prestigious award bearing a woman's name for the first time and Helen accepting the offer of junior partner for the rival Design Group, she had found plenty of opportunities to use her innovation on maximising space.

James still had in his possession a glossy magazine, showing in detail, how the under-floor office operated. Sectional, front panels of the steps to the higher floor level, lifted and cleverly slid back onto grooved runners; exposing the cavernous storage-space within. A1 size drawing boards, easels, files and folders, laptop and even an easily assembled desk; all could be easily stored and withdrawn – on wheeled platforms – to be set up in the light and airy space which doubled as extra lounge area. Masterfully executed in solid, natural oak with two large muted-coloured rugs, strategically placed, to soften and add a hint of homeliness; it never failed to engender, that all-important 'wow' factor.

Allowing his thoughts to wander, James compared the differences between his sister's home and Lyn's. Both were tastefully contemporary in style although each building had existed for at least a hundred years; Lyn's end-of-terrace, Victorian town house was much lower down the property ladder than Helen's country dwelling, but in all honesty, he preferred the cosy ambience of the former. The arrival of brandy and coffee, just as the nearby church announced through resonating peels that it was now ten o'clock, cut off his pleasant meandering of the previous evening.

"What a load of shit." Vinny shut off the television and poured himself another beer. How was a guy supposed to think straight when a bunch of toffee-nosed women kept filling his space with their catty remarks? The film had been on since eight o'clock, and because it contained 'Devil' in the title; and because he'd read snippets about how good a film it was; and because Vinny was convinced, because of the aforementioned, that it was bound to contain some sex or violence, he'd carried on watching for two hours, hoping to give his mind a break from the emotional turmoil he'd suffered since lunchtime.

After the run-in with Lyn Porter he'd spent hours trying to find out where Charlene was. His first visit to the Gym in the early afternoon told him one thing only – Charlene wasn't there and hadn't been since she left their employ. He had been hoping to squeeze information from Sandy, the receptionist who had worked opposite shifts to Charlene, but the frosty female on the desk at the time told him that Sandy was off-duty till six.

Several times he'd been tempted to phone Carl, only to chicken out at the last minute, knowing that he didn't like being contacted at the weekend unless it was an emergency. To Vinny, this was the worst kind of emergency, but instincts told him he needed to sort it alone. Searching the flat and the shop had produced nothing; he'd even turned on the computer, glared at the multi-coloured images before him and decided against proceeding any further; five frustrating minutes were spent trying to turn the damn thing off, until eventually, after pulling all the plugs Vinny stormed out of the shop and slammed the door.

His return to the Gym at six hadn't got him any closer to finding Charlene. In desperation, he'd pressed a twenty-quid note into Sandy's warm, chubby hand as an incentive to checking Charlene's file for telephone numbers of next-of-kin. There was only one – her Mother – and *she* hadn't seen nor heard from her daughter in over eighteen months; and from the tone of her voice, she couldn't care less if she never set eyes on her again. Having tucked the twenty-pound note safely in her pocket, Sandy had helpfully suggested that Vinny try her mobile.

"She's never had a bloody mobile," he'd said with an involuntary thump of his fist on the counter, "gave her bad headaches or something." Vinny was growing tired of the cat and mouse malarkey and there was no way he was going to hand over more cash without a definite result. He'd turned to go but was stopped in his tracks by Sandy's casual remark.

"It never bothered her using her mobile when she worked here." Two long strides had brought him back to within inches of Sandy's pink-cheeked, smiling face which had altered to a frown when Vinny squeezed her arm.

"What's her number?" he'd demanded after reaching for the pen and a piece of advertising blurb from the counter, hoping that at last he'd found the answer to his prayer.

"I don't know her number, she was always very secretive about it; but I would have thought that you, being her boss or partner or whatever you are would know it, and stop squeezing my arm, it bloody hurts." Sandy had pulled free and walked along the counter to deal with a list of outstanding requests from her immediate boss; leaving Vinny feeling more frustrated than ever.

Chapter 11

Sunday Morning

Lyn threw back the covers with fierce determination. She'd heard and read many times about the so-called 'crossroads' of life but never any mention of staggered junctions. Part of her wanted to return to the ways of just a few months ago; back then, she'd felt comfortable with her life and where it was heading. Trouble was, too many things had happened, especially in the last few days, and deep down she knew that returning to those old ways was impossible. Today was to be spent preparing for the rest of her life. Amidst the devastating worry, the erosion of self-esteem and the corrupt behaviour of a former colleague, she had been given the opportunity to better her life and only she could make it happen.

On returning home the previous evening, a message from James Fairbank had waited all day to be heard. A sense of warm regard contained in the message, had helped to brighten Lyn's evening and quell the rising sense of foreboding that had dogged her since her confrontation with Vinny. She'd played the message four times – making sure innuendo wasn't lurking behind the good wishes – but still hadn't deleted it; and even now in the cold light of early morning she couldn't quite bring herself to press the 'delete' button.

After a hearty breakfast of scrambled eggs, bacon and toast Lyn set about organising and prioritising her day. Besides the usual domestic chores, two major tasks needed to be completed today. One physical, the digging over and clearing of the growing beds of her back garden – an arduous task, but one that would give mind and emotions a complete rest, as well as cancelling out the shame and guilt she'd felt about it's neglected state.

The other, which involved lots of mental planning and would be better done first – especially as the breakfast still weighed heavy in her stomach and the air outside would still be uninvitingly cold –was to carefully pack her suitcase for the week ahead.

Two hours later, desperate for a cup of tea but refusing to succumb until this all-important task had been completed, Lyn thumped down the stairs wielding the strapped up suitcase which weighed twenty kilos but felt more like thirty. Again she went to cancel James's message but found her finger pressing play instead of delete. While she listened again to his captivating voice she manoeuvred the suitcase to one side of the hallway, placing the train ticket on top, all ready for boarding a taxi next morning.

Vinny looked across the road to the spruced up café, where several people sat drinking coffee and reading their Sunday papers. Funny, he'd never noticed before that the café opened on Sundays. They must be desperate for the money, he thought, as he turned from the bedroom window of his flat; remembering with a shudder how he used to be dragged from his bed on Sundays for the sake of selling a few bunches of flowers to the old codgers visiting the cemetery. "But not anymore" he said aloud to the empty room as he slipped into his running suit.

The frustration and worry about his plans being torn to shreds by Charlene's disappearance had stayed with him throughout the restless night. Then, as if by magic, the answer came to him unbidden in the creeping light of dawn. Lyn Porter knew where Charlene was and *he* knew where Lyn Porter lived. He'd pay her a visit at lunchtime, and catch her off-guard. Pleased with his brilliant plan, Vinny decided to run several miles before returning for a late breakfast – maybe he'd give the café opposite a bit of business.

For the first half an hour, Lyn almost gave up and abandoned the laborious work of clearing her overgrown flowerbed. Normally for this job, she would choose a more conducive time of year; when the air was warmer and the soil more compliant to giving up its weeds. But, because she'd been idle and let the autumn months sail by without lifting a finger, and the spring months seemed like an age away, she battled on. With willpower garnered, it wasn't long before her fingers tingled with welcome warmth and the irritating dripping from her nose dried up; allowing her to take pleasure from the scents of the earth as each perennial, deep-rooted weed was extracted.

A robin, eager to retrieve the fat, wriggling worms that appeared on each turn of the fork, kept Lyn entertained as she cleared and broke down the compacted soil. Halfway through the fifteen-square-metre bed, Lyn straightened her stiffening back and decided to have a break. Kicking off her earth-laden boots at the back door, her attention was caught by the sweet trill of the robin perched cheekily on the fork handle, awaiting her return.

From the kitchen window, the effort of Lyn's labour was clearly visible. A large pile of weeds – being meticulously picked over by her feathered-friend – and a smooth, sooty-black carpet of soil, contrasting sharply with the scruffy neglect of the remaining fifty per cent, gladdened her heart and brought forth her own attempt at whistling. Suddenly a more intrusive sound cut through the rising sing of the kettle and Lyn's attempt at mimicking the robin. The sound repeated; this time for longer and seemingly more insistent. Lyn realised with panic that it was her doorbell and the only person it could possibly be, was James Fairbank – eager to convey his wishes in person. Preoccupied with how she must look, Lyn brushed herself down before opening the door.

Before she knew quite what was happening, Vinny had pushed past her, kicking the front door closed behind him.

"Sorry about yesterday Lyn, had a bit of business to attend to, but I'm all ears now for that little chat you wanted." Vinny's eyes fell on the strapped up suitcase. "Off on a nice little holiday Lyn? Hope you're heading for somewhere warmer than here"

Feeling completely flummoxed, Lyn told him that she was off to visit Sarah in Ireland. She started to add that it was none of his damned business where she was heading; but before she had chance to finish, the kettle sent out a loud, piercing demand. Lyn scurried back to the kitchen; giving Vinny the perfect opportunity to gain valuable information.

"I'd love a cup of tea Lyn, two sugars in case you don't remember," shouted Vinny, relishing his opportunity. He'd seen the train ticket obligingly positioned on the suitcase. Using Lyn's pen, he scribbled down the time, the destination and the reserved seat number. He tore this gathered information from her pad; disguising the noise by shouting

"Can't smell a roast cooking Lyn, always thought of you as a traditionalist." On returning the ticket, it annoyingly slipped behind the suitcase and as Vinny bent to retrieve it, his nose almost touched the small, flashing, red light of the answering machine.

What's he doing out there? Lyn thought as she feverously tried to make tea whilst listening to sounds buried beneath Vinny's cocky voice. She didn't have to wait long for an answer. James's calm voice filled the hallway.

"How dare you!" Lyn shouted, as she ran to defend what was for her ears only; but Vinny was determined and his strong arms held her back as the play button was pressed again.

"*Good morning Lyn, I'm sorry to have missed you or maybe you're still sleeping, having been disturbed in the night by the storm. As you know, I'll be away until Monday morning and… I really wanted to wish you a safe trip to London and hope that your weeks stay there will help to sort out some of your misgivings. I am sorry that our little get-together yesterday evening didn't help much, and hope that this lack on my part, won't affect the chance of us becoming friends. Remember you still have my umbrella so…*"

Thankfully, as far as Lyn was concerned, the message ended abruptly, just as it had done each time she'd played it. Most people's messages were short and speedily executed and never before had she found the recording time on her machine to be inadequate. On each previous occasion, the abrupt, inconclusive finish had frustrated, her, but not now. James would have finished the message with his name; and more than anything else, she wanted to keep her connection to him from Vinny the Con.

The joy and satisfaction that accompanied the earlier gardening was missing when Lyn continued. Her back ached and she really wasn't in the mood; but as penance to her stupidity, she laboured on. The robin and his merry trill was obviously entertaining a more deserving soul; the only sounds, were the thwack of the fork as it was aggressively plunged into the ground and an audible grunt from Lyn on its retrieval.

"Forget the tea Lyn; I've got what I came for." Vinny's last words, as she'd shoved him out of her house, played over and over in her head. After thinking about it; she was convinced Vinny had recognised James's voice and even if he hadn't, the telephone number of James's office was clearly visible at the top of her pad – where Vinny had torn away the lower page. He hadn't mentioned Charlene or her whereabouts. Yet he'd left with an all-knowing, self-satisfied look that was undeniably obvious – he thought James was the key to finding Charlene. The thought of Charlene's battered body haunted her mind as the bruises superimposed onto James's handsome face. In desperation, she'd dialled James's office, knowing full-well that he wouldn't be there and she'd have to leave a message.

"Hi James.., it's me.., thanks for your message. You probably

won't hear this until Monday, and I'll have already left. I will be in touch when I return from London and hope it won't be too late. Don't make any appointments with Vinny.., Sorry, I mean with Charlene Dais's accountant and if possible, don't sign anything until I get back. It's for your sake that I'm saying this; keep away from him and don't sign anything."

Immediately after sending the message Lyn regretted it. She'd placed James in a very difficult position without explaining why; trouble was, no matter how hard she'd tried, she couldn't come up with a plausible way of conveying her fears to him.

Vinny hummed a tune as he strode purposefully back to his flat. His instincts had been spot on; and he felt chuffed and amazed by how easy it had been to get the information he'd wanted. He was slightly disappointed that the message on Lyn's answer phone wasn't from Charlene; but even if it had been, it wouldn't have led him to her. The main thing was, he'd discovered where she was going; and the fact that she'd lied about where she was heading was proof enough to him that Charlene was in London. The only thing the message had told him was that Lyn Porter had a bloke in tow. He'd got a kick out of watching her squirm with embarrassment, as lover-boy ranted on. He'd sounded familiar, but then again all posh-talking blokes sounded the same. Vinny chuckled as he thought about the two of them in bed, having a nice little chat instead of getting down to the main business.

For a long time he'd thought that Lyn Porter must be frigid or gay; maybe this bloke's a gay too and they get off on discussing each others experiences. Still, he thought, it was lover-boy who'd confirmed the length of time she'd be in London, which meant he would be heading in the right direction. Gay or not, one day he'd like to shake his lily-white hand and tell him how his girlfriend squirmed as he gave away her most guarded secret.

Chapter 12

Sunday Afternoon

The long walk had been just what Charlene needed; peace and quiet and time to work out how she could foil Lyn Porter's greedy assumption that *she* could walk away from the deal with forty grand while Charlene, who had borne the brunt of Vinny's repulsive ways, got a measly five. She'd only been staying with her cousin for twenty-four hours but boredom and irritation had already set in. Karen was more than happy to accommodate her; especially after Charlene had pressed the two, crisp, twenty-pound notes into her hand. She'd also offered to babysit little Millie, whilst Karen enjoyed a night out with her old friends – a rare treat these days, Karen had said, as she tucked the notes into the pocket of her skin-tight jeans. But after spending Saturday night bathing, changing nappies, and trying without success to settle the fourteen-month-old child, Charlene had decided to break free from it, as soon as possible.

The swelling, both to her ankle and wrist had diminished considerably, and the freshly completed walk confirmed that the damage, although ugly with bruising, was minimal and could quite easily be hidden beneath clothing or make-up. Charlene knew full well that the rapid healing of her body was down to the long hours she spent keeping fit, a regime she'd adopted several years ago. She also knew that to let this regime slide, even for just a week, would cost her dear. Karen's tiny house wasn't big enough to swing a cat and the claustrophobic feel and smell of baby stuff everywhere, drove her mad.

Not wanting to burn her boats completely – just in case things didn't go her way – Charlene told Karen that she'd be returning to Torbay the following morning, just to finalise a few things, and all being well she'd return the same evening.

Karen's disappointment was obvious. "Millie's usually such a good baby; it must be her teeth making her cranky with you. I'm making a brew, you want one?"

"Thanks, I'll have coffee. Did you remember to get some last night?"

"Shit no, sorry; I never buy it because it's so expensive. We could do a bit of shopping later if you like; get a few bottles of Alco pops for this evening – be like old times Charl. I need a few bits for Millie: she's the one who keeps me poor you know."

"Don't you get any maintenance from Joe?"

"Na. Sides, it ain't worth all the hassle that's involved. Me and Joe *have* discussed it. But we'd both be worse off if we went down that road; my benefits are not a fortune but it keeps me and Millie going and the rent's covered. You should get yourself pregnant Charl; then they would have to find *you* somewhere; must be better than all that moving around. Hold Millie and I'll get that tea."

Millie was plonked onto Charlene's lap as Karen headed into the small kitchen. Within seconds, the baby's face crumpled into a tight anguished scowl. Charlene knew what was coming. Before Millie had a chance to release a barrage of ear-splitting wails – a sound that had dominated the small house since Charlene's arrival – she unlocked the hold button on the DVD remote and sat her before its colourful animated screen. The baby stopped screaming, captivated by the antics of the cartoon characters.

As well as being related – Charlene's mum and Karen's mum were sisters – there was a time when Karen was regarded as Charlene's best friend. But best friends should be there when you need them most, and Karen had let her down badly. Charlene's own mum had let her down too, but then she had always been weak when it came to men, so it was to be expected. Karen's voice cut across the painful memories.

"Oh by the way, I heard that bloke from the flower shop phoned your mum yesterday; asked if she knew where you were."

"Bloody hell Karen, I told you not to tell *anybody* that I was staying with you." Charlene's mind was made up; she would leave first thing tomorrow morning and get the job done before her mum and that bastard of a boyfriend of hers, came looking for her.

"You can't expect me not to speak to my own mother Charl; I know you don't get along with yours, but me and mum are good mates and I promise you, you being here, has gone no further." It doesn't need to, Charlene thought. Telling Karen's mum anything, was as bad as advertising in the local paper.

"Fuck you, Carl!" Vinny shouted into the mouthpiece of his phone after he had cut the connection. He was annoyed with himself for sounding like a nervous tart on her first shout. All he'd suggested to Carl was that they give the solicitor a few more days to stew before going in for the kill. Carl had gone ape-shit; telling Vinny not to forget who's brain was behind their little scheme and if there was any tweaking of plans, Carl would let him know. The mood Carl was in, Vinny decided against mentioning Charlene's unavailability to sign the contract, due to her mother being taken seriously ill. Stuff like that never cut any ice with high-flying financiers. He would just have to make sure that Charlene was found by the end of Monday.

With an air of determination, he set about carefully planning his moves for the following morning. He'd board the train at Exeter – which was much busier than Torquay – making it easier for him to blend with the early commuters without being spotted by Lyn Porter. He wished now that he hadn't been so keen to show his satisfaction, she was a crafty cow, and may well be looking out for him.

Carl was livid; he'd spent month's grooming Vinny for the part in a scam which stood to net him fifty grand, and now for some unknown reason the stupid bastard could cock the whole thing up for him. Why on earth would he want to delay signing, just when the trap was primed and set? Naturally Vinny had never been given knowledge of the larger stakes his flower shop was party to; the man is an oaf and sharing the intricacies of such business ventures would be wasted on the likes of him. But the phone call had worried him; if all this unravelled, God knows who could be implicated and his job would certainly be on the line.

By five o'clock, Vinny felt confident with his plan. His dark suit, which had lately become known as his accountant's attire instead of the original funeral outfit, was hanging airing by the open window where he had sponged one or two stains from the lapels. An empty laptop case had been utilised to carry the maps and timetables he'd cleverly gathered from the tourist-information-office, on his way back from Lyn's. He'd even bought himself a cheap pair of specs from one of the town's gift shops – plain glass of course, Vinny's eyesight was perfect – to give that little extra assurance of not being recognised. By the end of the afternoon, he was actually looking forward to mingling with the business commuters on their way to the city.

Chapter 13

Sunday Evening

The atmosphere felt anything but relaxed as James drove his Mother back home. The dark, quite roads, highlighted on either side by the piercing full-beam of the car's headlamps, created a welcome focus, as hedgerows, interspersed with skeletal trees, flashed by in a magical mix of bright light and dancing shadows. James's favourite travelling CD had been set in motion shortly after leaving Helen's – in an attempt to smooth the passage of the forty-five minute journey – but after a few minutes of the sweet-sounding violin-concerto, his Mother complained of a splitting headache and asked if he'd mind turning it off. He'd thought that she may want to clear the air by discussing what was really bothering her, but after waiting patiently for a while he'd turned to find her sitting bolt upright with her eyes tightly closed.

A wave of sadness washed over him as he turned intermittently and studied her lined-strained face. James was absolutely certain that she was indeed, in pain. She'd suffered from a mild form of arthritis for years but over the last ten years – since his Father's sudden death –her condition had deteriorated rapidly. He was also absolutely certain, that the major part of her pain stemmed from dissatisfaction; of having been let down by her children.

Jack's birthday party had passed in a whirl of robust boyhood antics and games. The exhausted adults were left eagerly awaiting the more sedate evening meal that would be washed down with several well-earned glasses of wine. The original plan was for James and their Mother to stay over; but it soon became obvious, after the hoard of children had been collected by their parents, Mother wanted to go home. Helen blamed herself for bringing up the subject of sending Jack away to school. Mother had voiced the opinion that this was selfish of her, and that her son and husband should take precedence over her job. Helen, already harassed by keeping control over the marauding youngsters, retaliated and accused Mother of double-standards "What was the point of you and Father sacrificing so much, for our education, if I'm to throw the results of that education away unnecessarily?"

"Of course having an education is important Helen, but so is having a good family life and making every effort for the family to progress to the next generation. Your poor father never got to see that – thanks to over enthusiasm for your work." After this remark Helen had disappeared for a while, leaving the rest of them in earshot, lost for words.

As the car glided to a halt outside the modest three bed-roomed semi-detached house, James remained seated. He knew he'd be invited in for tea, but really didn't want to stay.

"Please come in and have a cup of tea with me James, I know Helen's cooking a meal for you, I won't keep you long."

After his mother's slow progress to reach and open the front door James stepped into the unchanged world of his childhood. In every room there were reminders of the close-knit, happy family that he'd been fortunate enough to belong to. Helen was right, their parents had sacrificed so much for them; but this, as all things had come at a price, a price that he hadn't been able to pay. James especially, had always felt under pressure to produce a son to carry on the family name.

Somewhere in the far distant passed, according to his father and backed up by a book in the local reference library; the Fairbanks had been well-respected and apparently very well-to-do. Fired up with righteous indignation, at the wrong doings of a certain ancestral rogue, his father took it upon himself to restore the family prospects. Providing his children with the advantage of a good education, seemed the best way to begin this single-handed crusade.

Naturally James and Helen were only too eager to play their part and accept their parent's sacrifices; and both felt that they had made full use of the opportunity. Even their first small flats – deposits were miraculously provided via Father who never let on that he had borrowed the money or that it had taken years to pay it back. James's train of thought was halted as his mother shuffled into the sitting room.

"Sorry, it takes such a long time to do the simplest things." She carefully placed the tray of tea and biscuits on the coffee table between them. James had learned long ago not to offer help; she was fiercely independent and woe betide anyone who challenged that independence.

"Helen mentioned that you have a lady-friend; I'm sure she only told me to quell any suspicions that you might be gay – I think that's the right term these days isn't it?" James nearly choked on the gulp of hot tea and it took two attempts to voice his response.

"In my capacity as a solicitor, I'm offering the lady in question advice, that's all; and what's all this nonsense about being homosexual?"

"Well I heard she was someone you had a fling with when you first moved to the flat that your father bought. Why on earth didn't you marry her then you could have had a grown-up family by now. And, as I recall, it was *you* who announced to all and sundry that you preferred men to women."

James refused to be drawn into his Mother's mischief making ways. He gulped down the tea in one long swallow and stood to go.

"I promised Jack a couple of my fossil books, I'll just get them then I must be off."

JAMES W FAIRBANK-FIRSTBORN

The decorative plaque which his father commissioned on James's twelfth birthday was still fixed to the bedroom door. It had caused a lot of sibling rivalry at the time but as their teenage years advanced it became the butt of many jokes between Helen and James. In reality, it was no laughing matter. Years later, when they could well afford to take nice holidays and move into a more pleasant neighbourhood; their parents refused to even consider the thought of spending such large sums of money on themselves. They were clearly hoarding it away for the future generations of Fairbanks.

James expected the door to creak as he slowly turned the knob. It was pushed open without a sound. The odour from waxed, stripped-pine furniture was slightly overpowered by the sweet-smelling scent of washing powder. After his first term at university, returning to his old room gave pleasure and reassurance. But now, although nothing had changed within the four walls – including the smell – he could only feel sorrow. He found the books he wanted from the dust-free shelf and headed downstairs.

His mother was waiting by the front door and there was warmth in her embrace as she wished him a good night.

"I promise to bring Lyn over if the friendship develops into something more, but I must warn you Mother, she is past child-bearing age, and she is not upper-class." They both smiled. In his mother's smile, he saw the beginnings of acceptance. In her son's smile, she saw that maybe, this new friendship could bring companionship and even love to a very honourable son who had been used and badly let down.

As James drove back to Helen's, music filled the air of his car and Lyn Porter filled his thoughts.

Refreshed from the hot bath and washed hair, Lyn sat on her bed surrounded by a heap of colourful photographs. She'd wanted three particular snaps. Jill had asked her to bring photos of Sarah and any other interesting snippets of her life that she had not been party to. Unfortunately, whenever Lyn delved into the 'memory box', she'd get carried away on a wave of emotion-filled nostalgia; forgetting her main purpose and the time this indulgence cost.

She'd finished the digging of the flower bed in a flurry of cursed determination. The light drizzle had turned to steady rain; and after stuffing the pile of mud-coated weeds into her compost bin, she was soaked to the skin. Rain hadn't been forecast otherwise she'd have left the job for another time. But once started, she couldn't walk away from any task until it was complete.

One small job remained and thankfully this was undercover. She'd needed to fill the log basket. After kicking off her boots under the shelter of the back porch she'd reached for the empty basket, taking care not to transfer drops of muddy water from her clothing. With reverential care, partly because her back had been screaming for rest, but mainly because this would be the last of her precious ash logs, she'd placed them in the basket.

A mound of debris had collected over the years where the logs had stood and as Lyn swept it onto her dust-pan, several interesting items had come to light. The first was a set of car keys, red rusted with age and damp air. Lyn clearly remembered the furore when they went missing; it had caused a twenty-four hour delay for Martin, on an organised climbing trip. Lyn had studied two other items covered in dust and dead leaves. A porcelain rose, which had been her first Christmas present from Martin – now sporting two damaged petals – and a particularly bad school report of Sarah's – perfectly preserved in a sealed polythene bag. Making a mental note to have a friendly word with Sarah during the Christmas visit, Lyn had binned the rusty keys and the damaged rose.

Sunday lunch had been cooked and eaten much later

than usual. Vinny had been right about Lyn being a traditionalist; but considering the major changes that undoubtedly lay ahead, this tiny tweak in a long-standing ritual was negligible. Satisfied that her kitchen had been meticulously cleaned, including the fridge and waste bin, Lyn had turned the central heating on – a luxury that hadn't been indulged for months – and run a hot bath. She'd placed the 'memory box' of photos squarely on her bed, fearing that after a warm, relaxing soak, she'd probably have forgotten her promise to Jill.

Midnight

Lyn surfaced from a troubled sleep. Something had nagged at her subconscious mind as she finally switched off her lamp and slid under the thick winter duvet; but feeling exhausted and concerned about getting enough sleep before rising early next morning, she'd ignored the pull of concern. In the distance, chimes rang out, synchronizing with the time showing on the bedside clock. On the final stroke revelation!

She leapt out of bed! Four long strides found her holding her breath on the top stair. From here she could make out the dark shape of her packed suitcase. She didn't need the help of artificial light to see that the ticket was missing from where she'd placed it – on clear view, caught beneath the carrying handle. She must have walked by the case a dozen times during the evening, part of her mind registering that it wasn't there, why hadn't she taken notice? "Vinny, you thieving bastard she uttered through clenched teeth, "remembering the look of satisfaction on his face.

Knowing it was useless but needing to do it anyway she flicked on the lights, bounded back into the bedroom and upended the contents of her large handbag onto the bed. No ticket. With rising panic she ran downstairs; unconcerned that all her lights were blazing and the thundering noise may well disturb her elderly neighbour. "Oh shit!" The anguished howl resounded through the narrow hallway as Lyn collapsed in a heap, at the bottom of the stairs. In her panic to reach the suitcase, she had stubbed the big toe of her left foot on the newel post.

Several changes to meticulously-made plans seemed inevitable. Her mind begged for attention; while she lay on the floor racked in pain and disbelief at what was happening. Suddenly the whimpering ceased. Lyn noticed a fragment of paper trapped between the skirting board and the suitcase. With pain and disbelief momentarily forgotten, Lyn reclaimed the elusive ticket. "Yes! Yes! Yes!" Her sense of relief was immense; and as she hobbled back up the stairs, she kissed the ticket over and over again.

Matt handed James the replenished brandy glass and kissed Helen goodnight. Mondays were always particularly busy at the hospital and he liked to arrive early. Retiring to his bed after midnight on a Sunday evening was not ordinarily done, but today hadn't been an ordinary day. Pride and love overflowed at the thought of his ten year old son. However, the feelings were tempered by a mixture of uncertainty and sadness that before his next birthday, he'd be seeing much less of him.

"I won't be long darling, just need to sort a few things out with James." Helen raised her hand to stop the protestations that James was about to deliver. The journey to and from Mothers had taken him much longer than she had anticipated; which meant their supper was eaten much later than intended. James, as always, was very apologetic but didn't give any reason or excuse as to why he was delayed. Helen had her suspicions. Mother knew that there were no secrets between her children; and took advantage of this fact, by releasing snippets of information to only one or the other.

"Helen I know you and Mother had 'words' earlier; but I swear to you, she didn't discuss your differences with me. In fact she was silent on the whole journey – in pain no doubt." Obviously not wanted to enlighten James either, Helen cleverly changed tack.

"She'll be eighty in three months time James, how do you think we should celebrate this special day; it will have to be a surprise, she would never agree to any fuss."

"Perhaps we should respect her wishes, and besides, you've barely cleared away the mess and upheaval of Jack's party, give yourself a break."

"Sorry, I'll leave it for now, but remember all birthdays containing a '0' are special; Jack's today, Mother's in three months time and yours in seven months.

Anxious to change the subject from upcoming celebrations, which for him were an ordeal and a total waste of money; James bluntly asked "What was the argument with Mother all about?" A heavy sigh, and watching Helen gulp her shot of brandy in one go, was the only response he thought he would be getting; until out of the stillness of the early hour, in an unsteady voice she unburdened her soul.

"God it's such a relief that this day is over." She said rubbing her arms as though the temperature of the sitting room had dropped. It hadn't. Looking earnestly at James she continued. "Normally, grieving at the death of a loved one is obviously heightened on the anniversary of the loved one's death, at least for the first few years. Perversely," she continued after exaggerating the word perversely and pausing for a while, "I grieve for Daddy on my son's birthday; and it's definitely not getting easier." She reached for the brandy bottle but to James's relief thought better of it.

"Anyway, whilst you and Matt were entertaining the boys, Mother was adding to my guilt. You'd think that sending Jack to one of the best boarding schools around would be just what father had dreamed of. But, her only contribution, to a decision that Matt and I have deliberated over for months, was that she'd see even less of Jack than she does now." Helen excused herself whilst she went to find a fresh box of tissues.

This bone of contention at not seeing enough of her grandson was deeply entrenched. Mother had naturally wanted Jack to stay over from time to time as any grandmother would. But, by refusing to allow Helen to revamp James's old bedroom into a suitable room for two young boys – Helen was convinced Jack would be bored stiff on his own – Jack had never been allowed to stay.

James could still clearly remember the massive row between them shortly after Father's death. Mother was away visiting her terminally-ill, older sister. During that time, although heavily pregnant with Jack and as a surprise early gift for Mother's seventieth birthday, Helen executed a complete make-over on her old childhood bedroom. Everything was stripped out and dumped. In its place, a reading /hobbies room was created, where Mother's books, needlepoint and various other creative activities could be carried out in comfort. The wooden shack at the bottom of the garden, hitherto used as a hobbies room, was stripped out to be utilized more appropriately. Mother had never used either room since. In fact, Helen's old bedroom is the only room in her house that isn't given a daily dust and clean.

Helen returned pink-nosed from the constant blowing. "Sorry James. It's been a hard day and I'm bushed; I hope all goes well with the bank tomorrow and they allow you sufficient time to get things sorted. Incidentally, didn't you say John Haydon was completing on the florists during this coming week? Only I know for a fact that he'll be in Edinburgh all week. Some big charity convention, and as he's on the board, he'll be expected to attend. I'm still baffled as to why such an astute businessman would agree to pay all that money for premises in a run-down area. Still, what do I know? I'm just a selfish, inconsiderate daughter who happens to be a workaholic."

After a good night's rest James knew Helen's self pity would be gone. He was intrigued however, about John Haydon's Edinburgh trip. "The owner of the florists is very eager to complete before next weekend, and I am hoping to have a new tenant assigned to flaunt at the bank manager." James's upbeat statement didn't correspond with the foreboding that surrounded this transaction.

"I need to leave early tomorrow Helen. I'll help myself to coffee and eat breakfast later at the office." He hugged his sister and kissed her forehead before releasing her, looking for a warm smile to match the one his Mother gave. Disappointment accompanied him as he wound his way around the steel and wood spiral stairway to bed.

Chapter 14

Monday 7-10am

Charlene took several tentative sips of the piping-hot, take-away coffee. The right side of her mouth still felt tender but the damp chill of the early morning was beginning to seep into every fibre of her body and it needed to be arrested. There was a twenty-three minute wait for the train to Torbay; but now that the Bristol to London Commuter had departed, the waiting room was almost empty and she could at least sit down. Heading for the far corner, which was clear of drafts caused by opening doors, she settled down to mentally rehearse her plans once again.

Originally, she'd intended to leave her suitcase at Karen's and return for one more night; and not because she cherished her cousin's company. Arriving at the Solicitor's door first thing in the morning with a suitcase, several faded bruises and no pre-arranged appointment would surely raise suspicion. She couldn't do a thing about the bruises, except apply more make-up on arrival, but her suitcase could be left securely at the station. Professionalism was essential in carrying off her plan and after the previous evening she was even more determined to succeed.

With Millie fast asleep, Charlene and Karen had been all set for enjoying a quiet night watching soaps and having a few drinks, when out of the blue Charlene's mum had turned up. It was nine thirty and Charlene had been really annoyed although she didn't show it. There were only two of the six Alco-pops left and her Mum had reached for one without any prompting.

"How long you staying?" the older woman had asked without looking at her daughter.

"Not long" responded Charlene as she'd handed her a clean glass, taking notice of the deepening wrinkles that were adding years to a woman who scoffed at anything that involved healthy living. Her mum had held the bottle to her lips and swallowed half of its contents; releasing a loud rattling belch as she'd handed the glass back to Charlene, before saying.

"No point in making extra work for Karen, she's got the responsibility of a babe to bring up as well as keeping house." Charlene hadn't responded, so her mum continued.

"Why you here Charl, you lost your job or what? You look like you been in a fight with someone, is it the guy who phoned me up? He seemed very eager to know your whereabouts. There's a bed at home, provided you pay your board and keep your hands to yourself."

Charlene had felt sickened at the thought of her offer; but still she'd said nothing and continued to sip slowly from her glass. Karen, uncomfortable with the change in atmosphere, rattled on about everything and anything that had entered her head. With the last bottle of Alco-Pops drained, Charlene's Mum had produced a flattened pack of cigarettes from her jeans pocket and looked pointedly at Karen for a light.

"Oh, I'm sorry Aunt Vi," Karen had stammered, "but you know I can't let anyone smoke indoors, what with Millie's asthma; poor little devil's had a wheezing chest all week."

"Jesus Christ Karen, you're getting as soft as Charl! I'm leaving now anyway, I'll just pop up and see my Millie for a few minutes while you make a brew; you don't begrudge me that do ya?"

Charlene hadn't been able to hold her tongue any longer. She'd barred her Mum's way to the stairs and pleaded with her not to go up and risk waking the sleeping child.

"She's my niece and the nearest thing I'm likely to get to a grandchild, so mind your own business and get out of my way."

Charlene had given up, knowing that to argue would just end in a slanging match and waking the child anyway. Karen had tried to make amends, by offering to make Charlene a coffee from the expensive jar they'd bought earlier; but she'd soon realised from Charlene's lack of response that telling her own Mum about Charlene's visit had been a bad mistake.

More than five minutes had passed and there'd been no sign of a waking baby and no sign of Charlene's Mum returning for her cup of tea. Suddenly, alert to a familiar creak, Charlene had leapt from the sofa and crept stealthily upstairs, finding her Mum rifling through the suitcase which had been concealed under the bed.

"I don't think you'd squeeze into any of my clothes Mum, but you can borrow my socks if life's got that desperate." For a second time Charlene had been pushed aside and on reaching the lower floor her Mum responded.

"Just remember my girl, you left with money that didn't belong to you; and sooner or later your step-father will recover what's due to him." By the time Charlene had checked and re-packed the suitcase, her Mum was long gone. Millie had slept through the whole sordid scene.

7-39am

The taxi dropped Lyn outside the large glass doors of the railway station with five minutes to spare before her train – the 7-44 to Paddington – was due to arrive.

She had intended to arrive at least ten minutes earlier but after the bizarre midnight experience, several of her carefully worked out plans had needed to be changed.

The big toe on her left foot was much larger than it ought to be, despite the cold compress and lavish attention she'd shown it before returning to her bed. This single, split-second act of misjudgement had cost her dearly and even though the painful blow had led to the discovery of the rail ticket, the hefty price in compensation for that discovery was still being felt.

Jill was expecting to meet her, wearing fashionable knee-high black boots, and a scarlet coloured, above-the-knee coat. Not having seen each other in over twenty years, Lyn had thought it prudent to give a description of what she'd be wearing. Jill, on the other hand, had felt confident enough to simply say, "I'll meet you at the Paddington Bear statue." Lyn could count the number of times she'd been to London on one hand and she'd never been to Paddington Station and wasn't even aware that Paddington Bear resided there, albeit in hardened form. But not wanting to show the extent of her ignorance, she'd agreed, knowing full well that a tongue in your head was all you really needed to find your way around.

Unfortunately, Lyn's most striking winter outfit had been relegated to the suitcase in the hope that it may be worn later in the week when her toe returned to normal. In its place, she would arrive in sensible brown shoes, brown trousers and a camel-coloured wool jacket that she'd had for years and hoped with all her heart that Jill hadn't seen before. This derangement of plans and alteration of what to wear had cost her precious time that hadn't been allowed for; which meant forgoing a further telephone message to James, giving a fuller explanation and including Jill's telephone number.

A garbled voice announced the train's arrival as it swept almost silently into the station. A sea of humanity surged forward from every quarter of the platform, leaving Lyn still trying to make out what the garbled voice was saying. Feeling sure that she'd heard the word Paddington gave her enough confidence to join the heaving mass.

Once aboard, she realised with dismay that her reserved seat was two coaches away. For the first time in her life, she felt the panic of a claustrophobic! Her throbbing toe, screaming to be released from the oldest, widest and softest shoes she owned, was far more bearable than the crush of unfriendly bodies that prevented her and her suitcase from moving forward. A part of Lyn pleaded to be relinquished from the hell; the door to freedom was in easy reach and the train hadn't yet started to move. But she stood her ground and concentrated her mind on what this all-important trip was about. Resigned to the fact that she couldn't even move into carriage B, so trying to negotiate the length of two coaches would be insane, Lyn pushed her suitcase to the edge of the gangway and used it as a welcome seat.

Determined to block out the surrounding unpleasantness of the trains interior, Lyn focussed on the passing scenery of South Devon. The beauty of the landscape, although locked in its dormant, winter state, helped to calm her frazzled nerves; and her toe felt marginally less painful now that the weight of her body was more evenly distributed.

A light tap on the shoulder brought Lyn's attention back to the mayhem. She turned with a start to find the face of an African woman, barely inches from her own. A strong smell of spearmint overlay the scent of jasmine as the woman spoke, looking Lyn straight in the eye.

"Would you mind looking after my son? I need to use the toilet which is at the end of the next carriage." She pushed forward a little boy who looked about four or five years old. Lyn nodded automatically and moved nearer to the edge of her suitcase to allow the child to sit down. The frazzled nerves returned as the tall woman was swallowed gradually from view. Would he understand English? Would he scream for his mother after a minute or two? How would they pass the time? Maybe she wouldn't come back! These thoughts and several more, equally worrying, passed through Lyn's mind, but were quashed instantly as the child looked at her and said in clear, unbroken words.

"What is your name? Mine is Wilcox. Let's play 'I spy with my little eye'; mummy and I always play that game when we are on the train."

Ten minutes passed in the delightful company of the small boy who was not yet four. Apart from several rounds of 'I Spy', Lyn learned that Wilcox and his mother were travelling as far as Exeter. This trip was made three times a week to enable his mother to carry out her work in a private hospital – apparently she was a mid-wife – and allow Wilcox to attend a private pre-school nursery. Several times Lyn wondered how his mother would feel about all the personal information her son was doling out to a perfect stranger. There was no mention of a father in the child's life and Lyn didn't want to ask, in case the sweet, natural rapport that had developed between them became affected. Without prompting, Wilcox also disclosed that his mother was twenty-nine years old and her name was Jasmine. Lyn was tempted to show that she'd noticed her name-sake-perfume but felt sure that this information might prove too subtle, or even too boring for such a bright young mind.

Jasmine returned with a beaming smile, a sincere thank you and concern that Lyn hadn't been bombarded with too many rounds of, I Spy. There was no mention of whether her son had volunteered the family details and Lyn certainly wasn't going to snitch. Within five minutes, both women were chatting like bosom pals as Jasmine verified all that had previously been revealed; while Wilcox retrieved a sketch book from his little satchel and contented himself by drawing the items from the I Spy game.

During their conversation Lyn mentioned that she had

a reserved seat in coach D and really didn't fancy sitting on a suitcase all the way to London – especially after paying such a hefty price for the ticket. At Jasmine's suggestion, Lyn pushed her way through the two carriages to see at least where her seat was located, whilst Jasmine and Wilcox sat on her suitcase. She was told that she would have to make a supreme effort to reach it at Exeter before a further batch of London commuters replaced the people that were disembarking.

"Mondays are always like this because lots of business people have second homes in Devon and they spend their weekends here even in the winter." Jasmine's voice held no trace of criticism she was merely stating the facts.

With a giddy sense of relief the seat was at last located. It was also confirmed, by moving text on a panel above the seat, that it was reserved from Exeter to Paddington. The relief disappeared and was replaced by concern as Lyn realised the seat was too far away from the luggage rack and her Gran's conditioning voice was just below the surface of her conscious mind. *Why would you want to go to London Lynda? It's full of foreigners, cut-throats and thieves.* She pushed further down the carriage till the luggage rack was reached and found to her delight that the nearest seat to it was not reserved from Exeter.

As the train pulled into Exeter St. David's, Jasmine carried the case above her head and Lyn held the soft, brown hand of Wilcox as they made their way along the slowly moving, crowded aisles that led to Lyn's chosen seat. Hugs all round brought a lump to Lyn's throat and as Wilcox withdrew his little arms from the tender embrace he thrust a picture into her hands. A quick wave and they were gone.

8-45am

As Lyn marvel's at the child's perfectly-proportioned drawing of a gentleman carrying a briefcase and umbrella, Vinny lifts his cheap imitation glasses in order to read the seat number where she was sitting. Neither is aware that here sat the hunted and here stood the hunter. Vinny's complete attention is focused on finding a particular seat and sitting as close to that seat as possible to observe without being noticed. It's the next coach where he is heading, but engrossed in the role of detective, he wants to know beforehand how the numbers run. Pushing forward impatiently, not caring that this simple, selfish act, causes a heavy overnight bag to crash down on an elderly woman's shoulder, he makes his way down the aisle. With the aid of his laptop case, one final push and he is standing in the space that connects to coach D. He can see at a glance that all the seats are taken. Caution kicks in as the train starts to shunt forward. He decides to delay entering until he is sure that his prey is not facing toward him; if the numbers run true to the previous coach, this shouldn't be the case.

Satisfied and confident in his disguise he slowly walks the length of the aisle looking from side to side till he finds the number that is ingrained in his memory. A toff, reading a newspaper, was sitting in the window seat where Lyn Porter should be. Not wanting to draw attention, Vinny refrains from swearing out loud. Again he walks the length of the coach. No sign of her! Reasoning that the train is so full she probably had to grab any seat she could; because toffee-nosed bastards wouldn't move for you, even if you had booked a seat, he decides to walk the length of the next coach. In fact, he decides, he'll walk the whole bloody length of the train if necessary.

This proved to be unnecessary. Vinny entered coach F and his eyes fell on a familiar item. Lyn Porter's red suitcase, with its distinctive black and white strap around the middle, was in clear view on the luggage rack. And there *she* was, sitting by the window on the closest seat to her luggage; hemmed in by a fat, suited toff. Her attention was on a piece of paper spread out across her lap and Vinny moved closer to investigate.

An inane jingle cut through the air causing heads to turn. Vinny cursed under his breath as he pulled the phone from his pocket. Seeing the caller was Carl he was tempted not to answer; but Lyn porter was going nowhere so he walked back through the automatic opening doors to take the call.

"Carl, what's up?"

"I'm reminding you to make that call to Fairbank. Remember to stress that you have another interested party who is happy to complete straight away; and by the way don't make the call to Fairbank until after eleven, got that?" Vinny's anger flares but he controls the urge to show it in his voice.

"I know exactly what I have to do Carl."

"What's that noise Vinny, where are you?" An announcement that the buffet car would be serving refreshments until reaching Paddington, made it bloody obvious he was on a train; so Vinny didn't bother denying it.

"I'm travelling to London, but don't worry, the phone call will be made and the deal will be done tomorrow." Silence for several seconds gave Vinny a sense of satisfaction but Carl's eventual reaction, reignited the suppressed anger.

"What the hell are *you* going to London for Vinny?"

"Minding my own bloody business Carl." The phone was pressed off. Vinny checked his watch. The announcement about the buffet-car reminded him that he hadn't yet had breakfast and knowing that he had loads of time to kill decided on enjoying a crispy bacon roll and coffee before making the all-important phone call.

9-25am

A light tap and the opening of James's office door caused him to abort listening once again to Lyn Porter's curious message. Sadie's large frame remained defiantly in the doorway and the disapproving look as her eyes settled on the untouched milky-coffee that was coagulating around the rim of the china cup, made him feel slightly intimidated.

He'd arrived ten minutes late; due to the heavy traffic which he'd thought he'd allowed for. Sadie had always refused to accept a key to the place and was quite poker-faced and half frozen when James had finally arrived full of apologies. She'd grumbled that she had better things to do than stand in the cold, damp air for over fifteen minutes.

"Make us some coffee Sadie that will cheer the morning," he'd suggested brightly.

"I don't have time for coffee drinking Mr Fairbank there's too much to do." James knew better than to argue with her; but five minutes after removing her coat, she'd brought him a cup, with a chocolate biscuit, and left it on his desk without saying a word.

Two messages had been left on his answer phone. The first was from John Haydon, informing James that he'd be in Scotland for a few days. The second was from Lyn Porter, a short bewildering message filled with concern – concern that seemed to be aimed at James. The coffee, along with the morning's list of urgent phone calls and paperwork were temporarily forgotten as James obsessively played the message over again.

"There's a young woman to see you, hasn't got an appointment but insists it won't wait. She looks vaguely familiar but when I asked her name, the cheeky madam said it was none of my business. I expect you'll be wanting fresh coffee for two" Sadie emphasised the word, fresh, and finished her announcement with a heavy sigh and a withering look.

"Just show the young woman in please Sadie."

James found it difficult to conceal his surprise. "Ms Dais, good morning, I trust all is well with you?"

"I think your cleaner was a little put out, but I don't give personal details to all and sundry. I'm sorry for arriving without an appointment but there's been a development and I need to act quickly."

"What sort of development?" James could just make out the bruising on her face which the clever application of make-up hadn't quite disguised. But the aura of determination was glaringly obvious and he leaned forward involuntarily, intrigued as to what was about to be revealed by this forthright female who was hitherto thought to be downtrodden.

"I'd like you to contact Mr Haydon right away and inform him that I want to finalise the sale of the shop today. I've got another interested party who is willing to match his price and my wishes. Also I want £40,000 paid separately to my account with the balance to V.C. Enterprises."

"May I be permitted to know what this separate payment is for? If Mr Haydon concedes to your demands, I, as his solicitor, would need to make quite plain in the paperwork the reasoning behind it, especially as you and your accountant have chosen not to be legally represented." He'd caught her off-guard but like the bruising she almost succeeded in disguising the fact.

"It's for a former employee of the shop; who invested money of her own two years ago. I've calculated a certain amount of interest in that sum so that she won't be out of pocket."

"So the money is for Lyn Porter?" James, feeling pleased that he could break this good news to Lyn – although it would have to wait until her return from London – wasn't prepared for Ms Dais's reaction

"How the hell do you know Lyn Porter? Like I said she's had no connection with the shop for two years." She could see James was taken aback by the outburst and added in a softer tone. "Look I didn't mean to snap at you, I want to do the right thing by Lyn, but I need to do it my way so please would you mind keeping this to yourself for a few days. Have you known Lyn long?" Her question was delivered with a coy, head-tilted smile.

"She was selling me bunches of flowers before you were born." James smiled as he answered but Charlene was under no illusion that this was the only information that was forthcoming on the subject of Lyn Porter.

Wanting to return to the crux of the matter, James warned her that he couldn't guarantee being able to contact Mr Haydon today; but he would do what he could.

"Is your accountant aware of this new development?"

"The business is in my name, I'm quite capable of signing a piece of paper on my own. Would you like me to call back later or have you a waiting room? I have to stress the other party are really keen, it would be a pity for you to lose out after all your work."

"Yes I have somewhere you can wait, would you like some coffee or maybe you prefer tea?"

"Coffee will be fine, thank you."

Sadie was summoned to escort Ms Dais to his upstairs sitting room and supply her with coffee. The two women scowled at each other and James felt relief as the sudden ringing of his office phone gave him a legitimate excuse to leave the strained atmosphere of the hallway.

"Good morning, James Fairbank speaking." There was a long spell of silence while James listened attentively to what Victor Connor – whom he now knew to be Vinny Conway – had to say. Although the man's voice was, as usual, aggressively loud, a whooshing, rumbling background noise made James question if he had heard him correctly.

"Am I right in assuming that you want the sale finalised tomorrow and not today?" He was about to enlighten him that Ms Dais was ahead of him but thought better of it;

remembering the bruising and the slight limp which could only have happened over the last couple of days. If domestic violence had been inflicted, it had certainly had a positive effect on Ms Dais's demeanour. Before Mr Connor had a chance to respond, a train announcement declared that its passengers would reach Paddington Station by 11-42.

"Are you travelling to London alone Mr Connor?" James wasn't quite sure why he felt the need to ask but he didn't expect the answer he was given.

"Not that it's any of your business; I'm travelling with Charlene Dais and neither of us will be available until tomorrow, got that?" Vinny had been really pissed off when Carl had ended his message with 'got that' it had an intimidating effect which, he decided, could be very useful when speaking to certain people. The connection was broken but James's phone remained held in position. His thoughts weren't centred on such trivia. Remembering Lyn Porter's number he pressed the six digits and waited. Seven rings connected him to her answer phone. Impatiently he replaced the receiver and opened the file on Floral Occasions.

Chapter 15

Monday 10-40am

The traffic had eased considerably as James drove along the main connecting road between Torbay and Newton Abbot. Something very underhand was going on and he was determined to find out what it was. Integrity in his business dealings had always been his number one priority and he wasn't prepared to sacrifice it for anyone.

After failing to reach Lyn Porter, he'd phoned John Haydon, fully expecting to be greeted again by an answering machine. Not so; on the second ring John had picked up, harassed and in a hurry to catch his flight from Exeter. James had explained briefly the nature of Ms Dais's visit and the strange conflicting phone call from her accountant – who happened to be travelling to London as he'd made the call. It was the last part of this passed on information that had riled his client, even though James had taken great pains to reassure him that the whole sordid episode was just a ploy to get him to complete as soon as possible; adding that he'd forewarned Ms Dais, he'd probably be unavailable.

Unexpectedly, James was told to go ahead with her

demands and to make sure that every single document bore her signature and was witnessed, before bringing the documentation over to John's office for countersigning and payment. Apparently John Haydon had been quite prepared to forgo the cost of the flight from Exeter and re-schedule for an afternoon flight from Bristol.

Pulling into the empty parking space alongside John Haydon's Mercedes Sports car, James turned off the engine and reached for his briefcase, and then thinking better of it, tucked it under the front passenger seat. John Haydon stood waiting on the forecourt of his offices and greeted James with a firm, pumping handshake.

"I made Alice park down the road, to save you driving around in circles, it's getting worse by the day for parking around here. I really am grateful to you James for dropping everything and… Where's the paperwork?"

James pressed his car key and the familiar clunk of the mechanism followed by the double flash of lights, reassured him that his car was securely locked. "I'll bring in the paperwork when you tell me what the hell is going on."

"Come on James, time is of the essence here, I've re-scheduled a flight for God's sake."

"Precisely my point, I've never known you to re-schedule anything before. You own millions of pounds worth of property, what is so special about this insignificant little shop?"

Unceremoniously, two glasses and a bottle of single malt whiskey were produced from a small cabinet; John Haydon poured a large dash in each and handed one to James. After taking a large gulp, he admitted to James that he'd been after that particular property for years. "I own the whole street you know; have done for going on nine years, but I could never get Fat Beryl to part with her shop – not at any price. *She* knew I was mopping up the other places one by one; I tried keeping a low profile but she was as sharp as a razor, good businesswoman too. When she finally kicked the bucket and left the place to that lazy, dip-stick of a nephew, I knew it was only a matter of time. I'd spent a whole lot of effort and money negotiating to buy the run-down garage behind the florists which has one and a half acres of parking and workshop space included, but a London-based consortium beat me to it; seems like the bastards are at it again."

"I find it hard to believe that a London-based firm would be interested in run-down businesses of the south west," James interrupted in a disparaging voice.

"Oh don't be so bloody naive man. Do you think I'm stupid enough to pay that kind of money to keep a no-hope florist shop going? Regeneration and development, that's where the clever money is; Torbay is ripe for regeneration and there's plenty of government support, financially. Trouble is, someone is feeding information to the London boys and obviously they've got wind of the florist shop which is very strategically positioned for several dynamic plans that have been put forward"

"So you mean to demolish it?" James felt betrayed, and more than a little foolish that he, as a so-called expert in conveyances, wasn't aware of any of this underhand dealing.

"Damn right I do."

"I'm your solicitor John, why didn't you enlighten me about all this before?"

"Don't take this the wrong way James, but the way things are these days you can't afford to trust anyone with more information than is necessary. For instance, I know you're in financial straits with the bank over your restoration project."

"How the hell…" James was stopped by John's interruption.

"Spies at the bank James, how do you think I got left behind on the garage deal? Look I'm sorry to press but we need to finish up here."

James collected his briefcase and removed the file of papers, spreading them across John Haydon's desk. Each had already been signed by Ms Charlene Dais and witnessed by Sadie, James's cleaner. John's secretary, Alice, joined them as he countersigned each document. The last paper, which James had typed himself before leaving his own office, referred to the separate cheque of £40,000 payable to Ms Charlene Dais for the purpose of passing on to Ms Lynda Porter. It also mentioned the allowance of five full days to evacuate the premises.

"Why has the cheque to be made out to the Dais woman if the money belongs to Porter?"

"Ms Dais says she wants to surprise her." James realised with embarrassment how feeble and ridiculous his answer sounded.

"I don't like surprises; you've done the searches James, has this Porter woman invested in the business?"

"Yes she has, although she was badly advised and borrowed against her home, but there is no doubt that she invested money in the business along with over twenty-five years of her life."

"Ah! Beryl's assistant! You know James, if Beryl had left the shop to Porter instead of the nephew, we wouldn't be having this conversation. Anyway there's no way I intend to write a cheque for one person when it rightfully belongs to another. And it's not because I'm a self-righteous bugger, I just want to make sure there'll be no repercussions down the line." James watched as John Haydon scribbled across three separate cheques with his signature barely more than a wavy line.

"V.C. Enterprises, whatever the hell that means, £280 grand. Ms Lynda Porter, £40grand, and incidentally, personally make sure she gets this James and get a signature to confirm it; I don't mean to point out your job but I am feeling a bit paranoid right now. Someone leaked the fact that I'd be off the scene for a while, can't be too careful." They've got three full days to get their junk out of there; I'll be sending a guy round on the fourth to change the locks."

Without a word James placed the two cheques inside the folder along with part of the paperwork. John Haydon handed him the third cheque which was blank save for John's wavy line of a signature.

"Who is this for?" James stared at the cheque feeling very uncomfortable.

"You know James, you're the straightest guy I've ever dealt with, and I'd trust you with my life. But I have to tell you, if you don't contact your bank very soon with a considerable sum of money, or prospects of the same, the bastards will pull the rug from under you. I know you don't usually send out accounts for a month; but take this as early payment and I'm giving you carte blanche to take a lot more if it means saving your arse.

"And how am I supposed to repay you John?" But John at that moment was calling to Alice to get her coat. James watched as his client kissed the newly-signed document before placing it in his safe.

A final handshake and the meeting was over, but as James unlocked his car, John Haydon called over to him.

"When you contact your bank James, talk to Carl in B. E. Division."

"What does B.E. stand for?"

"Business Enterprises. Bye, keep in touch!"

James headed back to his office leaving John Haydon punching onto his mobile phone as he waited patiently for Alice to bring back her Mini Cooper.

"Carl, John Haydon! The deal on the shop is signed and sealed. Yes I should have been well on my way by now, anyway just thought I'd let you know that the London boys were beaten on this one, their source isn't as clever as they'd assumed. No, the Dais woman came in alone to sign; she'll have the cheque by noon, see you anon."

11-15am

There was a time, not that long ago, when the thought of working and living in the heart of Torbay filled Charlene with joy; but the reality of it hadn't lasted long. She loathed the place now and on this freezing-cold November morning, anywhere else would be preferable – except, the small-minded Bristol suburb where she was dragged up. There were forty-five minutes to kill before being handed the cheque that would ease her nicely into the next phase of her life; money that would help her to avoid the likes of Vinny and her stepfather.

She'd had enough coffee for one day and the library seemed like the best bet for warmth and anonymity. If Lyn Porter, Vinny or his crooked friend got wind of what she was up to, she'd gain nothing. All she wanted was to sit quietly in the warmth, reading a magazine. Unfortunately, on reaching the Library, it seemed as though every dosser and old age pensioner had had the same idea. After spending five minutes in the library's one and only toilet – checking and reapplying the concealing makeup – she headed back into the grey misery.

Wandering in and out of stores devoid of customers made Charlene feel even more exposed. Resentment boiled as she thought about the old cow of a cleaner, almost frog-marching her from the building. Charlene had been more than happy to wait out the hour or so in the solicitor's beautifully furnished room, reading a very interesting article entitled, How to Keep Fit Whilst Cruising. The sour-faced bitch wouldn't have got away with it if the solicitor hadn't already left.

Still with time to kill, Charlene slowly headed back to the solicitors office taking a slightly longer route, and resigned to the fact she'd have to wait awhile at the door.

On arriving at the opposite side of the steep narrow street, four doors from his office, she could clearly see his open porch door – although there were still twenty minutes before their appointment. She'd heard the cleaner say on more than one occasion that she'd be gone by 11-30 and would drop the lock as she went. The solicitor had handed her a key insisting that she lock the door properly. Charlene quickened her step eager to finalise her plan.

As Charlene stepped into the porch, Sadie stepped out turning to insert the key in the inner door. Charlene held the door open with one firm hand and one firm foot – both chosen instinctively due to lack of injury. Sadie, whose thoughts had been on Alf – her husband – who was expecting her home long before now, nearly jumped out of her skin on realising she was not alone.

"What the bloody 'ell are you doing back here? Your appointment's not till twelve."

Shock and confusion caused Sadie to drop her bag, her gloves and the key-ring which held two keys. Charlene bent to help; making sure the door remained open as she pushed her whole body against it.

"Leave it," Sadie screamed liked an alley-cat, "I'll do it myself! Go away until your appointment is due."

Charlene withdrew from collecting the hoard of useless rubbish that was scattered around the porch, but not before retrieving the key-ring holding two keys which nestled out of sight in her closed left fist.

"It's not a crime to arrive early for an appointment; I, am linked to an important client of Mr Fairbank's and I'm sure he'd be very upset to learn that I've been left, quite unnecessarily, waiting in the cold." If the old crab still insisted on leaving, Charlene would simply let herself in and tell her boss it was his cleaner's idea – after all she wouldn't be seeing either of them again. Sadie's face reflected the worrying thoughts that played out within the sixty-four year olds head. With a force of strength that belied her age, she pushed wide the heavy door and held it open for the young madam who had become the bane of her day.

Once again Charlene sat on the comfortable, antique chair and reached for the magazine with the half-read article. Sadie sat bolt upright in an opposite chair, watching her suspiciously.

"I'm sure hubby will be waiting for you to present his dinner on the stroke of twelve, don't let me keep you, I'll be fine." The cleaner remained tight-lipped and anchored in position; until a sound outside, sent her running from the room.

11-43am

As James reversed into his marked parking bay, he noticed the porch to his office is open. A rush of exasperation cancelled out the calming effect of the return journey from John Haydon's office. The traffic had been extremely light, allowing him fifteen minutes of precious time to prepare for his noon appointment; plus the soothing bars of his favourite CD had allowed him to rationalise that other peoples business and how they chose to conduct that business, had nothing to do with him.

Exasperation turned to annoyance as Sadie confronted him on the porch step firing all kinds of accusations concerning Ms Dais.

"Sadie, will you please calm down and allow me to enter my office; you told me you needed to leave at 11-30, promising to lock both doors before you went."

"I couldn't get finished on time Mr Fairbank, thanks to madam in there." Sadie cocked a raised thumb behind her and continued in a flustered voice. "Cheeky mare insisted on another coffee before she'd leave then arrived back twenty minutes before she's supposed to; Alf'll be beside himself with worry but I didn't dare leave her alone."

"Why, couldn't you leave her on her own Sadie?"

"She's a conniving so and so, I wouldn't trust her an inch; and you'd be well advised to do the same. I'll see you Thursday." Sadie pushed past him and marched down the road towards home.

James had known Sadie for many years. She could be cuttingly-blunt at times, but her commitment to her job was unquestionable; but, James was beginning to wonder if the time had come when cleaning for him twice a week was becoming too much of a burden, especially now that her husband had retired. After dropping his briefcase just inside the office door he mounted the stairs, leading to his sitting room, two at a time.

"Ah Ms Dais, as you can imagine, your unexpected arrival earlier has thrown my morning's plans into disarray; please bear with me for a few minutes longer whilst I organise the finalising paperwork. May I offer you coffee?"

"No, please you've been very good about the whole thing and I do appreciate your efforts on my behalf; Sadie has been really attentive in supplying me with refreshments, but she dashed off before I had a chance to thank her properly. Incidentally, she dropped these as she left, I hope they're not the keys to her house, she'll be worried sick when she arrives home." Charlene gloated inwardly, as his bright smile was replaced by a look of consternation. He slipped the keys into his pocket and said nothing. Charlene was left with a mixture of disappointment and admiration.

Having finished reading the magazines article, she relaxed back into the antique chair fantasizing on a life lived as a solicitor's wife; but the solicitor interrupted her thoughts, anxious now to proceed.

"What difference does it make, if the money is going to Lyn Porter anyway, why shouldn't the cheque be made out to her personally?" James was finding it difficult to mask the aggravation of the last few hours. He'd escorted Ms Dais down to his office no more than ten minutes after arriving back He'd forgone any refreshment himself during the morning save for the whiskey which had hindered rather than settled him, and he was desperately in need of a break. She was very sweet and demure when he'd offered his arm in support as she'd limped down the stairs. James had explained the altered time scale from five to three days for vacating the florists shop and apartment and this was graciously accepted; however John Haydon's insistence on Lyn Porter's name for the £40,000 cheque completely changed the atmosphere.

"Look I didn't mean to blast off at you James, may I call you James, and I'm Charlene by the way." Charlene rose from the opposite side of his desk and offered the hand that was bruised and still slightly swollen, smiling with satisfaction when his eyes dropped from her face to their conjoined hands. His grip was gentle but firm and after the brief hand-clenching she regained her composure and resorted to plan B.

"James, I'm going to be completely frank with you. I appreciate the fact that you're not my solicitor but I feel instinctively that you're to be trusted... and there's no one else I can talk to. Lyn Porter promised me £5,000 if I retrieved the money she was undoubtedly owed, she knew she'd never get the money from Mr Connor, you know what accountants are." Charlene added nervously, "and if you don't believe me, give her a ring, I have her number but I'm sure you have it too." Charlene had noticed more than once how his face had brightened at the mention of Lyn Porter; and that nothing she had just revealed could be denied by the woman.

"I'm afraid it's impossible to verify anything with Ms Porter because she's on her way to London for several days – apparently, travelling on the same train as your accountant." James noted her reaction; and confident with the conviction that this information came as a complete shock, he continued. "Why do you think they would travel together to London if they are at such odds with each other?"

Charlene detected a hint of jealousy. "Perhaps there's more in their relationship than any of us are aware of. I think they were an item at one time; maybe the flame has been rekindled. I'm never surprised at the change in people when money lands in their lap. Would you mind me using your phone to ring Mr Connor? I need his advice on when and where to bank the larger cheque."

James pushed his phone closer to Ms Dais and walked to the far side of his office. He wanted to allow her privacy, but he also felt compelled to hear what was said. Charlene sat attentively, her strumming fingers on James's freshly-polished desk revealing the tension she felt. The receiver was replaced without a word being uttered.

"His mobile is switched off and in all the time I've known him that's a first."

James broke the uncomfortable silence that followed.

"What does V. C. stand for in V. C. Enterprises?" He was beginning to feel sorry for the woman, and wondered if he could advise her on how she might rescue her £5,000, which he felt sure she had been promised.

"When Mr Connor signed the shop over to me – incidentally, Carl, a friend of his at the bank suggested he do this – we agreed that selling the shop and investing the money into up and coming projects was the way to go. V and C, I was told, stood for Vinny and Charlene; but now I'm not so sure. For the sake of my own well-being, I'm leaving the area but I really do need the £5,000. Can you understand now why it was necessary to have the cheque in my name; I promise you, I would have sent the balance to Lyn straight away."

The forlorn look on her face produced a mix of emotions in James and for a brief moment he mentally witnessed his own hand filling in the open-cheque from John Haydon to the sum of £5,000. The telephone rang startling them both and James moved hurriedly to his desk.

Chapter 16

Monday Noon

For the third time Carl had tried to reach Vinny but the bastard's phone had been switched off. Pacing back and forth, in the over-heated office he shared with two lesser colleagues, he had tried to piece together a plausible excuse to offer to his London associates. They wouldn't be pleased, and not only did he stand to loose a tidy sum, his credibility would be shot to pieces. Looking at his watch and unhooking his jacket from the chair he'd headed for the back entrance to the bank. Once inside his car, he dialled John Haydon's solicitor. The number was engaged. With a roar from the cars engine, Carl skidded out of the small parking area at full speed.

With the entrance to James Fairbank's office, clearly in view, Carl parked his car twenty yards down-hill on the opposite side of the road; and pressed the re-dial button of his mobile.

"Mr Fairbank? Mr James Fairbank? I'm Carl from your banks B. E. Division. I believe we have a mutual friend – John Haydon." Carl noted the guarded tone in Fairbanks voice. "Yes, I spoke to him earlier and promised I'd give you a ring; are you free to speak? Fairbank's tone had turned from guarded to hostile but his response had also told Carl what he needed to know – his client was still with him. "Not a problem, I'll call you later in the afternoon, bye for now." Carl cut the connection and slipped the phone in the inner pocket of his jacket keeping his eyes riveted on Fairbank's front porch.

He didn't have long to wait. Charlene emerged pulling up the collar of her coat against the cold midday gloom as she proceeded downhill towards the town centre.

12-10pm

Vinny's confidence as private detective was disappearing fast. Everything had gone to plan except for two things and these two things had fouled up his plans good and proper. For starters: why had the stupid cow decided to sit in a carriage where no one was allowed to make or receive phone calls – a so-called quiet area. For the ticket price he'd paid, he'd felt more than justified in doing whatever he liked. The old farts who kept pointing to the signs had probably only paid a third of the amount. But when a big, burly guard marched up to him with the alternative of moving to another carriage or switching off, he didn't have a choice.

He'd settled down well back from his prey but keeping her in clear view. The newspaper he'd bought earlier came in very handy on the odd occasion she'd decided to look around her. And fortunately, he had managed to make the call to the solicitor which should at least, put an end to Carl's whining. All in all things had got back on track. Vinny smiled at the clever pun in spite of what had followed.

Twenty minutes before the train was due to arrive at Paddington – on time according to the smug announcements – the train slowed to a halt in the middle of nowhere and remained in this no man's land for fifteen minutes. Aggravation developed amongst the passengers and some started to wander about in the hopes of finding anyone who might tell them what was happening. Lyn Porter was one of the wanderers. One minute she was there, sitting in front of the bright red suitcase, next minute, both she and her case had disappeared from view. Whilst standing, to follow the frustratingly slow moving, snaking line of people that headed in the direction that Porter must have gone, an announcement crackled through the carriage, stopping everyone in their tracks. Apparently, some selfish bastard, having decided to throw himself under a train up ahead, had caused all this inconvenience for everyone else; but fortunately detouring onto another track was now possible. The train was expected to arrive thirty-five minutes late, and the not-so smug voice added that on such an occasion as this, mobile phone use would be permitted in coach F. The announcement ended and the train shunted forward, catching everyone off-guard as they reached in pockets and bags for means of contacting friends and relatives. A thin-looking business woman, standing just in front of Vinny, pressed a stiletto heal in the centre of his polished black shoe as she fought to regain her balance. With an almighty push and squeal of pain, Vinny sent her careering down the isle along with several mobile phones belonging to passengers in front of her.

Before she had a chance to see her attacker, Vinny sat back in his seat and concentrated on his own phone.

Several 'missed-calls' registered – all but one was from Carl – but Vinny was in no mood to respond to any. Stopping and starting continued but it was clear they were nearing the end of their journey and if he lost sight of Lyn Porter at the platform, he'd have no chance of catching up with her in the massive station. He was just about to return the phone to his pocket when the distinctive sound of a text-message-received, vibrated in his hand. The train was in stop mode so he read the message from Carl.

'wat the fuck r u up to? charl has completed. ring me.'

Vinny read through the text several times convinced that Carl was having a laugh. Checking the sender of the missed call, that wasn't from Carl, he could now see at a glance that it came from the solicitor's office just a short while ago. Beads of perspiration formed on his brow as he pressed 'return call'.

Three rings and the bright and breezy voice made Vinny curse inwardly.

"Good Afternoon, James Fairbank speaking, how may I help you?"

"This is Charlene Dais's accountant you phoned me a few minutes ago?" Vinny didn't want to give anything away in case Carl was pulling a fast one – he had been much less friendly over the last couple of days.

"It was Ms Dais who tried to contact you from here; probably, to inform you that the completion on the florists shop has been concluded satisfactorily. And Mr Haydon will take full possession after Wednesday… Mr Connor, are you still with me?"

Vinny forgot all about Lyn Porter as the ramifications of what had just been said hit home. The solicitor asked him something else but his mind was still reeling and he hadn't quite heard. James repeated the request to speak to Ms Porter, which flummoxed Vinny even more.

"What the hell has Lyn Porter got to do with this?" Passengers, eager to leave the train slowed as they filed by Vinny; gaining satisfaction that this brute of a man seemed to be having a hard time. The solicitor's voice remained annoyingly calm.

"You said earlier you were travelling to London with Ms Dais, which I'm sure was a slip of the tongue on your part because Ms Dais was here with me at the time. I happen to know that Ms Porter is travelling to London on the same train as you; and as I have some news for her, would you please be so kind as to put her on the line."

Vinny couldn't put her on the line even if he'd wanted to, she was long gone and so were all the other passengers. "Sorry mate, she doesn't want to speak to you." Vinny flipped his phone shut and stepped out onto the almost empty platform wondering which train would take him back to Exeter.

12-25pm

Feeling chilled to the bone and more disgruntled than she could ever remember, Charlene sat in a cold, impersonal railway station for the second time in just a few short hours. The retrieved luggage was arranged, to form a makeshift barrier between her body and the open door, which she had grown sick and tired of closing. If all had gone to plan, she would now be on her way to Brighton, driving a rented car with the heater on full bore. Charlene's Dad, who had run off with another woman when she was ten, owned a nice little holiday apartment overlooking Brighton Pier. She'd visited the apartment on several occasions when she was much younger and Dad was still eaten up with guilt. And believe it or not, Charlene still possessed a key that her Dad had ceremoniously presented to her stating, 'you can visit whenever you like Charlie'.

She felt bitterly disappointed about losing out on the forty grand; but was consoled by the fact she was still in pocket with the five grand that she was genuinely owed. At one point, she'd felt almost certain that the solicitor was going to cough up the money out of his own pocket, especially after her sob-story; but the phone call broke the spell and all he did was offer to send it on to an address of her choosing. What a laugh, she thought without smiling. To have an address at all, would be a miracle right now. Even taking the train to Brighton was risking spending money she couldn't really afford to lose; but she needed time to heal and exercise, before presenting herself to a richer clientele. Physical blemishes were not tolerated if you happened to be on the staff payroll. If Dad has sold the place or changed the locks she would have to book into a cheap B&B for awhile – using up even more of her precious resources.

She'd thought she'd been given another swipe at the five grand when Carl picked her up outside the solicitors. Although he'd masked it pretty well, Charlene sensed his anger and frustration, at her jumping the gun, and she had to admit he unnerved her. She'd looked back for reassurance to the solicitor's office, where James Fairbank had stood watching her leave his premises; but from this angle she couldn't make out his tall frame. Carl wanted the cheque of course – tried to say that Vinny had sent him to make sure it was safely and quickly deposited. Charlene had told him straight that she wasn't parting with anything until she'd received five grand for all the trouble this little scheme of theirs had put her through.

"That's more than fair Charlene". He'd said in a sugary voice that had unnerved her even more. "I have joint authority for V.C.Enterprises; I'll deposit it and write you a cheque straight away."

Charlene had laughed out loud in spite of her nervousness, telling Carl that if he wanted the cheque, he'd have to produce the money first – in cash.

"Cash it is Charlene. I am a little hurt that you feel you can't trust your lover's best friend; and I still need to pay the cheque in before I can withdraw anything. The account is empty at the moment, fortunately, in my position at the bank, I can vouch for John Haydon's cheque clearing without delay, and five thousand cash shouldn't raise any eyebrows. Feeling she had no choice in the matter, Charlene had handed him the cheque sealed in a crisp, white envelope and at his instigation remained in the car which was conveniently parked at the rear of the town centre bank.

On his return, barely five minutes later, Carl hadn't even tried to mask his anger. The forty grand, which, Charlene explained nervously, had been held back for Lyn Porter, had sent him into a rage of accusations. Charlene offered up her bruises, and whined that she didn't have a lot of choice, then let slip that Lyn Porter and Vinny for some unknown reason had gone off to London for the week. The look on his face frightened her more than any threat she received – including her step-father and Vinny. Self-preservation kicked in. She left the car without being asked, knowing full-well, there was no chance now of receiving a penny. He'd driven off at full speed, leaving Charlene standing in the middle of the sparsely occupied car park, as rain started to fall.

12-30pm

In spite of the low temperature outside, Vinny found clasping the chilled pint of lager, particularly comforting. After checking at the information desk, he'd reasoned that the fifty minute wait for the next train to Exeter, wasn't enough time to leave the station; but was too much time to sit twiddling his thumbs in a boring, waiting room. His morning paper had been read from cover to cover and had been dumped on the floor as he left the train.

Relaxing into the leather sofa of the elevated bar, he was determined not to allow Carl's dominating message to get to him. At least one thing was clear; Charlene hadn't left Torbay at all. Maybe she was staying with a friend unknown to Vinny, or, maybe she was shacked up with some other bloke. Either way the deal was sealed – at least on the shop. He raised a toast to himself and downed an almighty swig, half emptying the glass. He knew he'd have to contact Carl sooner or later; he just needed a bit of time and space to get his story straight about why he was travelling to London. He wasn't stupid, Carl needed Vinny's money and Vinny needed Carl's expertise and contacts to spring the trap. A couple of relaxing beers and a more relaxing train ride back was just the ticket to put him back on track. Vinny slapped his thigh and smiled at the same old pun before taking another large gulp of cold lager.

Sweeping his eyes around the huge station, they suddenly halted on a very familiar object. The bright-red suitcase, easily identified as Lyn Porter's because of the black and white strapping, was propped at the base of a huge bronze bear. Barely six feet away from it, Lyn Porter stood with her arms wrapped around a fat woman with short blonde hair. Fascinated, Vinny watched the pair, his instincts telling him that he'd been right about her all along. She was queer! And here was the living proof. Not only were they cuddling; and that went on long enough, but Lyn Porter was actually licking or biting the ear of the fat bird. If only he'd brought his camera, Vinny thought excited and sickened, who knows what could be gained from this knowledge. Moving to the next table gave him a better view but his concentration was broken by a sudden muffled noise from his jacket. Cursing under his breath, Vinny retrieved his phone.

"Hi Carl, I was just about to ring you; there was an emergency on the train and we all had to turn our mobiles off, bloody inconvenient for…" Vinny was halted in mid-sentence and fell silent as Carl, in a hissing voice, that sounded more chilling than the lager, told him to stop rambling like an old woman.

"What the fuck are you doing in London, whilst your tart of a girlfriend is succeeding in ripping you off? Forty grand has also been lopped off the purchase price of the shop, for the Porter woman; and after all my fucking efforts to keep her out of the loop I'm none too pleased Vinny; how about an explanation."

Vinny descended the steps to the main area of the station at break-neck-speed, talking in jolts as he went. "I'm dashing for my return train, Carl; I'll be back by early evening we'll talk then." Carl started to respond in a high pitched voice, reminding Vinny of his Mum in the days when he refused to go to school, but loosing forty grand was more important than anything Carl had to say. His phone was switched off and pushed deep into his pocket as his eyes feverishly swept the main cavernous area of the station. People were milling everywhere. For a few seconds he felt completely disorientated and was about to return to the upper floor to pin point where she'd stood. But as any private detective knows, if you lose sight of your prey for an instant, you're buggered.

12-45pm

Lyn had felt boss-eyed from searching through the hundreds of people that criss-crossed the floor space surrounded the famous landmark. She'd had no problem finding the statue of Paddington Bear: the first person she'd asked had pointed, without word or change to their marching step, to where the massive sculpture stood. It was very close to shops and refreshment bars; but miles away from a public toilet, which Lyn was desperate to use. She should have gone before leaving the train; but concern about missing her friend after the thirty odd minute delay, had forced her to hang on.

By the time Jill appeared, panting and flushed in the face, the hanging on had turned into urgency. The welcome embrace was lengthened as Lyn whispered in Jill's ear, "I'll pee my pants if I don't visit the loo soon." Twenty-five years of adulthood dissolved as the giggling pair embraced again before heading straight for the public conveniences. The shock of having to pay to have a pee was soon forgotten and replaced with blessed relief.

"I was concerned that I might not recognise you but your face looks just the same." Jill was guiding their way to the underground giving Lyn the odd pointer in case she chose to travel alone during the coming week.

"I wish my body was still the same, I'm lucky to squeeze in a size sixteen these days, but your figure's still fantastic Lyn; and, your hair as gorgeous as it used to be. It's really great to see you." For the second time Jill hugged her childhood friend as they descended a long run of moving stairway, with Lyn's suitcase positioned precariously end-on between them.

Following Jill's lead, they travelled along countless corridors and escalators, before boarding a half empty train for Baker Street. No sooner had they'd settled to continue their chatter, Lyn joking that she may well need the help of Sherlock Holmes in the next few days, and at least she knew his address and how to get there, than they were getting off to board another train for Finchley Road.

With her suitcase safely in the boot of Jill's car, Lyn

settled in the passenger seat for the final leg of the journey. Jill had warned her that she wouldn't be chatting much whilst driving. Weaving in and out of cars, taxis and buses with barely inches in between, Lyn understood and marvelled at her friend's calm acceptance of the seemingly chaotic traffic; and felt sure that sharing her personal burden with Jill had been her best option.

Chapter 17

Monday Afternoon 3-30pm

James arrived precisely on time for his pre-arranged appointment but was asked, by the serious-looking receptionist, to take a seat as Carl was running a little late. He'd had to admit that Carl's midday call had caught him off-guard; and initially he had shied away from contacting him again that day. However, after enjoying a spot of lunch, two cups of his favourite blend of coffee accompanied with chocolate biscuits, he'd phoned for an appointment, determined to confront his deteriorating financial situation. To his great surprise, Carl had indicated that he could see him within the hour. Not wanting to be unprepared for a second time, James had requested the later time of 3-30.

It had taken about forty-five minutes for James to complete a three-month projection of income; excluding any rents from a possible tenant. The figures weren't good, by any stretch of the imagination, but considering the dire state of the property market, they weren't that bad. With time to spare, he'd decided to walk the one mile, downhill journey, which would bring him to the rear entrance of the bank. The heavy showers, forecast to last throughout the afternoon, had abated and James felt the fresh air and exercise would help him to concentrate on the importance of the interview.

Caught up in thoughts surrounding the imminent meeting, James had barely registered the distinctive, black sports car that was partially blocking his entrance to the path leading to the front of the bank. But something had made him stop! He'd stepped back and looked again at the cars rear-end. He recognised the two last digits of the number plate; the only section visible from where he'd stood, watching Charlene Dais.

For fifteen minutes, James watched a lengthening queue of people impatiently waiting to be dealt with by two, overworked cashiers, At least a dozen other bank employees, darted in and out of offices or sat hunched over paperwork at various points around the large, open-plan foyer. One such person, after speaking briefly on her desk-top phone, approached James where he sat in the quietest, furthest corner of the foyer.

"Carl's ready for you now, I'll show you to his office."

James thanked the young woman and followed her lead. She wore a badge stating her name was Mandy, James had never used a persons Christian name without invitation and he wasn't about to be coerced into doing it now.

"James come in, take a pew." James recognised at once that this was the same tall, blonde-haired, young man that had been waiting for Charlene. He also recognised the voice which held the slight hint of Scandinavian.

"James Fairbank, thank you for seeing me today." James reached across the untidy desk and briefly gripped the proffered hand, hoping to be enlightened of Carl's full name. He wasn't. Instead, he was informed that everyone at the bank preferred to be on first-name terms, making it a much friendlier environment to work in. There were two other desks within this over-heated, environmentally friendly office; one of which was occupied by a much older, plumper gentleman who Carl referred to as Chaz, and to whom he now spoke.

"Take a walk for half an hour Chaz; we need a little privacy here." With a heavy sigh, Chaz pulled himself into a standing position and shuffled through the door without a word. James tried not to show the intense dislike that was already developing towards this man named, Carl. He opened his briefcase and removed a folder, explaining to Carl, that it held his projected income for the next three months. Dismissing the folder by a wave of his hand, Carl walked over to one of the two picture windows and stood with his rear end towards James. With his hands clasped easily behind his back, he spoke in a slow, purposeful, monotone voice.

"We are both busy men James so I'll get straight to the point. Firstly, we are not here to discuss your day to day business. You are a conveyancing solicitor and we are experiencing the worst property crash in decades; it stands to reason that your income will be at an all-time low. I'm giving you my time, free of charge may I add, at the request of our mutual friend, John. In short, you owe this bank over £200 thousand and in view of the economic situation; they want it back in full." Carl swivelled to face James but remained standing, in front of the window. James felt sure that had the light been on Carl's face instead of his back, a derisive smirk would be clearly visible.

"And, as a mutual friend of John Haydon's, what do you propose?" James heard the cynicism in his own voice. Carl returned to his seat and leaned forward across the desk in a conspiratorial manner. James figured, this man was no more than twenty-eight to thirty years old, and yet his calculating eyes, a cold steely-blue trained in the art of intimidation, seemed twice that age. Carl continued in a less strident voice.

"Well, it goes without saying that you need to sell the burdened property; unfortunately, there are no buyers out there because under present circumstances there are no loans to be had." Carl leaned back in his broad, leather chair raising his clasped hands to support the back of his head. James remained silent and passive waiting for him to continue.

"This is where I can help James. I have contacts with a property consortium that may, and I have to stress here that nothing's definite, want to purchase your property."

"And if I have no wish to sell my property?"

"Wishes and facts are two different things James. This bank owns the property in question and unless you have the money to buy it from them, i.e. by paying back every penny of the outstanding loan within the next few days; they will just take possession of what they regard as rightfully theirs. If that happens, and believe me it will if we don't act quickly, all your efforts and the original outlay will be gone." The hint of a derisive smirk unmistakable as Carl opened his arms to mimic the release of a long-held burden, rather than the tragic loss of an expensive enterprise.

Wanting to be out of the stifling heat and obnoxious

company of this man, James asked. "If I do decide to sell *my* property, and I'm not saying that I will, who conducts the valuation?" Again, Carl stands and moves to his position looking out of the window.

"It's simple enough James. The consortium will pay two thirds of the current market value; but I have to emphasise what I'm sure you already know, the market value of property is dropping by the day. A wise fellow, like you James, would act quickly." Carl returned to his desk, realising the interview was over. James had already replaced the unopened folder back inside his briefcase and was buttoning up the coat he'd refused to remove.

"It's a lot to take in James but the facts are very simple. If you allow me to help you, all your debts will be cleared and you are guaranteed a cash sum to tide you over the coming year. And every thinking man knows that this recession is on course to slump much further. If you don't act, the bank will call in the debt and you will be left with nothing to show for your past endeavours. If you try to sell or auction privately, too much time and risk is involved, forcing the bank to move against you. You really are between the proverbial rock and a hard place. Think about it James. When you are ready to sign just give me a ring.

James avoided accepting Carl's offered hand by continuing to fiddle with the buttons of his coat before marching out of the office with a cursory nod of the head.

3-40pm

As James was sitting opposite the most reviled person he'd

ever had the misfortune to be connected to as a mutual associate; Vinny was heading back to Exeter on a half empty air-conditioned train.

The initial excitement and relief of the completed shop sale began to wear off as Vinny realised the implications of having nowhere to live in two days time. Carl had indicated that getting the solicitors place at a knock-down price would be like taking candy from a baby, and could be done in days. But how easy would it be now with forty grand less in the pot? Also, how the hell did Carl know about Charlene turning up and signing away such a large lump if he wasn't involved? Charlene had never liked Carl, said he gave her the creeps, but she must have been staying somewhere close, and it wasn't Lyn Porter's place.

Vinny's head hurt as his mind revolved round and round the subject with no possible answer. He knew he'd have to phone Carl, but he'd wait a little while longer. Boredom started to set in as he reached across the seat opposite for a discarded magazine. Opening it half-heartedly at random, his eyes fell on **'Today's Horoscope'**. Running his chubby, nail-bitten finger down the page he stops at **'Scorpio'**.

'Don't be fooled by what you see as coincidences today. These things are meant to be. 'Just do it'-this should be your mantra from now on.

"What a load of bollocks!" Vinny hadn't realised he'd spoken out loud until a middle-aged couple several seats in front turned and gave a tut of disapproval. Ignoring them, he turned back to the magazine. On the opposite page were letters to an Agony Aunt – Vinny's favourite reading matter. He studied carefully the first and longest letter.

> **Sally from Kent was asking the Agony Aunt's opinion on hiring a private detective. Apparently, Sally suspected her husband of having an affair. Naturally she wanted to nail the bastard, but didn't know how to go about it. She'd heard that unlike America, private detectives in England could practice without a licence or qualifications and she was anxious to find a reputable guy.**

Agony Aunt's response was equally interesting and Vinny concentrated on every word.

> **She agreed that, as the law stood, anyone in England could set up their own Private Detecting Agency; although many are affiliated to governing bodies. I feel it only fair to warn you though, she said at the end, going down this route could prove to be very expensive and suggested that Sally talk things through with her old man.**

"Yea right. Yes my darling I've been bonking a much younger bit of stuff for the last six months. I'm surprised you haven't asked before now!" Vinny's second outburst was conducted in a high-pitched, posh dialect, which sent the middle-aged couple hurrying into the next carriage.

Unaware of the commotion ahead, Vinny read it through again before carefully tearing out the page. He turned back to the 'Scorpio' horoscope and re-read the words, carefully taking in their meaning. This too was torn out, reverently folded and placed with the Agony Aunt page in his laptop case.

In a rare flash of inspiration, Vinny knew for sure where his future lay. He was never destined to be a flower shop owner – that was just a means to a very logical end. Bathed in renewed confidence he punched in Carl's number on his phone, anxious to know about the amount and whereabouts of the all-important cheque.

Carl answered on the third ring, and made it pretty obvious that he was pissed off with Vinny. Vinny cut into his ranting and asked point blank where his cheque was and how much exactly was it for? Vinny heard, as he had done several times before, Chaz, being sent to get coffees. When Carl's voice returned, it was hard and hissing but Vinny clenched his fist against the intimidation that he knew would follow.

"Our cheque", Carl hissed, emphasizing our, is safely deposited in the joint account of V.C. Enterprises. Unfortunately as I said earlier, due to your stupidity, Lyn Porter managed somehow to extract £40,000. Your tart, Charlene creamed off another £10,000 and I've removed my expenses, which total approximately £50,000. If my mental math serves me well, I make that a clear £220,000 in our account. Still far more than the dump of a shop was actually worth, but not enough to satisfy your dream of moving up in the world. Your insane decision not to follow my instructions to the letter has cost us both dearly Vinny;

and I have every intention of recouping what is rightfully mine. Call me when you're back in Torbay; I can't abide trains, even listening to them as background noise makes my blood boil."

Vinny's head reeled from the deluge of information; but what was abundantly clear; the expected sale price had shrunk by £100,000. He leaned forward in his seat willing the train to travel faster.

4-00pm

Lyn ran a finger along the overflowing shelf of books in Lauren's bedroom, recognising several titles from her own childhood. Seven of the Harry Potter books took pride of place in the centre of the shelf with a pair of carved book-ends to keep them upright. Out of curiosity, for Lyn had neither read any of the books nor seen any of the Potter films, she took a copy at random and flipped back the jacketed, cover. Noticing that it was a signed, first-edition copy, she replaced it with care and continued her unpacking.

Twelve year old Lauren had departed the day before, for a three-day study trip to France; and Lyn had been offered her room for the next two nights. According to Jill, their guest bedroom was out of bounds due to a leaky roof, which their builder promised to fix before Lauren's return.

"Doesn't she mind, that a perfect stranger will be taking over her most personal space?" Lyn had asked as she'd watched Jill push Lauren's clothes to one side of the neatly arranged wardrobe; then empty two of her drawers, carrying the contents out of the room, to God knows where.

"Don't be silly Lyn, you're not a stranger; *you* are my oldest friend. I must leave you to unpack though; I have to collect the boys from school."

After unpacking the necessities for two days only, Lyn returned to the large family room and filled the kettle in readiness for her friend's return. Jill had been anxious to catch up on as much news as possible, warning that once the boys were home, all hell would be let loose and you wouldn't get a word in edgeways. But, she had avoided asking Lyn, why, after all this time, she had suddenly decided to spend five days in London. Maybe, sensing that changes were happening, and the changes could be hard to discuss, she was waiting for Lyn to make the first move. All conversation so far, had centred on each others domestic life.

Jill and Derik – her husband of nineteen years – had tried, without success for years to have a baby. Apparently nothing was physically amiss with either of them and their doctor implied that the stress of trying too hard was probably the reason. Having almost given up, Lauren was conceived and born when Jill was thirty-four. As far as Derik was concerned, the family was now complete; but when Lauren turned four and started school, Jill wanted to try for another before she turned forty. William and Thomas – the terrible twins – were born three weeks after Lauren turned five. Whilst drinking a chilled glass of Pinot Noir with their Pasta lunch, Jill had confided that since the boys' arrival, her work as an interior-designer had drastically diminished. She still had clients, from the heady-days of the eighties and nineties, contacting her for advice and possible commissions on all kinds of projects; but almost all were passed on to trusted colleagues.

Lyn replaced the photograph showing a happy family of five enjoying a sunny day in the garden. Lauren was dark-haired, tall and slender like her father. Will and Tom, squeezed protectively on Jill's lap, were blond, carbon copies of their mother.

A hint of loneliness crept over Lyn. Remembering how she'd enjoyed the company of Jasmine and Wilcox and how easy it had seemed to become their friends, she made a mental note to try harder to keep in touch with people she had met. Jill had raised the subject of man-friends and Lyn had had to admit that there had been very few since Martins death but… Jill, at this point had topped up her wine glass and nudged her to continue. She'd told her about James, but stressed she'd only met him a few days ago.

"A few days are all it takes Lyn, there's a gleam in your eyes when you talk about him, give him a ring and keep in touch." At the time, Lyn had laughed and said it was the wine that was responsible for her gleaming eyes. Looking over to the telephone, she was now tempted to make a quick call and explain the message she'd left.

An almighty bang stopped Lyn in her tracks! The bang was followed by another as the two young boys, one after the other, slammed back the kitchen door as they entered from the garden.

"Boys, calm down please," called out Jill as she trundled into the kitchen loaded down with shopping. Panting and red-faced, she plonked down on the nearest chair.

"Hi Lyn, I'm Tom, Hi Lyn I'm Will, Mum said we can shake your hand instead of kissing you. We hate kissing people, it's yucky!" Both of Lyn's hands were grabbed and pumped up and down several times before the lads scampered up the stairs to their room.

"Gorgeous aren't they? But damned hard work; I can't understand why I'm so fat, they keep me on my toes from morning till night."

Overhead the pair sounded as though they were demolishing the place but Jill unloaded her shopping and accepted a cup of tea as though everything was normal.

"School's not too far away thank goodness; and cutting through the park allows them to let off steam, doughnut with your tea Lyn?" Lyn clutched her full stomach to emphasize that the hearty lunch had been more than enough till dinnertime. Taking a hefty, wooden spoon from a large jug of utensils, Jill walked over to the bottom of the stairs and clouted the bottom of the banister three times before shouting, "treats boys!" A sound, very similar to a train at close quarters, filled the room as Will and Tom thundered down the stairs. Two small trays, each containing a doughnut and a glass of milk were set down in front of a television positioned in the far corner of the family room. Sanity returned as the set was switched on.

"Your home, what I've seen of it, is beautiful Jill." Before Jill's return, Lyn had walked around the ground floor of the large, modernised Edwardian house; enjoying the light airy feel of the place. The colour scheme throughout was a tonal mix of cream, beige and brown; but each room had a different primary colour incorporated – either by cushions and a centrepiece bowl, as in the case of the sitting room, where accents of bright, orange, added to the warm-welcoming-feel. The dining room had an eye-catching, zingy-green rug which mirrored the patina of several bronzes on display; and the family room's egg-yolk-yellow couldn't help but make you feel happy and comfortable.

"I can't wait to see your workspace," Lyn continued after enthusing about the cool aquamarine chosen for the kitchen, but decided not to press when Jill cleverly moved to the subject of what she'd planned for dinner.

Chapter 18

Monday Evening 6-00pm

It was another world! It was Derik's world. Lyn wandered slowly around the purpose-built workshop that was positioned in the bottom corner of the large garden. Bars at the windows and heavy locks on the doors proclaimed two things: items of value were kept inside and small boys – filled with mischief and curiosity – were kept outside.

Lyn had been shooed out of the kitchen by Jill after offering to help with dinner.

"Domesticity, dominates my life now, isn't that right Derik?" Derik hadn't answered. Lifting a bunch of keys from a pot on the highest shelf in the kitchen he'd quietly walked out of the back door; but before closing it, had asked Lyn if she'd like to see his workshop. Intrigued by his job-title – Conservator of Antiquities – she'd accepted readily.

Derik had arrived home ten minutes earlier to a noisy boisterous welcome, and after a few minutes of romping with the boys, had greeted Lyn and said how much he'd been looking forward to meeting her. His greeting had been much more formal than expected; shaking the hand of this serious-looking, dark-suited man, reminded Lyn of the two family funerals she'd had to arrange. However, after changing into jeans and sweatshirt, the hunched-shouldered seriousness melted away; and once inside the five-metre-square workshop, he became positively animated.

Several large containers were positioned along a stout work-bench, running the length of one wall, and before being allowed to peek under the lids of each one, Lyn was given a very brief lesson on the procedure of treating ancient, copper-alloy items for Bronze-Disease. She was fascinated, not so much by the various cleaning methods – the immersing in dangerous chemicals for days on end and the subsequent finishes – but by the very objects themselves. Derik lay before her an intriguing mix of decorative items from the time of Boudicca up to the period of Oliver Cromwell and several centuries in between.

"Who owns these pieces?" she asked fingering the exquisite carving on a large Anglo-Saxon brooch that was partially gilded. Derik gave a heavy sigh before answering.

"In the past, the majority of items being conserved, have been for public museums – collections donated over time and individual items given or purchased at auction, nearly always require the attention of a conservator – but these days, it's the private collector who is keeping me in employment. Cut-backs are being felt in all sectors, and museums are no exception. After a meeting today with the governing bodies of three major museums, I am now virtually self-employed."

Lyn was suddenly propelled from a world of Medieval Armour when, out of the blue, Derik said.

"I was sorry to hear about *your* situation Lyn; Jill knew how much the florist meant to you."

For a few seconds Lyn didn't know how to respond. There had been no contact with Jill since they were nineteen, except for a forty-five minute phone call four nights ago, and she certainly hadn't mentioned anything about her present circumstances. In fact, knowing things were bound to change drastically after this week, she'd deliberately steered clear of the subject. "How did you know?" was the only response she could manage.

Sensing her discomfort, Derik made light of the fact that Jill's Mother kept her daughter up to date on all the changes that were taking place in Torbay; adding, that instead of filling Jill's head with local gossip, she ought to be encouraging her daughter to pay more attention to her fading career. The workshop's, wall-mounted telephone rang twice and then stopped – Jill's signal that dinner was ready.

After the earlier hefty lunch, Lyn wasn't sure she could do justice to the promised 'rack-of-lamb', served with redcurrant sauce; but every scrap of the delicious meal was eaten; although she had to decline the follow-up of sticky toffee pudding. Volunteering to supervise the boys prior to and including their bedtime reading, Derik marched them out of the dining-room and the three of them disappeared upstairs. Carrying a tray of coffee with a selection of chocolates arranged on a small, porcelain platter, Lyn followed Jill to the sitting room, agreeing to clear up after their meal had settled.

"Right Lyn, no more pussy-footing around, what brings you to London?"

Jill's frank and straightforward way of dealing with anything was what had attracted her as a friend in the first place; and that friendship had remained until leaving school. Lyn smiled and reached for her handbag knowing that the time had come to be just as frank. After explaining to Jill about the two mysterious letters and how they'd come to light, Lyn carefully untied the narrow pink ribbon and held up the first letter.

Its discoloured white envelope still showed a clear post-mark – N.S.W. Australia, November 3 1962. The name and address on the envelope was completely legible save for the number in the first line of the address which was obscured by spotting. Lyn pointed out that the neat handwriting was similar to that on the back of a photograph which had also been discovered.

Mrs Ethel Cartwright
? Old Lane, Mile End
London.

Just as carefully, Lyn removed the single sheet of wafer-thin paper and handed it to Jill.

Dear Mother,
Pierre has at long last secured a good job; making it possible to rent a place for the three of us. We will soon have enough money for a trip to London and to get married. We are really looking forward to being reunited with our 'little flower' and can't thank you enough for all your help.

Looking forward to seeing you before Christmas, your loving daughter.

Jennifer.

"Jennifer was your mother, am I right?" asked Jill in a voice that was low and gentle.

"Yes but I have no recollection of her." Lyn handed the small Polaroid photograph to her friend, before opening the second envelope.

Jill studied it intently, read the inscription on the back and handed it back to Lyn. "She was beautiful Lyn; it's like looking at you when you were about eighteen; in fact I have a photo of the two of us in one of my many albums, I must dig it out and let you see."

Lyn removed the second letter, post-marked London and dated December 14th 1963. The good-quality, letter-headed paper was sent from a solicitor's office in Liverpool Street. Before handing it to Jill, she confessed that her Gran would never go near a solicitor's office even if her life depended on it. Jill said nothing but read the few lines twice over.

Dear Mrs Cartwright,
We have been instructed by Mr & Mrs P.Beck, of New South Wales, Australia, to seek out and make contact with you.

Please telephone Mr David Markham as soon as possible in order to arrange, at your convenience, an appointment at our Liverpool St. office.

Yours sincerely Robert Markham Senior

"What is it that's bothering you Lyn?"

Lyn explained that this letter was sent four months after her parents were supposedly killed in a traffic accident. Either Gran had got the dates mixed up or..."

Jill found her tongue and cut Lyn off in mid-sentence. "Your Gran was as sharp as a tack, Lyn, so don't continue making excuses for her, she's dead and buried and I for one am not sorry."

"She was the only family I had Jill, before marrying Martin; I know she had her funny ways, but she sacrificed a lot to bring me up."

"You'd have been better off adopted out, the selfish old bat wouldn't even allow you to develop your talents by going to college."

"And are *you* continuing to develop your talents Jill, now that your sons are at school?" Lyn would have done anything to retract the catty remark, but the words had escaped without any conscious thought and all she could do was apologise.

Jill, to her credit, brushed aside the apology and admitted to the truth behind the outburst.

"Let's not get off on the wrong foot Lyn; but your Gran hated my guts because I asked too many questions, about too many things. She tried to break our friendship many times; and I'll bet you didn't get a single one of the letters or cards that I sent after I left for college."

Lyn remembered how hurt she'd felt at not hearing from her friend. Twice she'd tried to find out Jill's address by writing to her Mother. Gran had always offered to post off any letters that Lyn wrote. Squeezing Lyn's hand before pouring the coffee, Jill suggested putting all past bad feelings aside and concentrating on the facts at hand.

"I'll do what I can to help Lyn and I can make a start tomorrow; using the internet, can save such a lot of time and trudging around. There's a strong possibility that your parents are still out there; isn't that wonderful?"

"Why is it wonderful? According to my birth certificate, I'm Lynda Cartwright, adopted by Ethel Cartwright – meaning I was never wanted by the beautiful and glamorous Jennifer, anyway." Tears pricked at the corner of Lyn's eyes causing Jill to call a halt to any more talking until after coffee and chocolates.

7-15pm

The gym was almost empty. Vinny had no problem parking directly outside the large, tinted glass doors which reflected his movements as he aggressively slammed his car door without bothering to lock it. Carl was already here; his smart, black car – gleaming under the gyms illuminated sign – increased Vinny's anger, and put him on his guard. Apart from a smart new address, Vinny had promised himself a set of decent wheels – a six-year-old family hatchback was as embarrassing as a flower shop; and was a standing joke with Carl. But Vinny was done with joking.

Vinny had regarded Carl as his best mate; he'd trusted his word on not needing to check every bit of paperwork that held Vinny's signature. He'd actually allowed him to open the account in the name of V.C. Enterprises; believing that the initials stood for Vincent Conway; not once had it been mentioned that Carl would literally have a hand in Vinny's bank account. How easy it is to fool someone, he thought, as he recalled the evening he promised Charlene that together, they were going to make a fortune; but they had to do what Carl suggested.

Carl was sitting in the farthest corner of the gym's

refreshment bar; the back of his blond head just visible from the entrance. Not a position Vinny would choose – instinct dictated that you keep your back to the wall – but Carl always had his reasons for every calculated move, and this put Vinny even more on his guard.

"Evening Vinny, I expected you over an hour ago; stop for a bite to eat did you? *I* haven't eaten since breakfast."

Vinny was still at least five metres from the table and his eyes hadn't left the back of Carl's blond head since entering the building. Nerves fluttered in his gut but he willed himself to remain calm.

"You obviously don't do much driving in the rush hour Carl; I've driven straight here from Exeter. Now let's cut to the chase, what's all this crap about my money being plundered?" Vinny sat down opposite Carl without ordering a drink. Two empty cans of Red Bull were pushed to one side of the table with the dregs of another being swirled around the glass gripped in Carl's hand.

"Your turn of phrase is very apt, Vinny; I've been chasing around on your behalf for months; you have let me down badly so I'm cutting loose and taking my share." Carl's gaze never left his opponent's; and his voice, although calm, was as cold and calculating as the icy-blue eyes.

"What fucking share, I never said anything about…" Carl grabbed at the lapels of Vinny's one and only suit, cutting him off before he'd said what he desperately wanted Carl to hear.

"That's the trouble with you Vinny, you never say anything; do you think I'm a fucking mind reader? I could have made my share by selling your property to a confidential buyer in London; which brings me again to the question, what the fuck were you doing in London? Before you answer, consider the fact that I hold your cheque, and once it's cleared I'm free to take as much as I like. The paperwork is all above board and signed by you."

Vinny lunged towards Carl but the taller man caught him by the hair and pushed him aside easily. As Vinny marched out of the bar, Carl called after him.

"Do be careful as you drive by my car; any dents or scratches will have to be paid for by V.C. Enterprises."

7-45pm

Three hoots from a car-horn brought James out of the sombre mood that threatened to engulf him once again. From the light of an outside lamp he was able to make out his sister, struggling with a bag of take-away food, as she locked her car door. Realising with a start that he'd forgotten to switch on the oven, as promised, he made to dash up the stairway to his kitchen; but the sound of Helen's heeled boots on the doorstep, followed by a tattoo of raps from the heavy brass knocker, halted him on the first step.

"For God's sake James, why are there no lights on? Here take this from me; I don't think we'll need the oven it's still piping hot."

Helen had phoned her brother earlier to ask if she could pop by after delivering a set of drawings to a Torbay client. James knew it was his sister's way of finding out the latest on his financial situation; and as she'd promised to arrive bearing gifts in the form of a meal, which James had no appetite for, he'd felt obliged to agree.

"I know you have always done it James, it was a standing joke when we were kids to leave you alone in the dark until your bad mood passed, but you scared the hell out of me just now." Helen stubbornly waited for a response.

"I can reason things out better in the dark; shall I set the table or shall we eat in the kitchen?" James's evasiveness only added to Helen's frustration.

"We'll eat in the kitchen and I promise not to say a word until we've both satisfied our hunger. Just bear in mind James, Matt and I are family and we are concerned about the situation you are in. We'll talk through the problems and see what can be done. And don't insult my intelligence with remarks that sitting in the dark helps you to think; sitting in the dark helps you to hide from the truth. Believe me, I know from experience."

James couldn't be bothered to respond. Instinctively, he removed a bottle of red wine from the rack, and half-filled two glasses before remembering that Helen never drank any alcohol when she was driving. Apologising, he emptied hers into his own glass and took a large gulp. By the time his sister had sat down with the two plates of food, James was topping up his glass again.

As promised, silence reigned apart from the chinking of metal on porcelain. Thanks to the wine plus six hours of ingesting nothing but coffee, James's appetite returned and he ate until his plate was empty. Feeling physically better, and knowing that there was no escape, he decided to lay all the facts and the happenings of that day before his sister. Expecting Helen to be as shocked as he was, in regard to John Haydon and his cavalier manner of buying property with the underhand agenda of demolishing it; he found her response irksome.

"The whole area is run-down James, it should have been demolished years ago, sure John Haydon will make money from the new development but people's lives will be improved, you have to look ahead and see the bigger picture."

"All I see are deception and greed; and I have to confess, it hurts when a person I regarded as a friend is not only part of that greed, but deliberately keeps you in the dark."

"And what about the greed of the florist's owner; if somebody offered me way over the odds, for a property or business that was running to seed, I'd regard myself as being very fortunate."

"You sound as though you condone this underhand practice Helen; did *you* have prior knowledge to what John Haydon was up to?" James raised his arms in apology at the horrified look on her face. In one single day, he thought, a whole raft of trust and regard, he previously held in certain people, had disappeared; and the most hurtful, had been finding out about Lyn porter and Vincent Conway – the supposed villain in her life – travelling to London together.

"I promised Matt I wouldn't be too late, so let's go over your options." James sensed Helen's growing impatience. Tipping the remaining wine into his glass, he settled back for one of her many lessons on economics.

When Helen had drawn up the plans, to return the ugly partitioned building back into a splendid Georgian House, she had voiced misgivings about James wanting to find a single tenant for the whole four floors. Lots of wrangling had resulted in a flexible compromise, which, according to Helen, would give James a much healthier return on his investment.

The first floor, commanding the highest rent, would mirror James's own apartment – two large double bedrooms, both with on-suite bathrooms, sitting-room, dining-room, well-fitted kitchen and spacious hallway incorporating several storage cupboards. The ground floor was best suited to office space. Two large rooms, independently secured, sharing a small kitchen/utility area at the rear. The basement rooms, which in James's view was best suited as secure storage of files for the possible solicitor he was hoping to attract; had been the biggest bone of contention. By installing a neat shower room and adequate kitchen, Helen had argued that a two bed-roomed flat with a small paved back courtyard and parking space – advertised as the Garden Flat – would prove far more profitable than storage space that would probably never be needed. She'd continued her argument; pointing out that the second floors two large rooms were more than adequate for storage; unless of course you want to create a small penthouse apartment with a stupendous view. James had cut short her mounting excitement; knowing full well that the only service on the top floor was electricity and costs were already spiralling out of control.

"I do accept Helen that in the present economic climate, I would most likely have to split the property into two or maybe three units and as you said at the time it will be very easy to self-contain the basement and first floor from the offices, but, I do think we are completely missing the point here. "The bank is calling in my loan, so your advice is, well, academic."

"Oh for heaven sake James, where is your fighting spirit? Come down from the high moral stand and grub around in the real world like the rest of us! Are you prepared to allow an egocentric, opportunist bank clerk to rob you of what you've worked hard for?"

"So what magic do you have up your sleeve dear sister?" The cutting remark found no purchase on Helen's tough skin.

"For starters," she said in a magnanimous voice, "it's hopeless in these economic climes, trying to secure a tenant. Property ownership is embedded in the British psyche. Why would anyone, pour money into the pocket of a landlord, when they could pay out a similar amount in mortgage repayments and eventually own the place. Times have changed James and those of us who don't change with them will go under."

"I'll think over what we have discussed." James kissed Helen lightly on the forehead; his head was a little dizzy and he wanted to be alone."

"James, the time for thinking is over, arrange for a meeting with your bank manager first thing tomorrow. Matt and I are prepared to draw our savings for you to use but we can only manage twenty per cent of what you owe."

"Helen you know me better than that, I can't take your money."

"And we are not offering to give it, it would be a loan at 2% interest; the bank is offering us no more, but I'll bet you are paying four times that rate for your loan."

James followed his sister down to the front door and checked the locks. On returning to the sitting room, he sat down heavily in his favourite chair after turning off all the lights.

Chapter 19

S tanding under the full force of the powerful shower, Vinny turned the dial to cold and allowed the chilling needle-like deluge to fall directly on his head. He'd had no sleep at all – spending the night alternating between packing his stuff and wondering what the hell he was going to do. Around 4-30am, when his body was at its lowest ebb and his mind had almost given up the fight of see-sawing between anger and worry, three small words drifted up into his mind. 'Once it's cleared'. Carl had said the words without thinking; after all, everyone knows that a cheque takes at least three to five days to clear; and the bigger the cheque, the longer the greedy bastards hang onto it, thought Vinny realizing that he'd been thrown a life-line.

Filled with renewed hope and vigour, He had re-read the two magazine cuttings before replacing them reverently back inside his wallet. Never before had he felt so sure of the way forward. The money from the shop would set him free and allow him to follow the destiny which was his by right. Aunt Beryl had known in her heart that he was never cut out to run a flower shop; and now that Lyn Porter had her money back, he was sure the bad dreams of his aunt chasing him with a knife would stop. *I'll cut your gonads off if you ever do any harm to Lyn.* However he would need every single penny that remained to fulfil his needs; and there was only one person who could help him do it.

After towelling himself down Vinny plunged himself into a gruelling regime of press-ups, knowing that he would need to shower again before getting dressed. There was still at least two hours before he could set his plan in motion; but it was necessary to stay awake and alert for the rest of the day.

8-45am

With no signs of a hangover and feeling surprisingly refreshed, James headed down to his front door to collect the daily-delivered, pint of milk. Mindful that nothing lasts forever, James had happily paid over the odds for the luxury of this particular, long-standing, English tradition.

After unlocking the heavy porch door, something stopped him in mid-stoop as he bent to retrieve the bottle of milk. Propped on the opposite end of the step with eyes closed and mouth open – emitting a low, rumbling snore – sat a man who was obviously homeless or drunk. On closer inspection, recognition dawned and James shook the shoulder of Vincent Conway – alias Victor Connor.

"Mr Connor, you'll catch your death sleeping in such low temperatures, are you waiting to see me?" James didn't particularly like the man; but in all conscience he couldn't leave him on the step until nine o'clock. Vinny swore softly as he shook the muddled drowsiness from his head, and then remembering where he was and what he had to do, apologised several times for swearing and littering the solicitors step – brushing it down as he stood to show that he meant every word.

James watched as Vincent Conway tried several times to fit his large chubby finger through the delicate handle of the cup With another apology, he wrapped both his hands around the heat of the small, china vessel and drank the coffee almost in one go. Silently, James refilled his cup wondering what had brought him to his office so early. He didn't have long to wait. During the sipping of the second cup, Victor Connor, who readily owned up to being Vincent Conway, unburdened his greatest fear that Carl would make off with most, if not all, of his money.

"I do sympathise Mr Conway, but I can't, in all honesty, see what can be done; after all I followed Ms Dais's instructions to the letter."

"I know that mate, and I'm not blaming you, but from what I've told you, and by checking the paperwork, it's obvious the shop was mine. It was Carl's idea to bring Charlene on board; to prevent Lyn Porter from getting her investment back. She's got her money and believe me, I don't begrudge it, but I need your help buddy, to stop what is mine, ending up in the wrong hands."

James found the newly-acquired, obsequious manner of Vincent Conway even more loathsome than his former brutish arrogance; but he knew for certain that he, too, was caught up in this vile web of deceit and corruption; and gaining knowledge was his only hope of protection. It was almost nine o'clock. He'd resigned himself to making an appointment with the bank manager – Helen would be phoning that evening for a progress report and after his appalling behaviour of the evening before, he needed to offer her something. "Like I said earlier Mr Conway, I can't see what can be done; what do *you* propose?"

"Phone Haydon right now and get him to stop the cheque; make up some cock and bull story that you lost the first one or you made a mistake, anything, so long as it's cancelled right away."

James took a while for the proposal to sink in. The audacity of this man caught him completely off-guard but still he remained silent; enjoying, in a perverse way, the thrown down gauntlet. "And what would I stand to gain from such a humiliating action?"

"A cash-buyer for part of your property James, or can I call you Jimmy, sounds much friendlier don't you think?"

"You can call me Mr Fairbank, and please remember, I am not your mate, your buddy or your friend and I doubt very much if you could afford any part of my property."

"Fair enough, Mr Fairbank it is; but we both know that the bank has been squeezing your balls and is about to call in their loan; all I need is a small flat with office space to carry out my profession. *I* get an address in 'The Terrace'; *you* get your loan paid off."

The thought of having Vincent Conway as a neighbour filled James with revulsion; but what was even more worrying, was the thought of what the apartment might be used for. He didn't even try to hide the derisive tone in his voice when he asked. "And what profession might that be Mr Conway?"

"Private Investigator, Mr Fairbank."

After a ten minute phone call to Edinburgh, James had gained the best possible outcome from the situation. He'd had to convince John Haydon that the cheque had been made out incorrectly – taking full blame for the over-sight. Instead of 'V.C. Enterprises', it should have read 'V.C. Investigations'; rendering the present cheque useless and the recipient to be hopping mad. Speed was of the essence and James suggested that John phone his bank straight away to cancel the useless cheque. To save further embarrassment and to keep the recipient happy, he would use the blank cheque from John to right the mistake.

As James walked back into his office, where Victor Conway sat biting on his nails, he was surprised at how easy it had been to deceive; and how integrity disappeared when you were backed into a corner.

"The cheque is cancelled Mr Conway, I suggest you open an account straight away in the name of V.C. Investigations; but be sure to use a different bank. I'll make an appointment to see you back here at eleven. Don't engage with anyone about this."

In response, Vincent Conway slapped James on the shoulder and promised to be back on the dot. As he stepped out onto the pavement his eyes wandered admiringly over the vacant premises; and his eagerness to view all four floors of the sumptuous property put a spring in his step.

A chilly wind blew around Vinny's ears as he headed towards town; but a heavy weight had been lifted from his shoulders. Jimmy Fairbank had proved himself worthy. He was now regarded as Vinny's best mate. In his new role as a 'private dick', having a solicitor next door could prove to be very handy. And no doubt Jimmy would need his help from time to time in return.

9-30am

The sound of Jill entering through the garden door, rustling with carrier bags, brought Lyn's attention back to the moment. She still felt groggy from lack of sleep; but the half-drunk mug of filter coffee was helping to bring her back into the land of the living.

In spite of feeling exhausted when she'd finally climbed between the inviting, lilac-coloured sheets, sleep had eluded her for what seemed like hours. Posters – depicting various scenes from the Harry Potter films – were neatly arranged around Lauren's bedroom walls. The images, innocent enough when viewed in daylight, took on a more sinister appearance when the lights went out. Through a gap in the curtains, the moon – which happened to be full – played tricks with movement as clouds, wind and tree branches colluded to produce an animated display.

When sleep finally took hold, it was fitful and crammed with nonsensical dreams. Remembered snatches involved her Gran fighting a weird monster with a rolling-pin and as the monster dipped its head to devour the troublesome old lady, it transformed into Martin. Another hair-raising scene found Lyn locked in a dark, underground room. Continuous banging on the door seemed useless, but afraid of being left to die in that cold, damp, tomb-like space, Lyn's subconscious self refused to surrender and her feet took over from exhausted fists. Sweating and fearful she woke with a start; confused that the banging was continuing; then realised that Tom and Will were hammering on the door asking if she'd like tea in bed. She'd shouted for them to go away and leave her alone; not believing the bedside clock which showed 8-16.

"God, you look exhausted Lyn, we could leave all this research stuff until tomorrow if you like; and I'll see if the builder will come today. I'm sure you'll be more comfortable in the guest room."

"No, really Jill the bed is fine; I never sleep well on the first night in a strange bed. Tomorrow I have to go to Watford. I meant to say before now but there seemed so many other things to talk about." Lyn knew what was coming next: and she felt guilty in advance of the lie.

"Why on earth do you need to go to Watford?" Jill had been unpacking the carrier bags of shopping – done after dropping the boys off at school – but she stopped and gave Lyn her full attention.

"Oh it's just a maturing insurance policy that Martin started years ago." Lyn rubbed the upper part of her face, feigning an attempt to wake her self up more fully; but in reality, she couldn't look her friend in the eye.

"Watford's not the most exciting place, but we'll stop for a bit of lunch there and just make the most of the day."

"No, I don't expect you to waste a day there Jill, the only reason *I'm* going, is because they've messed me around for ages and I want to collect the cheque in person and get it into the bank."

Silence reigned over the next few minutes save for the noise of shopping being put away. A combination of guilt and weakened resolve almost brought Lyn to the point of blurting out the truth; but remembering the promise she'd made; and the risk that the chance to better her life could be lost, she remained tight-lipped.

"So, the only reason you've come to London is to collect a cheque from Watford and solve the mystery of the two letters?" Jill sounded hurt and disappointed. Lyn was desperate to change the subject.

"And I'm here to see you Jill! When do I get to look over your design studio?" Lyn stood and moved over to her friend; wrapping her arms around her paunchy middle.

"I must get you some breakfast. We've got a lot of footwork in the east end, I doubt if we'll get very far on the internet with the first stage of the investigation." Jill had broken free from Lyn's embrace and the atmosphere became charged with uncertainty.

"I'm longing to see your studio, Jill." Lyn tried to keep the statement light-hearted; remembering Derik's comment about her fading career.

"You've already seen it Lyn; Derik is making good use of a space that stood idle for a long time. Lauren was such an easy baby; there was no problem back then mixing work and parenting. She takes after her father, very studious and independent. Different story when my boys came along, there was no time or energy left over for anything."

"But they're at school now Jill; surely you can keep your hand in, even if it's only on a part-time basis until they're older." Jill had taken a biscuit from a nearby tin and was absentmindedly breaking bits off and popping them into her mouth.

"Truth is Lyn, I've lost all confidence. There was so much work around in the eighties and nineties; I was fortunate enough to pick and choose the plummiest assignments. Then along came all the make-over television shows; and every other college candidate wanted to be an interior designer and the competition became very intense. Don't get me wrong, there's a wealth of talent out there – young things, confident and beautiful with fashionable ideas."

"You were confident and beautiful, you still are beautiful Jill, but everyone gets older. Experience comes with age and having an eye for colour and design has got nothing to do with fashion; it's about satisfying a clients needs in a lasting way."

"I was hoping…I mean I thought that maybe you'd decided to move to London. Mum keeps me informed about what's happening back home and I know the new florists didn't work out and your old shop is up for sale. I thought maybe we could team up. I've still got several long-standing contacts and with your flair, Lyn, I'm sure we could make it happen." Jill had become so vivacious and not wanting to burst her balloon of enthusiasm, Lyn said "Let's just see where the next few days lead; I'm starving; and we have a family mystery to solve."

Chapter 20

Tuesday Midday

For James Fairbank, punctuality and good manners were synonymous: so it was of little surprise that at the prearranged time of 11-00 o'clock, Vincent Conway was nowhere in sight. It was pretty obvious the man would turn up at some point – James held his money and the prospect of his new abode – but because so much was at stake, James had felt sure that he'd be back, champing at the bit, as soon as possible. Now, as the clock hands became one, and were about to ring out their midday melodious chimes; James began to worry that something untoward had happened.

The thought of having Vincent Conway occupying any part of his newly-refurbished property had filled James with disconcertion. But the certainty of allowing his pride and joy of a property to slip into the hands of the bank, if he didn't act quickly and decisively, was so disturbing and had raised such strong feelings of anger – anger which hitherto had played no part in James's business dealings. Helen had been right; his blinkered view of the world had caused him to almost lose everything he'd worked for. His long-standing reputation for fair-play counted for nothing.

In fact, amongst the get-rich-quick, crooked entrepreneurs, his way of conducting business was scorned and ridiculed.

As James tore his attention from unproductive thoughts and checked again all the paperwork before him, his telephone rang, synchronising with the last few chimes of his clock. Picking up the receiver, he listened attentively as he swivelled his desk chair towards the window and the panoramic harbour view.

"I'll certainly do what I can Ms Dais, but I can't promise anything, as you know, it's out of my hands now. Yes I will, I've made a note of your number. Take care of yourself, Ms Da… sorry Charlene."

"Where the hell is *she* phoning from?" Vinny's aggressive voice gave James such a start that it cancelled out the expected relief of his return.

"How dare you enter without knocking and listen in to a private telephone conversation!"

"If that fucking old fashioned clock hadn't been clanging out a poor interpretation of Big Ben, you would have heard me coming in, and besides I have an appointment, remember." Vinny slumped down in the seat on the opposite side of James's desk with a look of thunder on his face. The reason for the look soon became obvious as Vincent Conway relayed, in colourful language, his frustration at opening a new bank account. Apparently he'd walked out of one of the main branches, telling them to poke their account where the sun didn't shine, after he'd been asked so many personal questions and been given such a high tariff of charges as a New-Business-Account.

James listened, inwardly flinching at every crude expletive, wanting this meeting to be over as soon as possible but knowing there was still a long way to go. After a while Vincent Conway ran out of steam and silence reigned for a minute or two. James looked expectantly at the other man but said nothing.

"Listen Jimmy, in the end my only option was to open a personal current account; the business account bit will have to come later. Is that a problem for you?"

James could see that the answer to this question was all-important. Vincent Conway had no idea that James held the power of making out the cheque to whomever he pleased.

"I suggest we look over what is for sale and deal with the money aspect when both parties are in agreement. Like I said earlier Mr Conway, The Garden Flat is the only part of the next door building that is for sale and the only floor that you could possibly afford."

Before James had barely time to finish his last sentence, Vincent Conway's face creased into a look of horror and disgust.

"Garden flat, what are you on about? I've just unloaded a fucking florist shop and I wouldn't care if I never see another flower again; so I'm hardly likely to want to grow the fucking things, am I?" A heavy fist, slammed down on James's desk, punctuated the end of Vincent Conway's outburst.

"Calm down Mr Conway, I suggest we look over the flat in question; and I'd very much appreciate you keeping your fists to yourself."

"Sorry Jimmy, I'm just a bit tired and stressed, you know how it is."

Over the next hour or so, James Fairbank and Vincent Conway formed a precarious allegiance. Vincent fell in love with the lower-ground floor, pointing out that its subway-like situation was perfect for a private investigator. His concerns, over being forced into tending a garden, were unfounded; a small paved terrace area – devoid of any greenery – was all that was left of a space that had been mainly turned over to an off-road parking-bay. He'd congratulated James several times on the design and quality of the refurbishment and had readily agreed to the price of £205,000, with two provisos. First and most importantly, or so it seemed to James, was the change of address name (how could anyone take a private detective seriously, working from 'a garden flat'.) Secondly, he needed to move in by Thursday.

James had agreed to the two provisos, stating that as from Thursday the Garden Flat would become known simply as No 4a The Terrace. He had several stipulations of his own but decided to wait and voice them at the point when he was about to write Vincent the all-important cheque.

Sandwiches, followed by coffee and chocolate biscuits, were enjoyed by both men in an atmosphere of cordiality. However, when the refreshment break was over and all the necessary paperwork signed, the ambience chilled a little when James – poised with cheque book and pen – lay down his stipulations.

"Vincent, there are several things bothering me and which I would like to clear up before we become neighbours. You might think that what I'm about to ask is none of my business; but I can assure you it has a lot of bearing and will provide me with a great deal of insight on matters that will affect me at some point."

"Fire away Jimmy." Vincent's few words of bravado belied the worried expression.

"First of all, I want to know how Ms Dais came by her bruising injuries." James held up his hand to still an immediate response from Vincent that was ill thought out and probably untrue. "I also want to know as much about Carl as possible – the circumstances in which you met and how much you know about his background." James could clearly see that Vincent was in no hurry to supply this information and wondered if any would be forthcoming. "Finally, and Vincent this is most important, why were you and Lyn Porter travelling to London together yesterday?"

The very moment James Fairbank mentioned Lyn Porter's name, Vincent Conway realised that *his* was the voice that had left the message on her answer phone. It was obvious he fancied her. Shame, but he deserved to know the truth. Trouble is, thought Vinny, there's no easy way of telling a guy that the woman he's got the hots for is a dyke.

2-30pm

Lyn found it almost impossible to focus her eyes on the small, italic print of the café's menu. Splashing with cold water, blinking rapidly and rubbing with the heel of her fists, had all been tried in an attempt to soothe the damage of overwork. With a heavy sigh, the menu was cast aside in favour of a large blackboard displaying 'Today's Specials' in large, readable, chalk letters.

With Jill working beside her, they'd scrolled through what seemed like, miles of microfilm; looking for details of a double fatality that had occurred during June 1964. Nothing had come to light in any of the local newspapers of the day. Both women had expected this part of their research to be easy and fruitful – a cushy rest after the slog of walking the streets of the East-End of London, looking up addresses only to find they no longer existed. In short, the morning's efforts had been a complete waste of time. Even the solicitor's office, Markham & Sons of Liverpool St, had disappeared and been replaced by a ten-storey, glass fronted, office block that bore no sign of a solicitor of any description.

"The chunky soup with chunky bread will do me," said Lyn, rubbing her hands to warm them and not yet ready to peel off her warm wool coat. The waitress scribbled on her pad and turned her indifferent eyes on Jill without saying a word.

"Make that two, please." Lyn had offered to buy lunch; and Jill didn't want to appear greedy by ordering too large a meal even though she felt famished.

Lyn smiled at her friend; and as the stony-faced waitress marched away, whispered conspiratorially, "we'll cheer ourselves up with an over-the-top dessert." Both women giggled and the disappointments of the morning seemed to melt in the warmth of their companionship.

"I know we've run out of time for today, Lyn, but I can carry on the research tomorrow while you're in Watford. I'll bang away on my computer and see what the internet throws up."

"I'm amazed that you're even the slightest bit interested

after all the effort of today, with nothing to show but freezing-cold hands and feet and fuddled eyesight." At the thought of her extremities, Lyn registered the tingling of her toes coming to life.

"It's pathetically sad I know," said Jill, lowering her eyes and fiddling with the cutlery, "but this is the most exciting time I've had in ages. My life in the last few years has revolved solely around the kid's needs; I never consider what I want anymore."

"As Derik is almost self-employed now, couldn't you team up with him; don't you find it fascinating being involved with all that ancient craftsmanship?"

"God no, I'd hate all that poking around in stuff that's been buried for hundreds or even thousands of years. No, I'm a child of the here and now and when I bring my skills back into focus, it will be with designs for modern living and the future."

Two bowls of piping hot chunky-soup arrived and all conversation ceased as appetites were satiated. Jill's bowl was empty long before Lyn's; giving her the opportunity to disagree that the morning had been completely wasted.

"As we didn't find a single reference to your parent's car accident – and God knows we looked hard enough – there's a good chance that it didn't happen. Which means, you were lied to and there's the possibility that your parents are still alive, so…"

"Or Gran got the dates wrong," cut in Lyn chewing a piece of meat that threatened to choke her because of the sudden outburst. After clearing her throat she continued. "It *was* a long time ago and she must have been beside herself with grief and worry."

"The solicitor's letter indicates a different scenario Lyn. I don't think the mornings efforts were wasted at all; your two letters and the fact that no accident occurred during that month, speaks volumes. Tomorrow, there are several things I intend to check out, and if they are as successful as today – who knows where you might be this time next year. I would like a generous portion of sticky-toffee pudding to celebrate our massive step forward to revealing the truth of your past."

Again, Lyn nearly choked on the last chunk of the chunky-soup. She didn't feel the slightest bit hungry anymore and she was beginning to wonder if coming to London had been such a good idea after all. Maybe after the necessary trip to Watford, she'd make an excuse to return home. "I'll just have coffee, but *you* have whatever you want Jill, you've certainly earned it."

"That's why I'm this size Lyn; I always reward myself with food, what rewards do you use that keep you looking so slim and beautiful?"

Lyn pondered over her friend's words as the waitress cleared their bowls and took their order for coffees and one dessert.

"I don't ever remember rewarding myself for anything, I choose what I want to do and just do it. Why would I need a reward for that?"

3-10pm

James checked his watch for the third time. He was already ten minutes late for his appointment with the bank manager and he still had at least five minutes of power-walking to do before he could reach the bank. Old habits die hard, he told himself, consciously slowing his step to a more moderate pace. Why on earth was he rushing and putting himself out for an establishment that had treated him so shabbily; culminating in the threat of robbing him of his property (and robbing wasn't too strong a word) thought James as his anger and his step quickened once again.

James had strongly advised Vincent Conway to avail himself of an independent solicitor to safeguard his interests – and give James a little more breathing space. He'd flatly refused. Too pricey and too long-winded had been his no-nonsense reply – a response which was perfectly true but James had said nothing. After twenty minutes of drawing his attention to page after page of documentation, James had been stopped in mid-sentence by Vincent's impatient voice.

"Look Jimmy," he'd said, slapping both his splayed-out hands across the document currently being read. "I've seen the flat and I want to buy it. You give me the keys and I'll give you the money; I trust you completely to do the paperwork properly, so just tell me where to sign."

Vincent Conway's attitude to legal documents must have been a big plus to the likes of Carl; but James had been loath to bring his name up again. His second laid down stipulation – wanting to know as much as possible about Carl; had caused the man to clam-up in fear – leaving James to wonder what kind of hold Carl had over Vincent Conway, Charlene Dais and possibly, Lyn Porter.

James apologised to the receptionist for his late arrival,

giving no clue or reason as to why his lack of punctuality had been necessary. Melanie, according to her badge, in response, gave him nothing but a cursory smile and an indication to follow where she led.

He was shown into a small, sparsely furnished room – its purpose obviously multi-functional. All four magnolia-painted walls were blank, save for one piece of ultra modern art-work – a lithograph of Llanberis. This, was strategically positioned, for the purpose of giving light relief to anyone left waiting in a space that was almost completely devoid of sensory stimulus. A cauldron of mixed emotions simmered within James as he tried to gain peace from looking intently at the simple, idyllic scene.

James heard the door open behind him but remained seated with his eyes fixed on the print. A polite cough followed by Melanie's voice grabbed his attention.

"Richard is on his way, but his diary is rather full."

"Don't worry, I won't keep him long; may I have Richard's full name please?"

"Richard McNeal."

"Thank you Melanie." James had never met the current bank manager; and he wasn't prepared to stoop so low as to address him by his first name without being invited. Twenty-five years ago when he first opened his business account at this branch Gerald Foxley ran a very tight ship; no first-name-terms for him until you'd passed through his fair but stringent interview and had reached the stage where you'd shared lunch in one of the nearby restaurants. He'd been pensioned off in 2001 and since then there had been at least three managers – all of whom, it had seemed to James, were far too young to have had enough experience in taking care of customer's finances.

The door opened and a short, ginger-haired man in his mid-thirties strode purposefully up to James and offered his hand. "Good afternoon Mr Fairbank; Richard McNeal, how can I help?"

James reached for the offered hand, which was gripped firmly but quickly released, and apologised for being late. Richard McNeal – in a soft Scottish lilt – brushed aside James's apology as he sat in the opposite chair and opened the file before him.

"We are both very busy men Mr McNeal so I'll get straight to the point. I'm here to settle the loan against my property and recover the deeds."

Richard McNeal's eyes lifted from the file before him and rested on James's face, looking for some clue as to what he was up against. "May I be permitted to know why? I've only been here two months and I'm trying to get to know our long-standing, successful, professional clients."

James was tempted to fire a whole list of accusations at the man; but held his tongue realising that he was completely in the dark over certain underhand behaviour that was being carried out almost under his nose. "Talk to Carl in Business Enterprises, he'll fill you in, and incidentally, may I have Carl's full name?"

"Unfortunately, Carl's no longer with us. He's based in London; but spends six-months at a time in various development regions around the South West; last Friday was his final day in Torbay."

"I had an interview with the man yesterday and he gave the impression that he'd be available today." James garnered all his will power to keep his voice level.

"Carl is a very conscientious worker; he likes to tie up any loose ends even if it means running over his allotted time and losing financially. Everyone knows him only as Carl," the bank manager continued, "he constantly jokes – if it's good enough for 'Morse'…"

"Well it's not good enough for me," interrupted James unable to keep a lid on his erupting animosity. "I would like to be furnished with Carl's full name and the name and contact number of his superior in London. I'll collect the deeds to my property in three days time when my cheque has cleared. I'm sure you'll find the amount covers everything, I've a stack of intimidating letters showing the figures and no doubt you will have access to copies. As far as I am aware, Mr McNeal, Carl's conscientiousness is limited to himself and possibly the bank. He is a bad egg and I intend to expose him."

Chapter 21

Vinny hunted through his pockets, cursing aloud, as he examined several scraps of paper but not finding what he wanted. Suddenly it dawned on him that what he'd been trying to achieve over the last two hours – putting his paperwork into some kind of system – is where he would find the telephone number he wanted. He had thought of putting the solicitor's number on his mobile phone but changed his mind. After all, responsibilities came with being a private detective; in future, personal telephone numbers would have to be memorised and codes worked out for written down private addresses.

Vinny had just switched on his mobile phone – normally done before he'd even climbed out of bed – but today hadn't been a normal day, he'd told himself, knowing deep down the real reason. As expected, his phone indicated that someone had been trying to reach him – two voice-mails and one text – all from Carl. Vinny refused to cave in to the fear that fluttered and taunted his bowels. His money was safe, and Carl was in London (thank Christ he wouldn't be back till Friday). By that time, he'd be well hidden in his new basement flat. Vinny decided he needed the solicitor's word that he would keep quiet.

The phone was picked up on the third ring and Vinny heard the solicitor give the same professional greeting even though his office hours had finished over an hour ago.

"You're not still working are you Jimmy? I've got some news on Carl; thought you might want to hear it. I know I wasn't very helpful earlier but we were both in a rush. Tell you what, I'll grab a take-away and a few beers and we'll continue where we left off, I need to bring a few boxes over anyway. Will seven o'clock suit you?"

"Yes that will be fine Vincent, thank you." James's head was still filled with the conversation he'd had with John Haydon less than fifteen minutes ago; and it was only the mention of 'news on Carl' that had enticed James to agreeing to share part of his evening with Vincent Conway.

James had been systematically rereading the letters from his bank, appertaining to threats of repossession if he didn't settle in full the outstanding loan of £210, 000 plus interest – an amount which increased on each demand. His telephone had rung before he had reached the final letter, but not before he had realized something very important about the sender of each intimidating correspondence.

The call had been from Scotland and John Haydon was very off-hand. Apparently, within a few hours of John cancelling his cheque to V.C. Enterprises, word had travelled fast through the network of banking associates, and Carl had taken a step closer to sealing his fate by phoning John Haydon directly, spouting all manner of rhetoric about the illegality of cancelling cheques.

"This whole business has made me look a complete arsehole in the eyes of my bank James, Carl was very upset when I told him I couldn't reverse the decision because a cheque had already been raised in a different name, and I felt even more of a fool when I couldn't even remember the name on the new cheque."

James hadn't been able to control the smile that creased his face when he'd heard this outburst from his old friend; but he'd felt compelled to pacify without giving too much away.

"Just remember John," he'd said, in a voice as reassuring as possible, "the property you badly wanted is yours now and nothing can alter that; and believe me when I tell you that your money has gone to the rightful owners. Enjoy the rest of your stay in Scotland and I'll explain everything more fully on your return." James had put the phone down quickly, not only to prevent John from entering into another tirade of self-pity over his miss-placed standing with the bank; but because he was eager to get back to what he thought he had discovered.

7-15pm

The twins were driving Lyn and Jill mad. The main controlling factor of the household – Derik – was out for the evening – giving a constructive talk at the local Metal Detectives Club, on how to conserve their copper-alloy finds.

"He could have cancelled Lyn, he knows they play me up at bedtime when he's not around, and I did tell him that I had a splitting headache." Jill's anger was being taken out on the pots and pans that couldn't be squeezed into the dishwasher.

"Come on Jill, it's not Derik's fault that our day went pear-shaped; besides, it's unprofessional to cancel something like that at the last minute. It's those little monsters you should be angry at." Lyn's thumb flicked at the ceiling where the overhead noise was almost unbearable.

Jill's headache had come on as they'd driven back across London. The traffic had been so congested it had been touch and go whether they'd arrive at the boys' school in time. Then, with less than a half mile to go, a minor accident caused a huge tailback, trapping the women in the middle of the jam. With instructions from a frantic Jill, Lyn headed off on foot to pick up the boys.

They'd led her a merry dance all the way home; especially after she'd refused their demands of treats from the local sweet shop – she was freezing cold, her legs ached from too much walking and the lads had a cupboard full of so-called treats at home. Their revenge and pay-back had gone on ever since.

"Tell you what Jill, take a couple of pain killers and go and relax in that lovely sitting room of yours. I'll read the boys a story and get them into bed."

"Oh if only life were that simple," sighed Jill, scraping the untouched vegetables from Will and Tom's plates before slipping them into a bowl of soapy water.

Saying nothing, Lyn stood with arms folded in the doorway of the twin's bedroom. Toys littered the bed and floor; and as she watched, more were added to their number. Both lads, holding a plump pillow and standing astride their beds, were having great fun taking turns to swipe each other; not caring that items from their nearby shelves were caught up in the pillow's line of fire. Lyn continued her stance in silence and they, knowing she was watching, continued their antics with increased zeal. It didn't last long. Unfamiliar with this scenario they decided to change tack and broke into a chant of "we want mummy" giving them a common aim to raise their voices once again.

"Listen boys," said Lyn, in a tone remembered from her own early childhood, your mother has a headache, if you want a bedtime story you have five minutes to tidy your room." Thankfully, Derik had helped by supervising their ablutions before he left, although Lyn could clearly see pen marks down Will's clean pyjamas and his left hand. Both lads let out a wale of protest and returned to the 'we want mummy chant.' Unperturbed, Lyn pointed to their large, wall-clock – showing Spider-Man scaling the numbers towards 7-25. "I'll be back in five minutes, if the rooms not tidy, no story." She closed the door quietly and retreated downstairs; finding Jill still in the kitchen.

"I've just about finished here Lyn, thanks for trying; I could here their chanting, bless em." Lyn almost forcibly guided her friend to the calming embrace of the sitting room and told her she'd be back in half an hour for a glass of wine.

At seven thirty precisely, Lyn re-entered the twin's bedroom. The crumpled duvets and the surrounding floor were clear of toys and each lad sat upright in their bed clutching a book and trying hard to suppress a snigger as they looked from each other to Lyn.

"Thank you for doing as I asked, boys, although I'm very disappointed that you shoved everything under the bed instead of replacing them neatly on the shelves." Both lads, in unison, had informed Lyn that Mummy would do that tomorrow and had then started to argue as to who should choose the story. A small, lightweight easy chair was moved to the far corner opposite the beds and after turning off the lights – except for the low-wattage bedside lamp between the two beds – Lyn settled in the chair and was almost lost in the shadow of the darkened room.

"I'm telling the story and I don't need a book, so please put yours on the bedside cabinet and we'll begin." There was a few seconds of shuffling followed by silence as two small faces looked expectantly towards the shadowed corner. Lowering her voice, but maintaining the remembered tone from her early childhood Lyn imparted the tale of:

The Blind Goblin
Once upon a time, in a far flung corner of the earth where people hadn't yet started to settle, there lived a very old goblin named Gor-don. Most goblins live for about a thousand years; but Gor-don was more than twice that age.

Will gave a low whistle and asked if it was going to be a scary story? Without waiting for an answer, Tom cut in, informing Lyn that they weren't allowed scary stories at bedtime. "Scaredy-Cat," whispered Will. Lyn interceded.

"Well, *I* won't tell if *you* don't. Now can I continue?" Two heads nodded.

Gor-don's eyesight had started to fail him over the last hundred years or so until one night he'd woken to find that he was completely blind and was unable to hunt for his usual food of bats and rats

Lyn heard joined voices in a loud "Yuck!"

Gor-don was forced to roam into the land of plenty; where children lived. Although he was blind, his senses of smell, taste and hearing were still very good; in fact, they were even better now that he couldn't see. Boy-children became his favourite food.

"Why not girls, they're supposed to be sweeter?" asked Tom defiantly.

"Because girls are protected from goblins by fairies; I thought everyone knew that," said Lyn patiently.

"I don't believe in goblins or fairies," said Will crossing his arms.

"Haven't you ever had a visit from the tooth fairy?" Lyn asked incredulity lacing her words. Will and Tom looked at each other but said nothing. Lyn continued.

After sleeping through the daylight hours and awaking at exactly 7pm, Gor-don would prepare for the night of feasting. By laying his large leathery ear to the ground he could listen for the shouts and squeals of mischief. Very soon an evil grin would appear on Gor-

don's ugly face, revealing his one and only tooth. Then, by turning his head in the direction of the noisy boy children, he would lift his huge snout to the air, sniffing out the delicious smells of sausages, hamburgers, and other things that filled the blood of children. The boy-children that hadn't bothered to wash or clean their teeth were the easiest to sniff out, and, the first to be drained of their blood – especially blood not tainted with vegetables – Gor-don hated vegetables. He would follow the scent, sneak into their untidy rooms and hide amongst the mountain of scattered toys until they'd fallen into a deep sleep.

"How did he drain their blood?" asked Tom in a small voice.

"Gor-don satisfied his hunger by pressing his one and only tooth into the soft flesh of the boys' wrists and sucking with all his might." Lyn witnessed four small hands disappearing underneath two, bright-blue duvets.

Months passed and lots of little boys died, and all the grown-ups were at a loss at what to do.

Not far from the land of plenty, high on a hillside where the only food available was cereals and vegetables that you grew for yourself lived a boy named Bo-ad. Naturally, Bo-ad had heard all about the mysterious deaths down in the valley; not from television or newspapers – Bo-ad's family were much too poor for such things – he'd learned of the tragedies on his weekly walk down to the valley to collect and return books from the school. During the day Bo-ad would work on the land and milk the goats. In the quiet of the evening, he would learn his lessons before retiring to bed with his latest book borrowed from the library.

On his next visit, Bo-ad asked to see the Elder of the Land of Plenty and shared with him the knowledge contained in Bo-ad's latest, borrowed book – 'All There Is To Know about Goblins.' The Elder met with lesser Elders and all decided that it was worth giving Bo-ad's experiment a try. After all, boys were still being sucked of their life blood night after night so they had nothing to loose.

A law was passed the very next day: banishing children's television between the hours of 7pm and 7am, encouraging parents to increase the amount of vegetables that children ate and making sure that noise levels were kept as low as whispers, during this crucial time of danger.

Within a week of sticking to these changes, no further deaths had been reported. Within a month, Bo-ad had been awarded the title – Bo-ad the Bold and a huge bag of gold coins were given to his family.

Gor-don, the Blind Goblin, grew increasingly hungry; forcing him to roam further into the land of people, listening for and sniffing out noisy boys who didn't eat their vegetables.

Silence reigned and Lyn sat wondering if the boys had slipped over the edge into the world of dreams and nightmares. Tiny whispers enlightened her to the truth. She quietly approached each half-hidden head and planted two soft kisses on each forehead – one from her and one from Mummy – who, she explained, was resting her aching head. At their whispered request, she left the low-wattage light burning and before closing their door, whispered her own request – Good night, sleep tight, remember how to keep Gor-don from taking a bite.

As Lyn entered the sitting room Jill greeted her with a smile. "Well done you, you haven't smothered them have you?"

"How's the headache, have the tablets kicked in yet?" Lyn sank into the comfortable upholstered sofa and accepted the glass of chilled, white wine from her friend noticing that Jill's glass was almost empty.

"I didn't bother with the tablets, this works quicker and tastes better. Cheers!"

Lyn took a large gulp, enjoying the almost instantaneous effect of the alcohol. Jill spoke of children's stories as Lyn's mind roamed freely around her life in Torbay and how it would change on her return. "Do you mind if I give James a quick ring?" asked Lyn feeling the need to hear his calm, reassuring voice.

"Sure you can, So long as you give me the title of the story you told my boys – I must order a copy off the internet. I haven't had this much peace in ages."

"You'll be out of luck, I made the story up."

Lyn left the sitting room to make her call in the kitchen area of the family room; but returned within a couple of minutes looking disappointed. "He's not there."

"If what you've told me about this guy is to be believed Lyn, I wouldn't be surprised if he didn't have a date with a different woman every night. He sounds very much like the proverbial 'eligible bachelor' to me and believe me they are very thin on the ground."

"James is not a womaniser; he's been hurt badly in the past and like me, he's become, well, self-contained."

"You mean he's become a loner. Well he's not alone tonight is he Lyn? Maybe his disappointing experiences with women in the past, has pushed him in the direction of trying the opposite sex, for solace during the cold winter nights."

8-15pm

"There goes your phone again Jimmy, second time in twenty minutes, I'll bet you've got loads of birds after you." The irony of Vincent Conway's words, were spoken partly in jest and partly to make up for the bizarre revelation that he'd just communicated to James; a revelation that had left him feeling hurt and confused.

Amongst the remnants of take-away cartons and empty lager cans, Vincent Conway had confessed to the reason why, he was travelling on the same train to London as Lyn Porter. Initially, Vincent had done everything in his power to avoid answering James's repeated question – claiming he was tailing her in his role as private detective; and James should know better than to expect him to break the code of client-confidentiality.

Eventually, by also playing the confidentiality card, only in reverse, James extracted the truth. A simple threat – letting John Haydon know about the sale of the basement flat; and who the buyer was – had Vincent singing like a bird. James smiled at his own turn of phrase and was quickly realising how terminology altered, according to whose company you were in.

Vincent had reluctantly exposed the fact that an episode of rough sex, something he and Charlene had often indulged in, was responsible for no more than a little light bruising; and he honestly couldn't say how her more serious injuries happened. Clearly embarrassed, he'd quickly moved on to Charlene's disappearance, and why she should go at such a crucial time. Lyn Porter had paid an unexpected visit to the florist, on the morning of her disappearance; and he felt sure that they had done some kind of deal.

"That's why I'd followed Lyn porter to London James; I felt sure that she'd lead me to Charlene." James hadn't been able to hide the disgust that he felt.

"So why continue to spy on a completely innocent person when it was confirmed that Ms Dais was here all the time; doing exactly what you wanted?" James had sensed that his accusation had caused a slight shift and nullified some of the progress he'd made. This had been confirmed in Vincent's caustic response.

"Completely innocent my foot! You might think you know this woman Jimmy, but I've known her for a long time. I wouldn't be surprised if she's in on this scam with Carl; why would she suddenly decide on a trip to London? Maybe she's with Carl as we speak." Vincent had ended this volley of information by smiling and tapping the side of his nose with his right forefinger. He'd then gone on to soften this information by implying that Lyn porter's sexual preferences were towards women, so he needn't worry that anything was going on between them in that way.

James had had enough. He'd learned nothing about Carl – other than what he'd already known. Vincent Conway had made it quite clear that he wouldn't, under any circumstance, join forces in order to expose his illegal, intimidating dealings – citing the fact that Carl was a son of the devil and you would never get anything on him that would stick.

James looked at his watch and sighed heavily. "I promised to ring my sister Vincent; that was probably her, it's almost nine and…"

"You go ahead Jimmy, won't take a minute to shove this lot in a carrier bag, it's been a nice little party; but I promise a much better one when I'm properly settled in. Tell you're your sister that she's invited too, and that I think she's a brilliant architect, especially as she's a woman!"

9-10pm

James opened his office door; and content that the air was clear of the unpleasant aroma of take-away food, closed the two windows. When Vincent had arrived, wielding the curry-stained carrier bag and asking for it to be kept warm whilst he unpacked boxes from his car, James had reluctantly agreed, but not before risking his office contents by opening two large windows, reasoning that a locked three inch gap would still deter most opportunist thieves.

He turned to his desk, expecting the answer phone to indicate that messages had been left. There was no flashing light. It was unusual for Helen not to leave a few words; but he couldn't think who else it could be. He dialled 1471, and was given a Greater-London number that was completely unknown to him. Checking his watch and his curiosity, James decided to leave his response till the following morning. After scribbling the number down on his pad he locked the office door and headed upstairs.

Surrounded by the warmth and comfort of his sitting room; James dialled his sister's number whilst sipping on freshly-made coffee. "Hello Helen, did you try to phone me earlier?"

"No, has something happened?"

"Well, I suppose yes you could say that." James had sensed the concern in Helen's voice and decided to stick to the salient points, in order to arrest her fears. "I'm out of debt with the bank. You were quite right about selling off part of next door. The Garden Flat is sold; although I had to change its address description to simply 4a, otherwise it was a non-runner." No responses came from the other end of the line and James was not surprised. Helen never responded verbally without carefully measuring her thoughts first and what James had just revealed, required more than a little thought. He decided to extend her silence. "I'm so pleased that we didn't go down the expensive route of topiary-shaped plants in pots. The new owner would have dumped them all in the nearest dustbin."

"Just hang on a minute James; can we take this a little more slowly please? You say you're out of debt with the bank because you've sold the garden flat. For that to have happened in one day, you would need a cash buyer carting his wealth around in carrier bags." Helen's voice had taken on a strident tone, a sure sign that stress had taken hold.

"Rest assured Helen, the deal is done and I'll explain everything when I see you."

"Don't you dare hang up on me James; what's all this nonsense about changing the address name, how did you come to meet such a philistine?"

"By climbing down from my high moral stand and grubbing around in the real world. It's getting late Helen I'll fill you in with all the details tomorrow."

"James, are you sitting in the dark?"

"All my lights are shining brightly Helen. Good night and God bless.

Chapter 22

Wednesday Morning 6-15am

Lyn awoke to absolute silence; and her faculties, unexpectedly, were razor-sharp. There was no need to be reminded of the importance of this day – a veiled part of her had been ticking off an invisible calendar; aware of the slow movement of earthly time. Exactly one week ago, fate had deemed to honour Lyn with a life-changing opportunity. Instead of a downward spiral into mediocrity and debt, she had been given a second chance to make something of her life.

Her mouth felt dry from too much wine the previous evening; if she were at home, there'd have been no hesitation in popping down to the kitchen and returning with a pot of tea to enjoy whilst sitting up in bed; but this was not *her* home. Reminding herself that, being bold, would now have to be part of the deal if her aspirations were to succeed; Lyn crept as quietly as possible down to the kitchen.

Silence continued until Lyn had almost finished drinking her second cup of tea. Then, whispers and a few soft bumps – only heard because of the close proximity of the next room – punctured the otherwise stillness of the dark, early, winter morning. At least the twins are awake and still captivated by the threat of Gor-don the blind Goblin. Lyn's thoughts, produced a wave of guilt which threatened to envelop her and then hide within dark corners to share the space of earlier laid down guilt; but she halted its easy progress and rationalised her motives behind the made-up tale.

After filling her cup for the third time Lyn settled back against the pillows and wondered, without any emotion, how competent a mother she'd been to Sarah. Trying to remain focussed and dispassionate, she had to admit that there had always been resentment between them. Martin had indulged her; and this was understandable because he worked away for long periods. When those long periods turned into forever; Lyn was left to deal with grief, a massive drop in income and the insatiable demands of a fifteen year old, over-indulged child. So naturally there was bound to be resentments (on both sides). But, Lyn had realised some time ago that *her* resentments lay deeper.

Gran had never allowed Lyn the freedom that her friends had taken for granted. School trips – especially to London – were always denied, as were any chance of holidaying abroad. Lyn knew money was tight for Gran, *do you think money grows on trees Lynda, there's barely enough to keep us clothed and fed.* Money had been tight for Lyn after Martin's death but she had always put Sarah's needs first. Whereas, Gran's denying's seemed to stem from a fear that Lyn had only recently started to question. And even if Gran had still been alive, Lyn doubted if any of her questions would be answered.

After discovering the two mysterious letters, Lyn's curiosity had propelled her imagination into several directions – none of which she could pursue at the time – thanks to her position as manager of a town-centre florist. But now, well now there was no excuse to try and discover the truth a few written words that had been lost and gathering dust for more than four decades. Yesterday's efforts had produced nothing as far as Lyn was concerned, causing her to wonder if she ought to abandon the whole idea of trying to uncover the untraceable.

Two loud thumps and a chorus of "hoorah it's seven o'clock" brought Lyn out of her introspective thoughts. A volley of hammering on Lauren's bedroom door followed.

"It worked Lyn, Gor-don didn't come; will you tell us another scary story tonight?"

Before Lyn had a chance to respond, she heard Jill's muffled voice chivvying the boys back into their rooms. Making good use of the opportunity, Lyn slipped into the family bathroom and locked the door.

"I'll drop you at Finchley Road tube station, you can pick up the Metropolitan line there, take you all the way to Watford; mind you, I don't know Watford well, which insurance company are you heading for?" Derik was half reading the morning paper and half listening to conversations that bounced around the breakfast table.

"A lift to the tube station would be really helpful Derik; I'll take a cab when I reach Watford." Knowing that Derik would be leaving soon, and wanting to make sure she'd left nothing behind in Lauren's room, Lyn excused herself by wishing the boys a good day at school and saying how much she was looking forward to meeting their sister.

As Lyn climbed the stairs, "Lauren's boring," could be heard by two young voices before a stern, older voice cut in.

"That's enough, not another word until your cereal bowls are empty" Lyn smiled as she realised Derik's voice was just as potent as the tale of The Blind Goblin.

9-20am

Convinced that the two unanswered calls from the evening before were from Victor Carlson – better known to the rest of the world as Carl – James had spent the last hour or so preparing for confrontation. He would return the call and hopefully obtain more incriminating evidence against him. To his great surprise, (he'd always regarded himself as being above such avenging emotions) he was actually looking forward to informing Mr Carlson that he was now out of debt with the bank; and, after speaking with Richard McNeal, he now knew that the threat of calling in the loan was instigated solely by him. Because of your behaviour toward me, the bank is losing interest at a time when it can ill afford... The phone rang, interrupting James as he scribbled down yet another composed rebuke.

"James Fairbank, good morning." James swivelled his chair toward the window where grey clouds scudded across the horizon and boats rocked on the ruffled water of the harbour. "I do hope you are feeling better Ms Dais, you didn't look well at all on Monday, and yesterday you sounded as though you were suffering from a bad head cold. James listened as Charlene sniffled and croaked her way through asking again if Lyn Porter had collected her cheque. She was anxious to get the five thousand pounds that she'd been promised, but there was no answer from Lyn's home telephone.

"I believe she is staying in London with a friend and won't be back until the end of the week; where are you staying?" James detected fear as Charlene declined to give her whereabouts, saying that Lyn Porter could reach her by phone. There was a slight pause before she continued

"James is it possible, I mean, could *you* pay me the money I'm owed, and get it back from Lyn when she returns. I wouldn't ask but I'm quite desperate." James pictured the bruised, forlorn young woman, who, for all he knew had nowhere to go.

"I can't promise anything, Ms Dais – sorry I mean Charlene – but I'll make a few phone calls and see what I can do. I'll do my best to contact you this afternoon. Goodbye for now." James slowly replaced the receiver, wondering where the poor woman might be.

He looked at the scribbled promptings before him; remembering that Victor Carlson was waiting for Charlene as she left his office; and his dislike for the man increased.

He grabbed the phone's handset and punched in the London number.

"Hello!" Exclaimed a woman's breathless voice; a voice that was completely unfamiliar to James.

"May I ask who is speaking?" he said, perplexed.

"No you may not, I've just run the length of my back garden to answer your call, so I think the onus is on you for introductions; and if this is a market research pitch, you can just hang up now because I'm not interested."

James's anger toward Victor Carlson withered into

confusion. "Forgive my rudeness, but someone at this number dialled my office yesterday evening, I'm James Fairbank, a Torbay solicitor." James waited with bated breath.

"Oh James I'm so sorry, whatever must you think. I'm Jill – Lyn's oldest and closest girlfriend."

"Nice to verbally meet you Jill; would you mind passing me over to Lyn."

"Would if I could but I can't, she's not here at the moment, won't be back until late afternoon at the earliest." Jill knew she sounded nervous, even though she was trying hard to be nonchalant for Lyn's sake.

"Where has Lyn gone, is it possible to reach her?" James suddenly realised if he could speak to Lyn about the forty-thousand pound cheque that he held for her; maybe he could help Charlene Dais recoup her much needed money.

"Lyn doesn't use a mobile James, as I'm sure you know. She has a very important rendezvous today which will turn her life around, I'll tell her you phoned and perhaps she'll call you this evening – if she gets the chance. Goodbye James nice talking to you."

James sat for several minutes deep in thought, then rose and headed for the kitchen, desperate for a cup of coffee.

10-45am

The A4 sheet of paper was still blank – except for the heading, which read: **Incriminating Evidence against Victor Carlson.** James felt hyperactive from too much coffee but had nowhere to channel that energy. His determination to present a, Damning Report, to Richard

McNeal was proving more difficult than he'd thought. Vincent Conway, who should have been his main ally – especially after James had pointed out the similarities in their initials; and that this similarity had been used to gain access to Vincent's money – but Vincent had been adamant. All he was prepared to do was give James the benefit of his own experience of the man – 'he's as slippery as an eel and will have covered his tracks; so don't waste your time and energy Jimmy'. If only James could secure Charlene Dais's money for her, maybe *she* would feel disposed to filling in some of the disturbing gaps that whirled around his brain.

His phone rang and he picked up before the first trill had ended. "James Fairbank."

"Good morning James, you're on the ball this morning, but you sound much more severe than usual, is everything alright?"

Having a cosy chit-chat with Helen was the last thing he was in the mood for. "Good morning Helen, as you can imagine after yesterday's whirlwind property sale, there's lots to do today."

"I'll be with you in five minutes. Needed to drop off some work over this way and of course I can't wait to hear all about your exciting news. Put the coffee on James."

James wasn't sure which was the most daunting – confessing everything to Helen or drinking yet another stimulating cup of coffee.

Helen backed expertly into the gap between James's Audi A3 and a gleaming, Harley Davidson motorbike. Looking cute in her fur-collared coat and matching hat, she catches sight of James watching her from the window.

She smiles and offers a little wave before her attention falls on the motorbike. Suddenly realising that he'd forgotten to include chocolate biscuits on the coffee tray; James leaves the vantage position of his window, and disappears into the kitchen. On his return, Helen is nowhere to be seen. Several minutes pass before exasperation forces him outside. Helen could just about be seen, with her nose pressed to the window of the next door, basement flat. She responded to James's shout with a question.

"Does that wonderful machine belong to your new neighbour?"

"No it doesn't, why are you looking through his window."

"Why do you think? I'm trying to get a handle on what he's like. When I redesign interiors, it helps, to know the sort of people that are attracted to that property, get the keys James and we'll take a look at his possessions; the glass is too misted-up to see much."

"Helen, the new owner has the keys – both sets – it no longer belongs to me; but you are invited to his housewarming so you will have every opportunity to scour through the place. It's freezing out here and the coffee is poured."

After yet another cup of coffee and two more chocolate biscuits, James had just about filled Helen in with how the sale came about He had intended to keep the details as scant as possible, but Helen had never been easily fooled. Voicing her main concern – allowing the buyer to have both sets of keys before his cheque wasn't even in the bank, let alone cleared – had forced James to reveal everything (well, almost everything.)

"So, you have a private investigator on the lower floor, it will be interesting to see who purchases the ground and upper floors; unless of course you still intend to hold out for a tenant; believe me James you'll wait a long time. Besides, it's been a long time since I've seen you so energised and positive; no matter how coarse this Vincent character is, he seems to be having a good impression on you. How's your love life progressing?"

"It's not; she's in London till the end of the week."

"What an intriguing coincidence; one wonders if Lyn Porter and Victor Carlson aren't connected in some way?" Helen's mischievous smile suddenly collapsed into a look of horror as she looked at her watch and gasped. "My God is that the time, doesn't it just fly by when gossip is being gathered" She gathered up her outer garments, pecked James hurriedly on the cheek before breezing out of his office, leaving him flushed and irritable.

To calm his nerves James removed himself to the empty room across the hallway; where the view of the harbour was even better than his. Pleasant memories stirred; but unanswered questions raised bittersweet feelings within.

Chapter 23

Lyn felt that her world was now filled with endless possibilities; but she knew this in itself could cause endless problems – if she wasn't careful. She had just eaten an exquisite luncheon accompanied by an equally-exquisite half bottle of French Champagne. The earlier euphoria had been calmed under the silken blanket of good food and intoxicating beverage. Several times over the last hour and a half, influenced by the opulent surroundings, she'd caught herself planning extravagant outings for unnecessary spending; but in reality, she knew that she was made of stronger stuff. Having collected her seemingly long-awaited cheque and paid it into her current account – fighting off all proposals to put the money on deposit – Lyn had vowed never to get into debt again.

From day one she'd predicted a celebration of some kind; you would have to be super-human not to, and this was hers – a meal in the most expensive restaurant she could find. Pity that it wasn't shared with someone else (she'd considered inviting a total stranger off the street, maybe an elderly person who lived alone) but thought better of it. In an age filled with mistrust and deception, she'd probably have been reported to the authorities. Besides, she had made the all-important 'promise', not to mention her good fortune to another living soul; even though the money was now safely in the bank, breaking a promise of such magnitude was unthinkable.

Eating in a restaurant as extravagant as this again was also unthinkable. The bill was horrendously large – the ten percent service charge would have easily bought a reasonable meal, including wine, in an average establishment. Lyn paid up with a smile, suggesting to the immaculately dressed waitress that the remaining two inches of Champagne should be enjoyed as further remuneration.

"That's very kind of you Madam; but we are not in the habit of drinking the remains from our customer's wine bottles."

3-00pm

Wrapped from head to foot in several layers of her warmest clothes Charlene trudged along Brighton's pebbly beach. Her plans had taken a turn for the worse. Yesterday a text had arrived from the cruise company stating that due to unforeseen circumstances, they required her to start work by the end of the week. What a cheek, she'd thought, refusing to acknowledge the message; her own circumstances were far from settled at this point in time.

For starters, she had been all set to rush back to Torbay today, grab the £5,000 cheque and head straight back;

having previously thought that there was a good chance of getting away with the little white lie she'd told the solicitor; but he'd wanted confirmation from Lyn Porter, and she knew that wouldn't happen. Also, she had just been informed by her nosey neighbour that Charlene's Dad would be arriving on Friday for a weekend break – which meant that from tomorrow Charlene had nowhere to stay. The offer of starting her new career early would have been a God-send; but for one simple fact. Charlene's physical state didn't match the person they'd interviewed back in early September. Bruising was still apparent although more muted; but it was still obvious to anyone that she'd either been beaten or had been involved in an accident – either of which would be off-putting to the agency. Also her nose seemed to be permanently blocked – mainly due to warm air heating of her Dad's pokey little flat. And to cap it all, she had a large, disfiguring cold-sore which was so painful it brought tears to her eyes whenever she accidentally touched it.

As the moist sea air gradually cleared the blockage in Charlene's sinuses, an idea began to form that might just work. Wrapping the thick, woollen scarf about her head, she turned into the wind and headed back to the flat.

"Hi there James, yes Charlene and I'm feeling a little better thank you. I've just had a phone call from Lyn and she has no objection to you paying me the £5,000. She understood my plight and was sorry that she couldn't give it personally but her business will keep her in London till the end of the week; but she will phone you again to confirm this – apparently she's tried several times already. I'll pick the cheque up early tomorrow afternoon, if that's

O.K; and James thank you again for all the support – you're a special kind of person. See you tomorrow."

P.P.O. that's all it takes. Persistence Pays Off every time; Charlene thought as she moved purposefully around the flat's bedroom making sure everything was as she'd found it. She would have to pay a visit to the cash point later; but not to worry; it will soon be replaced with good interest. Even in Torbay, during the winter months a small apartment – if rented for six weeks – wouldn't cost a lot; a tiny cottage, away from all the razzmatazz would cost even less. She would spend that time recuperating and getting back into her exercising; January 2009 will be the start of a new lifestyle, she thought, a lifestyle that includes warm sunshine and exotic places. Charlene began to hum a tune as she jotted down all the things that needed to be done before she left next morning. Top of the list: phone Cruise Agency – give them a bit of 'attitude'. Bottom of the list: replace groceries used; this was then crossed out alongside the words, sod it!

4-00pm

Vinny's list was much longer than Charlene's and contained items that he'd never even heard of, let alone understanding how they worked. He was in the middle of an out-of-town store that specialised in computers and accessories. Two blokes had already pissed him right off; he'd pointed to several things that he'd scribbled on the back of an envelope, (hoping to get a good discount for buying in bulk) but all they were interested in was asking stupid questions like: how many megabytes this and which software that. Then they had the cheek to tell him that he'd be wise to take a course on basic computing before he went shopping for accessories that he couldn't even pronounce.

The afternoon's well-planned intentions were going downhill fast. Vinny had earlier responded to an advert from the yellow pages to find out more about joining a professional body of private investigators– something extra to enhance his planned business cards and letterheads. The phone had been answered by Ronald – a pleasant enough bloke and Vinny had been pleasant enough in return. However, after a long period of spouting about the benefits of belonging to their society; He had interrupted and the pleasantries had abruptly ended. Vinny's main interest, was how much it was all going to cost and when Ronald furnished him with this information, Vinny told Ronald to fuck off and slammed down the phone.

He'd already spent a small fortune on magazines that were crammed with information on the requirements of the 'modern private detective' with tips on setting up your own agency; but to gain all this precious knowledge you had to apply on-line and Vinny hadn't yet cracked it. Every time he turned the florist's computer on, he was faced with one obstacle after another. A portable laptop was going to be his best bet along with a printer and fax machine (Christ Almighty, would he ever get his head around all this stuff.) He left the store empty-handed wondering where he could get a crash course on computing without announcing to the world what his intentions were.

The next morning, he'd be moving the rest of his stuff from the shop to his new flat; if he played his cards right,

Jimmy would give him a few lessons on computers, after all, he can't have much else to do, we're in the middle of a property slump.

4-30pm

"Hello Jill, for the second time today I've caused you the inconvenience of having to run for the phone and I do apologise most sincerely, could I speak to Lyn please?" James, expecting to be passed over to Lyn, reasoning that she must have returned at least an hour ago to have phoned Charlene, was treated to yet another breathless, dressing down from Jill.

"I already told you this morning James; she won't be back until early evening, and yes, you did bloody inconvenience me; only this time I had two bags of shopping as I ran up the garden." James heard a raucous exchange of children's voices in the background; amongst the hollering, they informed their mother that she'd dropped the doughnuts in a puddle of water. He apologised again and put down the receiver. All he'd wanted was Lyn's confirmation. He felt unhappy about writing a cheque that he could ill afford, and, was really not his responsibility to write.

After Helen had left, he'd tried his hardest to diminish the growing pile of paperwork in his in-tray – paperwork that was usually easily contained to a manageable level in spite of the fact that his secretary was away on maternity leave – but these were not usual times. His thoughts, normally organised and balanced, swung erratically between gathering incriminating information against Victor Carlson and concern that Lyn Porter might somehow be involved with him. If only women were easier to fathom; life would be much less complicated. His musings stopped him once again from completing the tasks he'd set out to do; in sheer frustration, he cleared his desk, switched the phone through to upstairs and locked the office.

Chapter 24

Wednesday Evening 6-50pm

"Where on earth have you been Lyn? The children have already eaten, there's no-way they could last this long, poor Lauren had been travelling most of the day with hardly a thing inside her and…"

"Jill please, calm down," interrupted Lyn as she peeled off her gloves, scarf and coat. "I told you that I'd be away all day and not to worry about cooking for me; I've had a good meal, honestly, you and Derik go ahead and eat."

"It's not just about feeding you, Lyn, I've got something really special to tell you, been burning to tell you since I found out and I've had to keep it all to myself. And that solicitor chap of yours has phoned three times trying to reach you, why don't you treat yourself to a mobile and stop being so mysterious." Jill withdrew into the kitchen and continued her vengeance on the cutlery as she removed one of the place settings. In a louder voice, she continued her reproaches from a distance. "I had planned for a really special meal with all of us together and now it's come down to just me and Derik."

Derik peered over his newspaper, giving Lyn a look that

wasn't easy to read. The hurt showing on Lyn's face was very easy to read – for anyone who bothered to look; but Derik's eyes were back on the newspaper. Jill's accusations did sting but determined not to let it spoil this momentous day, Lyn switched her mind to more pleasant thoughts.

After leaving the restaurant she'd wandered around the centre of Watford lost in thoughts of what was now possible. Up until now, her life had always revolved around others. First, her Gran, *always think of others before yourself Lynda; selfish actions will inevitably have an impact on those closest to you;* then Martin, even in his leisure time, *he* was more than happy to bask in a few days of complete freedom; leaving his wife in charge of home and child, whilst working full-time. And since Martin's death, Sarah had assumed the role of most needy. Charged with determination and fresh hope for the future she'd vowed that from this day forward, Lyn Porter was going to stand in her own spotlight and no one would be allowed to push her into the shadows again. She had been in no hurry to return to Jill's, hadn't even thought that it might cause her friend inconvenience or that she ought to phone her. There had been plenty of public phones around; but she had been far too wrapped up in her new plans.

Lyn closed the sitting room door on Jill's continued clattering and the overhead noise of Tom and Will. Jill's advice to use this room to phone James was welcome, but the overhead din could still be heard. Refusing to be fazed by it Lyn dialled the easily remembered number.

"I hear you've been trying to reach me and Jill says to apologise for swearing at you, although she didn't give any clues as to what you did to deserve it."

"Lyn what is that awful noise?" She glanced at the sitting room clock before answering.

"It should stop in approximately fifteen seconds time; how are you James, and what is so desperately important to warrant three phone calls?" Well aware that she sounded more bold than usual, Lyn waited patiently for his response.

"Well, you left me a strange message about not signing anything until you return and then you tried to reach me – twice it seems – so you go first." James's voice sounded light-hearted enough but Lyn sensed an undertone. She wasn't sure how to respond. The sudden halting of the overhead racket came to her rescue.

"My word I am impressed Lyn; you can tell me all about how that was achieved on your return. If your message and calls were about the florists, I'm sure you know from Charlene that the sale of, Floral Occasions, was completed on Monday. I'm sorry Lyn I know how much it meant to you but at least you have the money back that you invested in the shop and that was the main reason I phoned earlier. It is alright for me to write Charlene a cheque for £5,000 tomorrow…?"

"I'm sorry to interrupt here, but I don't know what the hell you are talking about." Lyn had to make a special effort to lower her voice; but the shock of hearing that the florist was gone – thanks to Charlene's betrayal – and she was expected to reward this betrayal. And what was James doing calling her Charlene anyway, was she missing something here.

At Lyn's insistence, James gave a brief account of what had taken place in her absence. The undertone was still there, causing Lyn to feel disappointed and irritated at the same time.

"As I see it Lyn," James continued in a soft considerate voice which irritated even more, Charlene let you down by not sticking to the arranged plan, but if it hadn't been for her, you wouldn't have got your investment money back. Is it alright to write her a cheque for £5, 000 tomorrow?"

"You can write her a cheque for £50,000 if you like James; but don't expect a penny of it from me."

For several minutes you could have heard a pin drop as Lyn sat looking at the replaced receiver. Gradually whispers from upstairs and the soft tinkle of cutlery cut through the silence.

"Shall I do the coffee?" Lyn asked, as she entered the dining room, "then we can catch up on each others' day."

"I'll have coffee too if that's O.K. Mum, it'll help keep me awake, I've got lots of writing-up to do." The tall, slender twelve year-old (who looked the image of her father except for the eyes) had followed in Lyn's wake. Jill fussed and complained that it wasn't a good idea for children her age to drink coffee, knowing full-well that her opinion would be disregarded.

"It's nice to meet you Lyn; I hope you found my room comfortable." Lauren glared at her mother at the end of the statement.

"Your room was very comfortable Lauren. I hope that my invasion of your private space hasn't altered its lovely calm ambiance; your mother was very reluctant to move me in there. By the way, how was your trip?" Lyn received a grateful smile from Jill before full attention was given to listening about the antics of Lauren and her school friends as they sauntered around the famous galleries of Paris.

By eight o'clock, Lauren was back in her room, Derik had disappeared to his workshop and Lyn and Jill had just about finished returning the kitchen and dining room to normal.

"Follow me I've got something I've been aching to show you since eleven o'clock this morning." Jill's face was flushed with excitement as she led Lyn to a curtained alcove. Drawing the curtain to one side revealed a neat combination of shelving above a computer desk and printer. As Jill switched on the computer and fiddled amongst notes she'd made, Lyn's eyes wandered over the shelves of files stacked above their heads.

"Are these contacts of yours Jill, Can I take a look?"

"Not now Lyn please, this is very important. Almost there, now sit here and close your eyes; and promise not to open them until I say." Jill shifted out of the computer chair and positioned Lyn in front of the screen. As instructed, Lyn kept her eyes closed, as she listened to keys pressed at expert speed. Eventually, Jill's voice, showing no trace of the earlier excitement; but overwhelmed with emotion, whispered in Lyn's left ear.

"There, you can look now."

Lyn's eyes focussed on the bright, colourful screen before her.

Jennifer Beck's Floral Paintings

For more than three decades, Jennifer's accomplished illustrations of 'The Flower' have captivated the eye of collectors and

gallery owners. Executed in pastels and acrylic, her exquisite work is on sale in most major cities of Australia.

There was a lot more to read but Lyn's eyes were fixed on the image who was undoubtedly her Mother. Even after all this time she was still recognisable, she was still beautiful. The portrait had obviously been done by a professional – the background lighting cleverly hiding the fact that she was entering into 'old-age'.

With rising excitement, Jill pointing out that although no phone number was available, an email sent straight away would, she felt certain, provide a contact number within the hour – over in Australia the day was just beginning.

"No, no I don't want to contact her."

"Lyn, what do you mean?"

"Exactly that, I don't want to contact her." Lyn's eyes remained riveted on the face of her mother but she felt nothing. Jill's voice gradually got louder and in exasperation she slapped the desk top in rhythm to each point she was desperately trying to get across.

"She's your Mother Lyn and you thought she was dead; why on earth wouldn't you want to contact her? What was all that footwork and eyestrain about yesterday if you didn't want to find her and contact her?" Hurt, disappointment and frustration welled up into tears that threatened to escape from Jill's deep-blue eyes.

"I just wanted to find out the truth Jill, but deep down I suppose I've known it all along. It's hard for you to understand because you have always had a normal family around you. Gran, in spite of everything was Mother and Father to me."

"She lied to you Lyn, spent her life lying to you."

Lyn felt something cold and heavy grip her inner chest. "And let's not forget that Jennifer, The Famous Artist, abandoned her child in order to swan off to sunnier climes with her continental sweetheart."

"Yes, but you know they tried to find you; the second letter proves that."

"*You* have just proved how easy it is to find someone Jill, that's if you really want to. I've made a decision to move on from the past and concentrate on my own future."

"Your future, it's always about you! I never realised before now just how selfish you can be Lyn. And what about Sarah, don't you think she has a right to know that her maternal grandmother is out there – at the touch of a keypad?"

A soft murmur and a flicker of movement from behind caused both women to halt their heated exchange. Will and Tom stood side by side, each clinging to their favourite bedtime toy. In the crook of Tom's left arm was a small brown bear sporting a homemade eye patch and a bandaged leg – a bandage that had been liberally spotted with red marker pen. Will's toy, held more casually by one leg, was an action-man-type-warrior with an evil-looking alien face. Both lads were clearly upset and spoke in whispers.

"Lauren says; if you don't 'cool it', she'll put her music on full bore. We don't think Gor-don will like her kind of music."

Jill took the boys by the hand and disappeared upstairs. On her return the computer was switched off.

"Clever you, I didn't think you knew one end of a computer from the other."

Lyn knew she owed Jill a fuller explanation, but now wasn't the time. Changing the subject she asked if she could say goodnight to the boys and explain that all this nonsense about the blind goblin is just a load of make-believe.

"Certainly not! Have you any idea how welcome the peace and quiet has been in the early morning and evening. Believe me it won't last Lyn; but maybe eating their vegetables will become commonplace before they realise it was just another fairytale. Derik says you deserve a medal and Lauren says you ought to be asked to stay permanently – rent-free." Both women smiled, but each was aware that a gaping chasm had opened up between them.

"You seemed very positive about something earlier, Lyn, care to share it with me if I promise not to throw it back in your face."

"We'll talk tomorrow, Jill, I'm sure I'll see things in a different light after a goods nights rest; I know it's early but I've got a fair amount of paperwork to read through."

"You're starting to sound like Derik and Lauren; and here's me thinking I'd have a whole week of stimulating conversations. Maybe I'll switch on the telly; there must be something less boring than sitting twiddling my thumbs."

9-15 pm

James had moved an armful of paperwork up to his sitting room in a determined effort to clear the backlog. He'd heard Vincent arrive at the basement flat over an hour ago, and was determined not to be drawn away from his task. With his office in darkness and the telephone switched to answer phone he'd managed to reduce the paperwork by half. Taking a well-earned break, he poured a glass of wine and moved to the front window. Being careful not to allow light from the lamp to show below; he peeped through an inch gap in the heavy drapes; sighing with relief when he saw that Vincent's car had gone. But after tonight his new neighbour would be here permanently and James was mindful that new ground rules would have to be made.

He was also mindful that Charlene Dais needed to be contacted, and soon. It was pretty obvious that she'd lied about getting Lyn Porter's permission to write a cheque that would be reimbursed; but it must have been sheer desperation that had driven her to do it. But facts had to be faced, although he felt sorry for the young woman, he couldn't afford to lose that amount of money; and he couldn't afford for her to turn up on his doorstep the following day, expecting it.

James dialled Charlene's number determined to get his point over before she had a chance to gain any sympathetic ground. Her phone gave eight melodious rings before it was passed to a messaging service. After listening to several unnecessary commands, a voice told him to – 'record your message after the tone'. James replaced the receiver and picked up his glass of wine. He didn't want to fill his head with anymore thoughts of women and their strange ways.

But as he sipped, the image of Lyn Porter filled his mind; forcing him to admit that she had seemed a completely different person to the one he'd remembered just a few short days ago.

Chapter 25

Startled by two loud thuds and a chorus of 'hoorahs'; Lyn was dragged from deep sleep. Squinting at the bedside radio-alarm she could see that it was precisely seven o'clock. Reverse counting, to when she'd last read the time, caused her to groan aloud. Barely three and a half hours had been spent sleeping – giving her troubled mind respite from the jumble of thoughts and accompanying emotions. She'd retired early for the specific purpose of thinking through the day's events and her developing ideas; but it was Jill's surprise that had caused the most turmoil.

She hadn't quite been able to understand the depth of negative feeling toward the woman – Jennifer Beck, (even in thought, Lyn couldn't bring herself to call her Mother.) Eventually two main points stood head and shoulder above the many others. Jennifer Beck was a successful acclaimed artist. Lyn Porter didn't even have a job, let-alone a career; and until yesterday, had been desperate and in debt. If Jennifer Beck had other children, (and the chance of this was more than likely,) how would they feel about their famous Mother's revelation? Lyn would be branded a 'gold-digger' for sure. In fact, their beautiful, talented Mother probably hadn't even told them about the shame of her earlier life in England. Either way, Lyn was bound to be rejected – again!

After, what seemed like hours of tossing and turning, Lyn had forced her mind away from all thoughts connected to her past; but even this hadn't brought her peace. Guilt had invaded the vacant space. Guilt at how she'd treated her best friend, who, after all, was only trying to help. It wasn't until Lyn finally made up her mind to offer up a compromise on the sensitive subject, that the arms of Morpheus finally opened.

Realising that this was her last full day in London and the last chance to make up for her inadequacies, Lyn crawled from beneath the warm duvet and headed straight for the en-suite bathroom. Every convenience had been tastefully catered for, from the comfortable, Queen-sized bed to the vast array of toiletries positioned on a glass shelf above a pile of fluffy towels. Jill's Mother was the most frequent user of this guest-room and it was clear from the many framed photographs that she was very much loved and appreciated.

After a long shower and feeling surprisingly refreshed, Lyn put on a brave face and descended to the family area where it seemed everyone was talking at the same time. Conversation halted as Lyn approached the breakfast table.

"Good morning everyone, I hope you all slept well." Lyn's forced jauntiness broke the uncomfortable silence as several voices returned morning greetings then relapsed back into silence; Tom's small voice cut through that silence.

"Lyn, why weren't you happy to find your lost mummy?" Derik chastised his son's disobedience; it had obviously been made clear that the subject was taboo.

Tom's head lowered in response to his father's rebuke; but his eyes remained riveted on Lyn's face. He needed an answer. "Thank you for your concern Tom, I've spent half the night wondering about the same thing. You see, since as far back as I can remember, I've always thought of my mother as an angel in heaven and when one day it's pointed out that she's just a woman like millions of other women, well it's a big shock, that's all."

"But you are happy really that she's been found?" Both lads nodded but waited for Lyn's confirmation.

"Yes of course I am, and I want to thank your Mum with a surprise of my own." The usual breakfast mayhem returned; causing Lauren to roll her eyes and leave her seat.

"I'm out of here, Dad are you ready to leave?" Derik checked his watch and with a smile told her he had ten more minutes before he became her chauffeur. With a heavy sigh she returned to her room. Lyn and Jill smiled at each other both aware that a difficult obstacle had been removed.

"I'll walk the boys to school if you like Jill."

"We'll both go; we can discuss your new plans and my surprise. We have at least half an hour, tuck in to the scrambled eggs and bacon while it's still nice and hot."

8-45am

James pushed aside the poached eggs on toast; his stomach was churning so much that he doubted its ability to digest the food. He'd been up since six o'clock, determined to finish the back-log of paperwork – the intended one glass of wine, of the previous evening had turned into three, forcing him to renege on the self-made promise of completing it. Twice, in the last half an hour, he had tried to speak with Charlene; but her mobile phone was switched off and he was loath to deliver such disappointing news by voice-mail. What should he do..? What could he do? The cheque was made out to Lyn Porter, and there was no written obligation to pay Charlene anything. Nevertheless he hadn't expected Lyn to sound so callous about it.

Determined to regain a modicum of control he dialled Charlene's number again; and again it clicked through to voice-mail.

"Charlene, I would much rather be speaking directly to you, but it's important for you to know as soon as possible that I won't be available today. Please contact me as soon as possible and I'll make an appointment for tomorrow. I hope my re-scheduling hasn't caused you too much inconvenience. Goodbye for now."

James squirmed with embarrassment as he heard the message played back and it took every ounce of his fading willpower not to delete it; but he needed to pick up the reins of his own business and leave others to theirs.

9-00am

Charlene tossed the empty cereal bowl into the sink and guided the movable, gushing tap over its inner surface; not caring that remnants of the uninspiring breakfast were starting to clog the drain; and splashes from water hitting the spoon sprinkled the tile surround. She was well-aware of the two 'missed calls' from James Fairbank, probably predicted correctly what the calls were about (he's a solicitor, he's bound to want everything in triplicate.) The voice-mail that had followed proved she was right; and now she would have to spend another day and night in this stinking, pokey flat. At least her Dad wouldn't be arriving till lunchtime next day; maybe she ought to wait for him and give him a sob story of her plight – who knows he might be good for a few pounds. He was never any good for anything else.

10-30am

A loud crash followed by a tirade of foul language wafted through the two inch gap of James's office window. He was so preoccupied with his paperwork he hadn't noticed the large, white van – emblazoned with the words – **I'm Your White Van Man** – parked outside the next door premises. He groaned inwardly as Vincent's intrusive hollering cut through the air.

Eventually, curiosity got the better of James as he realised that Vincent had a helper; someone who apparently wasn't much help at all – if the continuing foul language was to be believed. As quietly as possible, James opened the office and outer doors and peered over to where the shouting emanated. A youth, who looked no older than sixteen, was pinned against the corner of Vincent's front door; gripping as though his life depended on it, a cabinet of drawers and glass-fronted cupboards. Even from that distance, James could see the fear in the boy's young eyes as Vincent lambasted him over and over again.

Not wanting to get involved James returned to his office and closed the window. On returning to his paperwork he found that his focussing power had diminished; instead, a distant memory pushed forward and begged to be remembered in detail.

During a summer break, whilst James was studying for his 'A' levels, he acquired temporary employment as a 'van driver's mate', which entailed helping to deliver new white goods to domestic premises and removing old items if need be. Jock – the van driver and James's immediate boss – had two passions in life: an intense hatred of Englishmen and an even more intense hatred of nicely-spoken, well-educated Englishmen.

After three days of suffering at the hands of this bigoted bully, James committed the worst crime imaginable – in the eyes of his proud father – he deserted his post. An automatic washing machine, far too wide to fit through the customer's front door sent Jock into a fiery fury which bounced repeatedly in James's direction. The old lady produced tea and cakes in an effort to calm the situation. James, having had enough of the abuse asked if he could use her toilet and absconded out of the back door; noticing as he fled that the back door's aperture, was plenty wide enough for the washing machine.

On returning home, James's father was almost as abusive as Jock. Words weren't shouted and the chosen language was refined but the content cut just as deeply. Every marching step, back to the old ladies cottage, recounted his father's shame and the words that described that shame. Cowardly and unreliable were at the fore front and to make amends James was ordered to apologise and offer to work a whole week without pay.

As luck would have it, Jock was just finishing his second cup of tea as James returned via the back door.

"Where the bloody 'ell did you disappear to?" he asked, stuffing the last piece of cake into his mouth. The old lady stepped between Jock and the nervous looking James.

"He just ran a quick errand for me, while you was drinking your tea, is that all right Jock?" James looked to the old lady who smiled knowingly and winked unashamedly.

"I've found the answer to our problem," James announced, more with relief than fervour. "There's enough room to park the van in the back alley and the back door is wide enough to take this good lady's new machine."

It would be stretching the truth a bit, to say that James enjoyed the remaining weeks with Jock; but his abuse didn't rankle quite as much as it had. As to his father, the cowardly incident was never mentioned again.

Recalling the unpleasant episode, James decided that it was time to repay-in-kind the old ladies help. He opened the front door and leaned over the decorative railing.

"For heaven's sake Vincent, keep the noise down, people are trying to work around here." James looked up and down the smart terrace of mainly business premises; wondering how many of his neighbours could also hear the appalling language.

"Oh hi Jimmy didn't see you there. Come and give us a hand will you? This little tosser is absolutely useless. He's already smashed a glass door – fucking idiot – let it slip right through his lily-white hands."

"I'll give you a hand on condition that you refrain from shouting obscenities and desist from bullying that young man."

"Young man, this is no young man Jimmy." Vincent gave the lad a slap on the arm before continuing his onslaught. "This is a 'mummy's-boy'; he'll never be a man, young or old." The lad's face coloured bright red as he lowered his eyes to the ground.

James descended the steps and insisted that his conditions be met otherwise he'd leave them to it. Vincent agreed and introduced the lad as fifteen-year-old Wayne.

"Why aren't you at school Wayne?" James asked, not wanting the local authorities knocking on his door."

"Because he can learn more out of school helping me; and he was hoping to earn a few bob, but after smashing my cabinet front I think he owes me."

James could see at a glance what had happened. The pair had been trying to squeeze the piece of furniture through a doorway that simply wasn't wide enough. Déjà vu kicked in as James asked.

"Why don't you take the furniture in the back entrance Vincent? The door frame is wider and you won't have steps or these tight bends to contend with."

"Well planned strategy Jimmy." Vincent tapped the side of his nose with a nail-bitten forefinger, "Everything that's for this front room, was loaded last and will be unloaded first. *Then* we'll drive round the back and unload the rest."

"That's all well and good Vincent; but they have to fit through the door in the first place."

"They went in the fucking flat over the florist with no problem." Vincent hissed, realising that he'd already broken one of James's conditions.

James looked in more detail at the piece of furniture. "That's because this cabinet was in its original flat-pack stage."

Wayne sniggered and Vincent aimed a fist in his direction but James placed himself between the two. "The way I see it Vincent, you have two choices; either dismantle the cabinet or place it back on the van and use the back entrance. I feel sure the second option will be much easier."

Remembering the whole day he'd spent putting the flat-pack cabinet together and gluing the bolts in position so that they'd never come loose on him, Vincent mentally decided to go with James's second option but he still whined a protest. "Christ Jimmy this thing weighs a ton."

James pulled open one of the drawers and saw that it was crammed full of magazines and brochures; he looked at Vincent in disbelief.

"I ran out of cardboard boxes so I left the stuff in; what's the problem?"

"The job will be a whole lot easier if you just remove the drawers – including the contents – and carry them in separately."

"Shut it you!" Vincent aimed at Wayne, who was clearly enjoying the exchange between the two older men.

Within two hours, the van had been unloaded from the back entrance and coffee with chocolate biscuits, were being ravenously enjoyed. James had learned from Wayne that he quite liked school; but his priority at the moment was to replace his stolen bike. He also learned that coming from a one-parent-family, meant that there was little chance of getting financial help from his mother. He'd been promised £25 for helping Vincent but doubted if he'd see a penny of it.

"Well everything's in, I'll return the van and arrange things this afternoon." Vincent's eyes wandered over the boxes and randomly placed items.

"Pay Wayne what you owe him Vincent then he can get off back to school."

Vincent slapped a £20 note into Wayne's outstretched hand. "Come on Vincent, a deal is a deal."

"Oh yea, and what about my broken glass door?"

"It would have cost you a lot more than a glass door if you'd carried on the way you were."

Vincent cursed under his breath as he delved deep into his pocked and counted out £5 in coinage. "Here, now piss off." Wayne didn't need telling twice.

Chapter 26

Thursday Afternoon

Lyn and Jill had had a very productive morning. After dropping the boys off at school they'd gone on to an exhibition at Marble Arch – a venue that Jill used to attend annually before the twins were born. Lyn was introduced to several people, who, it was felt, could be useful contacts in her future business. Enthusiasm for her new venture grew as she moved from stand to stand; outlining her plans and picking up on every available tip and piece of advice.

Feeling a little reticent, Lyn had outlined her ideas at the breakfast table, half expecting Jill to say that they were ridiculous and unworkable. Fortunately, her friend – showing a completely different side to her nature – was equally convinced that the whole concept could work provided that they did their homework thoroughly.

Market research had begun the day before as Lyn wandered around the centre of Watford. By sheer chance she had come upon two independent florists. Each were devoid of customers and both, she could see by the fading freshness of the stock, were having a lean time. Walking into the first shop and striking up a conversation with the assistant had been a complete waste of time; she was a temporary fill-in and couldn't answer any of Lyn's questions. The owner of the second shop however, had proved to be very helpful and unwittingly had given Lyn the first stirrings of an idea that found its own momentum as the following hours had unfolded.

For weeks Lyn had desperately wanted to get back into what she loved most – being creative with nature's bounty – but, she'd come to realise that setting up a conventional florists shop was no longer the best option. Sitting behind a counter waiting for the odd elusive customer, whilst expensive stock withered, was not going to trap her again. This time she was going to aim high; go where money wasn't the first consideration, and only take on a project if *she* was given the freedom to indulge her talents. Suitable premises and a certain amount of equipment was necessary; but most of all she needed her friend. Jill's talent for colour, shape and balance would prove to be invaluable when assessing any prospective clients from the London-end. Weddings, Gala dinners, Concerts, Seminars and Exhibitions; all needed floral arrangements and all could be booked months in advance; allowing Lyn to purchase the best materials at the right time.

With an armful of business cards and magazines, Lyn virtually dragged her friend over to the exhibition's café area.

"Jill I need a coffee and a bite to eat; we've been on our feet for hours without a break."

"I know isn't it wonderful, I haven't even thought about food once, but you're right a coffee would be very welcome." They fell into the bright-blue, plastic, stackable chairs and looked around for a waiter. Realising that it was self-service, Jill made a dash for the counter leaving Lyn with an unspoken retort and the job of sorting through the pamphlets.

Within a couple of minutes, Jill returned with two coffees and a misshapen cheese sandwich wrapped in cling film.

"Where's yours?" asked Lyn realising that the coffee was only hot water poured over coffee grains and the sandwich was curling from dehydration.

"I'm saving my appetite for dinner; I'll pick up some tuna steaks on our way home."

"Oh my God I'd forgotten all about tonight!" exclaimed Lyn, remembering the surprise she'd organised, as a thank you to Jill and Derik – a table for three at an Italian restaurant within spitting distance of their home. Lyn revealed her intention; quashing all concerns about baby sitting the twins and keeping Lauren sweet.

"You don't seem very happy about my surprise; I thought it would be nice to celebrate the launch of our new partnership with a bottle of Champagne and a thank you meal."

"It's very sweet of you Lyn; it's just that…"

"What, tell me?"

"Lauren's not old enough to babysit and I was hoping that the surprise you mentioned to Tom was going to be associated with contacting your Mother. Both of you are involved artistically with flowers, don't you find that a wonderful coincidence; please say you were serious about contacting her?"

"Yes I am, but not until I've got the business up and

running and not until I've spoken to Sarah. I'm spending Christmas in Ireland; so there'll be plenty of opportunity to talk about Jennifer... my Mother."

Jill smiled and nodded with satisfaction. Glancing at her watch the smile disappeared as she thought of the traffic they were bound to encounter between here and home.

4-30pm

With a sigh of relief and the shadow of a smile, James cleared his desk and flicked two stray paperclips from his empty in-tray; but pondering on next months projected figures caused the smile to melt away. If he didn't find tenants soon for the vacant floors next door he would be forced to go on overdraft. Two more house sales had fallen through; both due to banks reneging on mortgage promises. A certain amount of work had been done for the clients; but James knew it would be months before he saw any of the money – if he saw it at all.

All too quickly he'd grown used to being out of the bank's grip. Having Vincent Conway in such close proximity wasn't pleasant; but it was preferable to the constant worry of escalating debt. Even so, he still had every intention of making a formal complaint to Victor Carlson's superiors – if, he could substantiate his claim with evidence. He felt certain that Charlene had witnessed the wrong side of this conman; but she was hardly likely to help now that there was no money for her to collect. A twinge of guilt was felt as James remembered their next day appointment.

The sound of banging from next doors lower floor reared thoughts of Vincent and the audacity of the man's latest request. After making sure that Wayne had been paid his due, James had collected his tray of coffee cups and had headed for the outdoor steps to return to his work; but Vincent had halted him in mid-stride, saying.

"Hang on a minute Jimmy, I want you to do something for me, I know business is crap, so it will save you wearing away your twiddling thumbs, *and,* give you a bit of company."

James had remained speechless as Vincent had gone on to disclose that he desperately needed a crash-course on computing and he felt that James was just the man for the job. At first, James put this presumptuous request down to Vincent's warped humour and assumed he was joking. Floral Occasion's had its own website and the florist's accounts were all computerised; but after voicing this, Vincent enlightened him to the fact that Charlene was the computer expert and as he was well aware, she had disappeared to God knows where.

After thinking about Vincent's predicament and Charlene's need for money and shelter; an idea began to develop which might just fulfil all their needs – including providing the evidence against Victor Carlson.

The trill of the nearby phone cut James's idea off in midstream.

"Hi James its Lyn; I want to apologise for putting the phone down on you yesterday; how's business?"

"You've only been away four days Lyn, not much has changed this end, (he lied,) how about you?" Her voice sounded kinder and less strident, maybe there was still a chance that Charlene could pick up her money and move on; but Lyn's next remark quashed that hope.

"I know how I must have sounded, but Charlene and I had a deal and the whole point of that deal was to keep the sale of the florists on hold until I return tomorrow. She broke her end of the bargain and you being a solicitor, well, need I say more. I've lost any chance of securing Beryl's Florists and need to move on with new ideas. Maybe we can help each other out in that direction. Can we meet tomorrow evening and talk about it? How about going to the Arsey Foods restaurant again? It'll be my treat this time?"

"Which restaurant," asked James, realising too slowly that she meant R.C.Foods and was continuing her little joke from their previous visit there. James agreed to meet; how could he not, he'd missed her every day in spite of the grave misgivings that threatened to invade his thoughts at every given opportunity.

Chapter 27

Thursday 6-00pm

"See you in about an hour then Jimmy." Vinny was eager to shut the door on the freezing cold draught that was threatening to undo all the efforts of the last hour.

"Seven o'clock on the dot Vincent or the food will spoil."

"Yeah, yeah, yeah," answered Vinny, shutting the door on James and the damp November chill. He'd been so busy and wrapped up in getting everything organised that he hadn't noticed the temperature dropping like a stone – the shifting, lifting and hammering had kept him warm. That morning, Jimmy had given him a brief run through of how the combi-boiler worked; but he hadn't taken much notice – it's only turning on the fucking central heating when all's said and done. But, it had taken forty-five soddin' minutes of reading through a fistful of blurb before the radiators began to 'hiss', 'click' and finally warm.

Vinny had thought the tapping noise was due to air locks and it wasn't until the tapping developed into banging that he realised someone was at his door. Insisting on remaining outside, Jimmy had invited him to share a bite to eat; said he was cooking a nice dinner and there was enough for two. Naturally, Vinny jumped at the opportunity, he was starving hungry and his cupboards and fridge were empty. The thought of a nice juicy steak made his mouth start to water.

An hour later as Vinny entered his neighbour's place via the back door the warmth wrapped pleasantly around his still partially chilled body; unfortunately the cooking smells weren't as pleasant. Frowning, Vinny watched as the solicitor, clad in a blue and white striped apron, began to stir a handful of something green into a steaming pan.

"Is that fish I can smell Jimmy?"

"Yes, a speciality of mine, 'fish stew with dill'. I get the fish stock from…"

Vinny cut him short, he wasn't the slightest bit interested in the whys and wherefore's; the only fish he liked was deep-fried in batter with chips. Vinny's disappointment plummeted further as his eyes wandered over to the salad and crusty bread.

"Don't tell me you're one of those 'health-freaks' Jimmy. I don't mind fish and chips on a Friday night but that smell tells me that this is too fishy for words."

James was speechless. He'd paid full attention to watching the stock and white wine reduce to just the right level before adding the fresh variety of fish and seafood. He was almost on the verge of turning the ungrateful so-and-so out when he remembered the main reason behind the invitation. "Sit down Vincent you must be starving; just keep an open mind, I'm sure you'll enjoy the food."

With a sullen expression, Vinny plonked himself down in front of the fancy table setting. "Charlene used to try and get me to eat this rabbit food you know." His hand waved casually over the glass bowl of young salad leaves, freshly tossed in a light dressing of lemon and extra virgin olive oil. "She gave up in the end. His voice suddenly became wistful. "Where is she Jimmy? I'd like to call her and I know you have her number."

"Vincent, she was covered in bruises and she hasn't made any attempt to contact you. I can only assume the two things are connected."

"I already told you that had nothing to do with me; she was fine when I last saw her."

Conversation halted as the two men tucked into the hot, tasty stew. Vincent emptied his bowl first and helped himself to seconds without comment.

Noticing Vincent's relaxation was quickly turning to tiredness James decided it was time to find out if Vincent was amenable to his idea. "I've been thinking about your dilemma regarding computer lessons Vincent."

"I knew you'd come round to my way of thinking Jimmy, I'll be a good student, I promise."

"Vincent, *I* haven't got the time or the expertise; the way I see it, you have two choices. There are local authority courses for beginners." James halted as Vincent raised both hands to cut him off.

"I'm ahead of you mate, I've already checked them out. Three hours a week spent in a class of old biddies who want nothing more than to learn how to email their nearest and dearest; or, two hours a week at an evening class with unemployed nerds who can't afford their own computer hardware. What I need is one-to-one tuition and I need more than just the basics."

"That costs money Vincent."

"I never said I wasn't prepared to give you a bung Jimmy." A hurt expression appeared on Vincent's tired face.

"Vincent, I haven't got the skills you need; and even if I had, I don't have the time."

"So what's my second choice?" Vinny reached for the last piece of bread and wiped it around the inside of the serving bowl that had held the stew.

"You need a secretary."

Vinny nearly choked on the bread. "I don't need a fucking secretary, I haven't got a business yet; besides they cost serious money. I notice you don't have a secretary."

"I do have a secretary, she happens to be on maternity leave at present."

"Well there's the answer; I'm sure a little extra cash will come in handy. What's her name?"

"Vincent, she is due to give birth within two weeks."

"So, she'll only be sitting down; I'm not expecting her to decorate or lay carpets."

With growing frustration James came straight to the point. "I know someone who is more than capable of doing the job, but I need to speak with her first. What are your terms?" In response to the blank stare James continued. "She'll want to know if it's worth her while."

Vinny moved toward the back door. Jimmy had donned his apron again and was clearing the table. There might be a pudding on offer but then again there might be a whole lot of washing up to be shared, better make a quick getaway. "Tell you what Jimmy; bring her along to my little housewarming on Saturday night. Your sister's coming, another female will balance things up nicely?"

9-50 pm

"I'll just dash on ahead and make sure everything's alright." Jill shot down the remaining fifty yards of their road – front door key already positioned between the chubby fingers of her right hand. Lyn and Derik continued at the same leisurely pace, engrossed in a conversation about redundancy, and how it affected one's self-esteem.

The Italian meal had been delicious but hurried. Jill's concern for the twins had irritated Derik and his irritation had marred the celebration.

"Well, have they been gobbled up by gremlins?" Derik asked as Jill descended the stairs holding the five-year diary that Lyn had given Lauren as a present.

Ignoring his sarcastic remark she held up the diary – minus its key. "Are you aware that your twelve-year-old daughter keeps a lockable diary?"

With a heavy sigh, Derik shrugged out of his overcoat and moved through to the sitting room.

"Am I invisible?" screeched Jill as he closed the door on the confrontation. She made a move to follow but Lyn caught her arm.

"I gave it to Lauren before we went out; I bought it yesterday in Watford along with a couple of books for the twins. Where's the harm Jill? *We* both kept diaries when we were teenagers."

"She's only twelve Lyn; and it's lockable; that's really sneaky."

"Did you leave your diary around for your mum to read?" Lyn knew the answer, it was one of their fondest pastimes – keeping ahead of Gran and Jill's mum to hide their latest penned shenanigans at school. She could see from the dawning smile that Jill also recalled the antics. "Lauren won't need to half-demolish her bedroom looking for a safe place to keep her written down thoughts from prying eyes."

"I'm her mother, I don't want her to have private thoughts that she can't discuss with me. You have just witnessed first hand how Derik refuses to engage about anything other than what's happening in his work; and I don't want Lauren to be like that."

"He is the main provider Jill, what's happening to him at work must be very worrying, he probably views everything else as trivia, try not to take it so personally. You have a wonderful family. You really are very fortunate."

"So what books did you get for the boys?"

"A double volume titled, Understanding the Mischief of Gremlins and Goblins."

Chapter 28

Friday Morning 6-45am

Feeling disgruntled, Charlene slammed the front door of her dad's flat and pushed the key back into its hidey-hole before bumping her suitcase down the three concrete steps that led to the rusty, creaking gate. A twitch from the curtains next door indicated that Dad would be informed, in detail, of all her comings and goings. So what, thought Charlene, giving the twitched curtain a little wave as she toed the gate open; she'd only dossed down on his lumpy bed for four nights and opened a few tins of out-of-date, cheap food. The antiquated heating system barely warmed the place and to be honest she was glad to be on her way. Most fathers doted on their daughters. Bought them a car, coughed up a deposit on their first house, even paid the mortgage repayments if they got into difficulties. No such luck for Charlene. She had always been left to more or less fend for herself.

The taxi drew alongside and a short balding man, with an incessant cough climbed out and flung her case into the boot. Feeling concerned about his state of health and still worried about her own, Charlene kept as much distance between them as possible but remained alert to any indication that he might start to smoke. Her sinuses were still giving her trouble and although the cold sore was less painful, the look of it was horrendous. She'd wasted over six pounds on, supposedly, invisible plasters that were barely big enough to cover a pimple. The snotty cow at the chemists refused to give her a refund because Charlene had opened the pack. Using what little strength she'd had to argue that you couldn't see the size until the pack was opened she'd been told that she'd have to come back when the manager was on duty; and that would be later today.

Giving the taxi driver exactly the fare showing on the meter, Charlene grabbed her case and hurried to meet her train which had just arrived and was shunting onto the platform. A double line of commuters surged forward and as the doors to carriage C stopped directly in front of Charlene, a look of triumph creased her face as she barged through a gap and was first in line to board. Commandeering the first available double seat, she positioned her suitcase in such a way that it was impossible for anyone to share it. She needed to think. She didn't want anyone, no matter how well-meaning, feeling obliged to make light conversation. It was obvious that the train would fill; she would close her eyes on the chaos and feign sleep; you would have to be a real bastard to wake up a sleeping woman who didn't look too healthy.

After ignoring several tuts, a quick peek as the train pulled away showed that she'd be left alone for the time being. The temperature of the carriage was warm reminding her of how cold the last four days in Brighton had been and her mistake in going there. It had cost her dear both in money and recuperation; but there was no point in recriminations, she had to make sure that the next six weeks didn't continue in the same way.

Gainful employment wasn't easy to come by during the winter months in Torbay and the credit-crunch had made it almost impossible – especially with lodgings included – but determination not to use any more of her savings set Charlene's mind working on a different track.

9-15 am

Victor Carlson, known to his new boss as Carl Ericson – a name verified on documents he'd held for over twelve years and had studiously kept up to date – was settling into his new office. Standing in front of the floor-to-ceiling window, which from a dizzying height overlooked the snaking path of the Thames, he assessed his position and aims for the next three years.

He was the youngest of five sons born into a family of fishermen. Two of those sons had been lost whilst doing what their father proclaimed to be 'their natural destiny' – rising at death o'clock every morning and using all their bodily strength to drag as much as possible from the cold, unforgiving, Scandinavian seas. Even as a boy, Carl was determined not to follow in footsteps that had been determined by his father; and two days short of his sixteenth birthday when his father dropped dead after a massive heart-attack, he'd recognised his first opportunity. With the assistance of his beloved mother, Carl managed to extract his share of the family business – not caring that his remaining two brothers had to borrow heavily to accommodate him. *His* destiny would lie in his own hands.

During an unforgettable lecture at University, it was pointed out that a man could only rise as high as his own aspirations. Carl's aspirations were aimed very high. By the time he'd reached thirty he was a millionaire twice over, owned three properties and a small hotel. At thirty-four, he wasn't quite sure of the extent to which his fortune had grown – his rule of re-assessing his position every three years had been cut short by eleven months – thanks to the bungling of Vinny Conway. No matter, Carl never forgot his friends and always kept tabs on his adversaries; and scores would be settled eventually.

11-45 am

After pacing up and down the area that Vincent regarded as 'the hub', he collapsed into the newly-assembled swivel chair and with a slight push from his right foot, swept his eyes slowly around the room. It all looked very impressive; the new black and silver laptop, printer and desk-top shredder in matching colours and two sets of filing cabinets – one black and of course one silver. The whole caboodle, except for the filing cabinets, sat neatly on a new desk which spanned the length of the room. Problem was, apart from the chair and the posh, energy-efficient desk-lamp; he didn't have a soddin' clue how to get the equipment up and running. Even the new digital phone had him stumped. Twice he'd tried to set its clock – which was necessary for the working of the answering machine, but the fucking thing had refused to do his bidding. He'd had to hold a tight rein on his anger to stop himself from flinging the piece of Chinese crap across the room.

Vinny had woken early, wondering where the hell he was; and it had taken some time before his confusion had transformed into excitement and impatience. With the rest of the flat sorted the day before, he'd decided to bite the bullet and splash out on everything he needed for the small office. With his car loaded up, he'd arrived back shortly after ten and it hadn't taken long to set the stuff in position.

Absent-mindedly he continued to swivel at a slow pace slumped on the one-man, merry-go-round. Jimmy had been right – as usual – there was no other way but to eat shit and hire a secretary. Grabbing his mobile from the window sill he punched in the now familiar number. "Jimmy it's me, I know you said you didn't want to be disturbed today but this is just a 'quickie'. I've decided to take your advice about taking on a secretary, give me her number and I'll organise it now." Vinny had detected a pissed-off sigh when the solicitor first picked up his phone; but his voice seemed friendly enough when he spoke.

"Vincent, I need to speak with this person first; she might have other plans or she might simply not be interested in working alongside someone she's been involved with be…" Silence followed as James realised he'd said too much. He'd been so engrossed in compiling his report of complaint against Victor Carlson that he'd been caught off-guard.

"I feel sure that I'll have an answer for you by the end of the day, now please I must finish my paperwork and prepare for two afternoon appointments."

"Tell you what, we'll have a couple of beers tonight and sort things out then, yeah?"

"Sorry Vincent, I have a prior engagement this evening, I must go now."

Vinny scratched his newly-shorn head wondering who the hell Jimmy had in mind as a secretary. Jimmy's gaff hadn't passed unnoticed and the only person Vinny could think of was Lyn bloody Porter. He knew Jimmy was sweet on her and she needed a job; the fact that she was due back from London anytime soon, slotted everything neatly into place. "I'm a bloody private detective" Vinny announced to the empty room; "surely you didn't expect to get away with pulling a fast one like that. Well sonny-Jim, it ain't going to happen, I'll go down to the employment agency this afternoon and find my own bloody secretary!"

Chapter 29

Friday Afternoon 1-15 pm

Breakfast that morning had been a little strained – Jill and Derik were obviously still locked in conflict – so when the offer of a lift to the station came up Lyn had grabbed the opportunity; not caring that all she'd eaten was one piece of toast. The train journey had been pleasant enough, due in part to the few scheduled stops and the vast amount of empty seats; but this in turn, Lyn suspected, was why no buffet carriage was available.

On arriving back home, she'd dropped her suitcase in the hallway, turned on the central heating and headed straight out for something hot to satisfy the growling rumble of her stomach.

Lyn sat, once again, at the window table, looking out on the boarded up premises that for years she'd regarded as her second home; in fact in the year following Martin's death, she'd regarded it as her sanctuary. During that harrowing time, Beryl seemed to be the only person in her life that understood what she was suffering. Even Gran's attempts of guilt-laden chivvying hadn't broken through the high, stone wall that Lyn had subconsciously erected against the outside world.

Fully aware that all such barriers were now demolished, Lyn was able to see the place for what it was; and only a slight pull of sentimentality remained for the woman whom she'd regarded as mother and best friend. There was no doubt about it, this area of Torbay was in dire need of investment; but it would take a lot more money and a lot more time than she could offer. The place seemed dead in comparison to the hustle and bustle of London. It was Friday lunchtime, and it wasn't that long ago that the place would have been packed out with customers eating in and waiting for hot food to take out. Two smartly dressed young women sat in the far corner drinking coffee and sharing a baguette; they were the only other customers. Catching a few words from their hushed conversation Lyn determined that they were concerned for their future employment.

The owner herself came to take Lyn's order; the welcoming smile only partially disguising the haunted look of worry. Lyn ran quickly down the menu, wondering how much was really available and more importantly, how much was fresh.

"I'm quite hungry and I feel like something hot, what would you recommend?"

"I'll get chef to surprise you, is there anything you don't particularly like?" she asked with a genuine broadening smile. It was hard to believe that this was the same toffee-nosed-mare from a week ago and Lyn wondered if the woman remembered her.

"Tell the chef I could eat a horse; is that enough of a clue?"

Stir-fried vegetables with beef and a steaming bowl of

Jasmine rice arrived fifteen minutes later and every mouthful was enjoyed. This particular dish wasn't on the menu but Lyn decided it would be a regular choice for her – provided the café could weather the financial storm and stay afloat. As the owner cleared away the empty plate and took her order for coffee, Lyn asked what was happening to the florist. Without hesitation, the woman informed her that the whole block was being demolished for redevelopment; then added bitterly, that had they known beforehand, they would never have bought and sunk so much money into this place.

Lyn's attention was suddenly drawn to the door. A young woman was struggling backwards, trying to drag a large suitcase through the aperture whilst holding back the sprung door with one foot. Instinctively, Lyn jumped up to hold back the door and it wasn't until the woman was safely through that she realised who she'd helped.

"Charlene, my God what's happened to your face?"

"It's only a cold sore Lyn; the scab got disturbed a few times and it grew bigger in revenge." Charlene had made the scab worse by applying then removing plasters that weren't big enough to cover her disfigurement; but she wasn't about to confess that to the last person she'd wanted to bump into. She'd only just arrived back and was hoping to find out where Vinny was, because she was desperate for somewhere to stay.

Lyn nodded at the suitcase. "Where are you going or should I say where have you been?" As expected, no answer was forthcoming so she changed the subject; pointing across the road she asked conversationally, "Why would anyone pay all that money for the florist and then just shut it down?" She now knew the answer but wondered if Charlene had been privy to this information.

"Thanks to me, at least you got something out of it."

It took a moment for Lyn to realise that Charlene was playing the same game. "We had a deal Charlene and you broke that deal"

Looking suitably contrite Charlene dipped her head and spoke in a small voice. "I was forced into doing what I did."

Lyn had been on the receiving end of Charlene's lies before, so she didn't take this piece of drama too seriously and said nothing, knowing that Charlene would enlighten her further.

"He threatened to burn the place down if I didn't play ball, didn't care if anyone was inside neither."

So that was it, thought Lyn, an 'Insurance Job'. The place was going to be demolished anyway, why not fill it with stock, put a match under it and walk away with even more money. Well it hadn't worked; there was no sign of fire damage and besides Vinny had never bothered to insure; said it was a con and a complete waste of money. "Who are you talking about, was it Vinny that threatened you?"

No! Vinny's never threatened me. I'm talking about that piece of shit Carl. He waited outside the solicitor's office and helped himself to Vinny's cheque. When he'd realised it was forty grand short..." Again Charlene lowered her head in dramatic fashion; Lyn waited patiently. "I took a beating for rescuing your money which is safely waiting for you; and you can ring James if you don't believe me." The use of the solicitor's Christian name hadn't gone unnoticed by either of them. "I dread to think what Vinny will do when he catches up with me. Do you know where he is?"

Lyn was trying to absorb what had been said and sort out the truth from the fantasy. A slight movement from behind and Lyn's coffee was placed in front of her. The owner looked at Charlene and her face softened.

"Hello Charlene, how is your father sweetheart?" The café owner wrung her hands as if expecting news that would prove embarrassing.

"He's doing well thank you, Estelle, the stroke wasn't as bad as they first thought."

"Well that's nice to hear; can I get you a hot meal? You look as though you could do with one and I'll put this in the office; we don't want anyone tripping over it; I've already got one claim on my hands for a woman who tripped over her own feet." Without waiting for an answer, the suitcase was carted through to the back of the café.

Charlene called after her. "I just want a coffee please."

"She's right, you need a good hot meal inside of you – I can thoroughly recommend the stir-fried beef – then a couple of days resting up at home."

"Lyn, I can't afford to think about my bloody stomach when I haven't even got a roof over my head; that was my home, remember." Charlene prodded the glass in the direction of what had been the florists; leaving the distinct impression of her fingerprint in the misted glass. "Now you know why I need to find Vinny and face whatever's coming."

"Charlene, he knocked you about!" Lyn's raised voice, caused the two women in the far corner to cease their conversation on the state of the economy in favour of listening to someone else's misfortune. In a lowered but earnest voice Lyn continued to cite all the reasons why she would be better off walking away from this man, and this area. Charlene cut her short and asked if she could doss down at her place for recuperation; before picking up her handbag and heading for the bathroom.

With a heavy sigh Lyn looked about her. Jill had been right, for any business to do well, the right location was paramount. In the past, this area was perfect for the businesses that thrived here; but change is the only constant in life and if you don't adapt to the changes you were done for. She reached into her bag and retrieved her cheque-book feeling duty-bound to help Charlene make her own leap into the unknown pool of change. On her return from the bathroom, Lyn handed her the cheque and advised her to locate to an area that had more to offer. Charlene thanked her and said she'd book into somewhere cosy for a few days then return to her Dad's, just to make sure he was continuing to improve.

2-45 pm

Charlene checked her watch; she should have been at the solicitors office quarter of an hour ago – so what, she thought, his help wasn't needed now. She'd left her case at the café, promising to return by late afternoon. Estelle hadn't been too pleased; but when Charlene explained that she had a couple of job interviews, she'd smiled and encouraged Charlene to use her own bathroom for a wash-and-brush-up.

Having banked the £5,000, Charlene headed to the main Letting Agency – a premises shared by the town's only remaining Office Recruitment Centre. Her eyes skated over the apartments and bedsits advertised in the window and she was horrified at the rentals – especially as it was off-peak season.

"No recession there! Rents have gone sky-high since the increase in repossessions; 'course it's the council – that means the likes of you and me that'll pick up the tab."

Charlene said nothing; the last thing she needed was to engage in a one-to-one with a grumpy old man. A loud tooting focused their attention on a car that had pulled to a halt directly in front of the agency. As the driver emerged a broad smile creased the round, paunchy face of Vinny.

"What are you doing here babe?"

Stumped for words, Charlene looked behind her before replying confidently. "I've been registering with the agency for office work." She saw his smile falter and continued with a little more humility. "I've seen the florists boarded up Vinny and I'm sorry for what I did but my hands were tied. Where are you staying?"

Suddenly, Vinny noticed the old man, watching and listening. "Piss off granddad!" With his arm protectively around Charlene's shoulder he led her to the car.

"Bit more private in here and warmer, Christ Charl you look like death warmed up where were you?"

"I was nursing my sick Dad."

"You told me you hated your Dad, said he was too interested in young girls."

"That's my step-dad; my real Dad's fine; a bit on the idle side but… I thought he was going to die Vinny, that's why I rushed to sign so that I could see him before…" Charlene lowered her head and blew into a paper tissue being very careful not to disturb the healing cold sore.

"Did he croak then?"

"No, I nursed him back to health, run myself into the ground doing it."

A mobile phone – indicating a left message rang through the interior of the car. Charlene and Vinny looked at each other and Vinny said.

"It ain't mine, I'm switched off."

"It'll be the agency blurted out Charlene knowing full well it could only be James Fairbank. They told me there'd be plenty of interest; but I've insisted I'm looking for a position with accommodation too."

"Fuck the agency, I've got you a position and you'll have your own room with en-suite shower. I've got my own place bought and paid for and a fully equipped office to run my new enterprise. You can be *my* secretary and I'm going to allow *you* to set up the new laptop and printer."

"Where is your new place?" Charlene asked, relief washing over her as she relaxed into his embrace.

"It's in a very fancy area and I need to lie low for a while, ok, so no running off at the mouth. Looking at the state of you Charl, you could do with keeping out of sight as well. I'm having a little house-warming tomorrow night – just one or two of the neighbours. In the meantime, I'd try one of those invisible plasters on your face; that scab's a bit off-putting."

5-00 pm

James stood looking in disbelief at the paper announcement positioned in the window of his neighbour four doors away.

FOR SALE
Spacious, Ground Floor, Commercial Premises
Off-road Parking for Two Vehicles

Two disturbing thoughts jostled for priority as James re-read the poster. This was bound to have an adverse effect on his chances for letting; and why hadn't Peter Radcliff – the accountant who owned the premises – given the business of selling the property to James. It was an unwritten rule along 'The Terrace'; you supported each other and kept business local. The answer to the weaker thought was obvious and underpinned all that had gone awry in the economy over the last year. It could be summed up in one, short sentence. The whole banking system – fuelled by unbridled greed and wanton risk-taking – was out of control; and everyone else was suffering as a consequence. Like the rest of us, Radcliff had to cut costs and the commission on such a prestigious sale was worth saving.

James had been late, yet again, for his 3-00pm meeting with the Bank Manager. Charlene Dais hadn't turned up for their 2-00pm appointment; and although James had almost convinced himself that the two calls to her mobile were due to concern for her well-being; in truth, it was disappointment that he would have no signed document as witness to Victor Carlson's illegal and abusive methods. So anxious was he to obtain such a clincher, that he'd also phoned John Haydon with the hope of establishing help for his honourable crusade. He'd declined without hesitation; feeling that he'd caused the man enough embarrassment; and especially after, in his opinion, Carl had done a wonderful job on increasing his profits.

Sitting in the same sparse room as before, James had laid out all the damning documentation on the man known only as Carl to most of his colleagues. As it turned out, even if the battered and bruised Charlene had been sitting beside him – singing like the proverbial bird – it wouldn't have made the slightest bit of difference. Victor Carlson no longer worked for this particular bank.

James had been getting into his stride; confidence in his quest growing, as he pointed to page after page of illegalities. Richard McNeal listened patiently then without the slightest hint of emotion said.

"There's nothing I can do Mr Fairbank, the man in question has been 'head-hunted' by another financial institution."

James had looked over to the simple, abstract print of Llanberis; searching for a blanket of comfort to smother the rising anger. Then he had exploded!

"Head-Hunted? The man's head should be served up on a block!" James's fist fell heavily on the small laminated table between them; causing the other man to flinch slightly.

"Can you at least furnish me with the name of this rival financial institution; or has the man fled to a country where financial regulation is even more lax?"

After learning only that his adversary was in the heart of London – enjoying an increased salary and the promise of huge bonuses, and, according to Richard McNeal, entitled to the laws of privacy; James had gathered up his damning-report and left without even bothering to collect his property-deeds. His emotions were in turmoil and it had taken a walk around the harbour and a visit to his barber to bring back a modicum of calm.

The call of his name brought him back to the moment. Standing in the doorway to his office, twenty yards away, a female form was waving her arm. The shadows surrounding the soft street-light couldn't disclose her salient features; but who else could it be. James quickened his pace.

"Charlene, why did you break our engagement, I've been trying to reach you by phone but…"

"Sorry to disappoint you James, Charlene never mentioned that you had 'an engagement'; when's the wedding?" Lyn couldn't resist the jibing pun even though she knew that Charlene was probably only using James for what she could get; and now that she'd got it she'd be miles away.

"My mind was pre occupied; sorry for the mistake. I thought we'd arranged to meet at the restaurant at 7-30." He was flummoxed and knew that it showed. Lyn looked composed, confident and very attractive. This added to his discomfort.

"I've been looking over Peter Radcliff's premises – nice place – seemed churlish not to pop in, say hello and pick up my cheque. By the way, I like your hair."

James noticed she was holding a folder; obviously containing details of Peter's property. Jokingly he asked, "Thinking of buying into 'The Terrace'?"

"Maybe; it's certainly got the ambience I'm looking for."

James selected a key from the bunch he was holding and thrust it into the brass escutcheon of his front door. From force of habit, he stepped back to allow Lyn to precede him into the porch; realising too late the embarrassment of their extreme close proximity whilst he fumbled for the inner-porch key. He dropped the bunch of keys and the "bugger" escaped from his clenched jaws; followed by an apology for the expletive. Simultaneously, they bent to retrieve it; and as they returned to full height – bodies brushing lightly against each other, familiar scent of after-shave and perfume mingling; their eyes locked for a few seconds only.

"With an outstretched, leather-gloved palm, Lyn held out his keys. "You're looking tired James; do you want to postpone the meal until tomorrow?"

"No! No I've been looking forward to it." James left Lyn in his office saying he needed to pop upstairs for her cheque.

Lyn laid the Radcliff folder on his desk and walked across the hallway to the premises she coveted most. After pacing its dimensions and running a tape over the height between the window sill and floor she was alerted to James presence – watching her from the doorway.

"The ground floor area is identical-in-proportion, to Peter Radcliff's; James pointed out as he joined her."

"And that's where the similarity ends. It's not as nicely restored, the view from *his* window is obliterated by the modern buildings opposite and the neighbours aren't as nice; it's just a pity that this place is only available to rent."

"Lyn I've no wish to deflate your plans, but it's only fair to warn you that this", he waved what was obviously her £40,000 cheque in the air, "is not enough of a deposit, and you have no chance of securing a mortgage in your situation."

"I don't need a mortgage James; I'm a cash-buyer."

Lyn plucked the cheque from his fingers pecked him on the cheek and made for the door. On opening it she turned to see a confounded, adorable-looking man. Before disappearing into the gloom of the early evening she said, "I must go, I've promised to phone my daughter; see you at the 'Arsey' at 7-30."

Chapter 30

Friday Evening 7-40pm

A fine mist had descended by the time James marched purposefully down to the harbour. Tiny, salt-laden, sea-scented droplets of moisture peppered his new hairstyle, his cashmere overcoat and brown – highly polished shoes. The effect of weather upon clothing went unnoticed by James; nor was he bothered that he was already ten minutes late. The events of the last week had brought about a seismic shift in the values that had shaped his life; burying the ones that he'd hitherto taken for granted.

It was a given that the entrenched disciplines he'd always adhered to were a legacy of his father and *his* father before him; but James had felt comfortable adopting them as his own. Who could argue against the benefits of self-control, integrity and chivalry, all qualities that seemed extinct in the human race at this point in time? Now it seemed inevitable that he too must travel the same downward path; if he were to survive the steep, economic down-wave that was tearing England apart.

After Lyn's departure, James had discovered that she'd

accidentally left the details of Peter Radcliff's property behind. Without shame, he'd riffled through the half dozen pages which gave chapter and verse of a property very similar to his own. Included print-outs of three photographs – taken at advantageous angles – proved Lyn right, the refurbishment, carried out five years earlier, was not as well executed as his own. But it was the 'asking price' that had kept James feverishly turning the pages until he reached the final line on the last page. P.O.A. Please Tel. etc etc.

Throughout his showering and dressing, one thing only filled James's mind. Should he phone Peter and ask outright for answers to the questions that were begging to be asked. Having decided, he'd skipped the glass of wine he'd promised himself before leaving for the restaurant and headed up to confront the accountant in person.

Peter had been candid about everything. The old, semi-retired dentist who occupied his basement flat, and had done so since before Peter bought the place twenty-four years ago, was paying barely more than a peppercorn rent. Peter had accepted this when he bought the place at a bargain price; reasoning that the frail-looking, old boy would soon be pushing up daisies. But he'd proved to be much tougher than he'd looked. The roof and back wall to the property badly needed attention and Peter had approached the dentist for help with the costs. He'd refused point blank, so while matey (Peter had pointed a finger to the floor as he merrily recounted the information) continues to earn a fortune at my expense, I need to move my office upstairs and sell off the ground floor.

He'd heard about the quick sale of James's basement flat.

God knows how, thought James; but he hadn't had the time or the energy to probe into Peter's social grape vine. After patiently listening, the moment of disclosure finally arrived. Peter had felt that a figure of around £320,000 would be a fair price for commercial space at such a prestigious address; bearing in mind that James achieved the wonderful sum of over £200,000 for the pokey basement. James hadn't bothered to argue that his basement had been extended at the back and was now a well-designed spacious flat.

The talking continued and James had to still his rising impatience. Peter apparently had been aiming for a similar position to James – hang out for a tenant, even if it meant riding out the recession – eventually it was bound to pay off; but the economic world had collapsed and Peter had needed a cash injection now.

The opportunity of a slight pause had been missed as James had taken on board Peters last words. Retailers, continued Peter, were the backbone of my livelihood and they are going bankrupt left, right and centre and that's another reason… At this point Peter had had the decency to look sheepish. He'd apologised to James, for not giving him the business of selling – said straight out – couldn't afford the commission. At last James had recognised an opening for more pertinent information.

He had asked if anyone had shown interest. Peter had continued to oblige, with the full facts of Lyn's perusal of his premises; the most interesting fact being that she had a partner based in London. Peter's assessment of this disclosure, gave him increased confidence that she may well close the deal; fortunately the weak pound is having a positive effect in London – due to the amount of business done with the Europeans. He also added that he found her accomplished in matters of business and extremely charming in nature.

James was panting by the time he reached 'R.C. Foods'; on entering, he allowed a few moments to catch his breath even though he was well aware, fifteen minutes had already been snatched from their evening together. Lyn sat at the same table they'd shared the week before, smiling brightly as she and Rick – the proprietor – discussed something funny. She wore a pale mauve, silk shirt – its sheen shifting in the flickering candlelight before her. Her hair hung loose about her shoulders and the same candlelight danced among the shining, highlighted strands. A single pearl, suspended from a silver or white-gold chain, was just visible between the 'v' of her shirt. An irrational thought darting into James's mind – maybe it was a gift from her London partner – and the vision was soured.

"I'm sorry for keeping you waiting Lyn, you left these behind and knowing how important they are, I left them on the hall table as a reminder to bring them along." At this point, James was about to launch into a fictitious tale of how Sadie – his cleaner, had tidied them away, resulting in him having to spend precious minutes hunting them out – in short, he was looking to lay blame elsewhere for his lateness, but after looking at Lyn's face, he lost the nerve and said nothing more.

"It doesn't matter James, you're here now covered in fairy-dust and smelling of the sea." Lyn saw confusion cross his face so she pointed to the tiny droplets on his hair and coat; sparkling in the candlelight. "As you can see", she continued happily, "Rick has been taking good care of me". She raised the glass of champagne that James had witnessed being topped-up. "This is now regarded as 'our table' James; although after our last, argumentative meal, I would have thought, shoved up in the far corner would have been more appropriate." Lyn didn't mention that she had brazenly asked Rick if James had any other 'special tables' for entertaining lady-friends; and that he had answered with a wink that she was the first in many years. It was usually men-friends – business colleagues, he'd added quickly. She had also mentioned to Rick that this meal was her treat and on no account was he to give the bill to James. That might not be easy he'd started to say; but she'd stopped him with the smiling threat that if her wishes weren't met, she would never come here again.

Small-talk filled the period of first course; but during the lull before main course, Lyn asked James outright if he thought the price of £400,000 for Peter Radcliff's place was a bit steep?

"He's not asking as much as that; is he?" James suddenly wondered if the accountant was pulling-the-wool over Lyn's inexperience in property values.

"That's what it says in here." Lyn waved the details that James had considerately placed in a clear, polythene folder.

"Price on application it says in there and £320,000 is what he told me." He knew he'd been caught out; her triumphant smile held the mischief of a trap set and sprung.

"Two bad marks against you so far James Fairbank – late by fifteen minutes and nosing into other people's private papers and conversations – no doubt Peter Radcliff relayed my future business intentions." The tear-drop-shaped pearl dipped into the top of Lyn's cleavage as she leaned forward for his response. With so many questions still unanswered James found it hard to match her optimistic mood.

"Peter said you had a partner in London, does it happen to be Victor Carlson – better known as, plain old Carl." James watched her reaction carefully but couldn't deny she looked confused.

"Who the hell's Victor… Whatever."

"He's the rogue who almost swindled you out of £40,000, and I know he's back in London, where else could you have got your hands on that kind of money Lyn?" Rick, sensing that an argument was brewing arrived with the main course. Before picking up her cutlery Lyn said in a lowered voice.

"Vinny's creative accountant didn't try to swindle me, he just offered a way for me to raise money for something I'd wanted to do; it didn't work out and Vinny, no doubt with the help of this Carl, found a way of cheating me. I should have known better, I do know better now and it will never happen again. Their greed and my ignorance was all that happened. I have my money back plus enough money to give me a fresh start. I've been blessed with good fortune James and I want to move forward."

"Was the money come by honestly?" He knew at once that those six words had irreparably damaged any chance of saving the evening; and the remaining silence while they picked half-heartedly at the food confirmed it.

Rick appeared with more wine; Lyn allowed him to replenish her glass but James refused and ordered a coffee

– neither had the appetite for dessert. Desperate to break the impasse but unsure of the way forward, James cleared his throat and said

"Your friend Jill, is she married...I mean were they her children I could hear in the background?"

"Jill and I go back a long way, she's a very talented interior designer, but since the birth of her twin boys, she's lost her way. Jill is my partner in London." The last few words were emphasized in the hope of putting James at ease. He sipped his coffee and averted his eyes leaving her to wonder what was passing through his mind.

An uninvited mental image found its way into James's head. Vincent Conway's lewd description of how the two women had greeted each other at Paddington Station jeered and mocked him. He forced the image to disappear. "Is she married?"

"Of course, like I said, she hasn't worked for years, poor Derik has been practically forced into becoming self-employed, and with twin boys and a twelve year old daughter to support, it's in everybody's interest that this venture succeeds. Having the right location is paramount to that success James and I've found what I need."

Not wanting to lose the chance of a buyer, but even more important, not wanting to lose this blossoming friendship James offered a compromise to the dilemma that faced him. "Did Peter Radcliff mention that I've sold the basement flat?"

"Yes, you obviously wanted to keep it to yourself, so I didn't probe, I suppose he's a 'public-school-educated-professional', like you; and I'd be lowering the tone."

James groaned inwardly at the thought of Lyn learning

the truth. Resigned to the inevitable and flushed with embarrassment he took her hand and held it between both of his. "I am prepared to sell the ground floor area Lyn; but it's only fair to warn you, your neighbours – and I'm including myself – may not live up to your expectations. The chap who bought the basement is having a small housewarming tomorrow evening. I'd like you to come along. Helen, my sister will be there and I know she's looking forward to meeting you. Wait until Monday morning to make up your mind; you may well decide that Peter Radcliff's is the better place."

9-50 pm

Lyn put a flaming match to the paper that supported kindling and the last two ash logs. The magnificent tree had been silent witness to her early years as wife and mother and burning them now was to be part of a therapeutic session that was long overdue.

Arriving back from the restaurant earlier than anticipated; she'd decided to call Sarah once again. The earlier call of 6-00pm was badly timed. She'd purposely sat waiting ten minutes for the clock to chime six because old habits die hard and calls must be made at the off-peak time. This penny-pinching had caused her to miss her daughter by five minutes – according to Fergus. She'd also learned from Fergus that Sarah had some wonderful news; "but she'd be wanting to tell you that news herself," he'd said, unable to disguise the excitement in his voice.

Walking over to the shelf that displayed her favourite

photographs, Lyn stood looking into the eyes of the only man she had ever loved. No father, grandfather, or even a casual lover had ever had to compete for this position. But now there were stirrings. Feelings, that Lyn had accepted as dead and buried; were igniting and warming a void that for too long had remained cold and hollow.

Taking hold of the framed photograph Lyn held it close to her chest and settled into the fireside chair.

"Martin," she began, helped by the alcohol that still raced through her body, "as you know I've never been one for talking to the dead. Gran scorned it." *Once you're dead there's nothing left but dust and ashes and no amount of God-bothering will alter that fact.* "On the other hand, several of my old customers swore by it, said it eased the way through grieving."

Lyn closed her eyes and transported her mind back to the last time she'd seen Martin alive. The happy, smiling faces of love and commitment – shown in the photograph – were absent on that morning. In its place were anger, resentment and insecurity, which had caused the pair to argue. As Martin had climbed into his car ready for parting, (and neither could have possibly known that the parting would be permanent) he'd insulted Lyn by saying she was growing more like the 'old bag' each day. In response, Lyn had blurted out. "I hope you fall off the bloody mountain and break your neck." Words said in the heat of the moment, could usually be retracted later, in the warmth of each others arms; and for nearly ten years Lyn had wished for nothing more. Relieved, that she could now face the memory of that final encounter in a more dispassionate way, Lyn continued to bring Martin up to date.

"As you know, money has been tight since… I mean you didn't exactly leave us well-provided-for, did you? You'll no doubt be pleased to know that Sarah's fine – married into a-well-to-do, Irish family of horse-breeders – so she'll have everything she desires. Oh incidentally, I hear we are to become grandparents in the spring; and if it's a boy, she intends to name him after you. Gran died almost penniless fourteen months ago; maybe you've bumped into each other; if so tell her I know all about Jennifer and Australia – no wonder she nearly had a heart-attack when you mentioned emigrating there.

Times have been very tough here Martin over the last few months, I won't go as far as to say you're better off where you are; but believe me, there were moments when the thought of joining you had seemed preferable to the misery and hopelessness of struggling on.

Then out-of-the-blue, something extraordinary happened. I acquired enough money to sort out my life. I was asked just a short while ago, if this money was come by honestly? I suppose stealing by finding *is* considered a crime of sorts; but how could anyone determine the rightful owner of a lost £1 coin; a coin that was used to buy a single lottery ticket. *I* picked out the numbers so the result of the good luck is rightfully mine. I haven't become an overnight millionaire; but the winning combination of five numbers plus the bonus ball – added to the fact that it was a four week rollover – meant that I could clear my debts, buy my own business premises for a new venture, and have a little in the bank to fall back on. As you know, I've always been secretive, but it's such a relief to share this with someone at last. The few people who know think the money's part of your life-insurance, and I don't intend to disillusion them.

Finally Martin, I hope that the ropes left behind weren't responsible for your fall or the fact that you were pissed-off with me. I've always regretted that our last goodbye was a missed opportunity to tell you how much I loved you. The thing is, I mean I want you to know that I've met someone who makes me feel, alive and hungry the way you…"

Suddenly, the loud trill of the telephone sliced across the engrossed one-way conversation; cutting Lyn's connection to Martin and dispersing the room's tranquillity with its continuing assault.

It was James, checking that she'd arrived back safely. At the end of the meal Lyn had offered a nightcap back at her place but James had declined. A taxi was ordered but on its arrival he had insisted on walking home – saying that the air would cool him down. Their conversation surrounding the Private Detective in the basement flat had caused James to become hot and bothered; blushing like a teenager over something he'd done or was about to do. He blamed the red wine and had quickly changed the subject.

"I would have felt happier paying the bill Lyn, especially as I was responsible for spoiling your evening."

"You didn't spoil my evening James; I got what I wanted – the chance to buy my dream property."

"Hold fire on that until after the weekend. When you've discovered for yourself, what I'm trying to say, I'll understand if you don't want to go ahead Lyn; and I really hope that we can remain friends. I'll see you tomorrow; good night, sleep well."

Lyn climbed the stairs to bed; the positive effect of drinking champagne had worn off and she suddenly felt weary. The logs had burned to ash and the cherished photograph had been polished and replaced on the shelf. Having a chat to Martin, hadn't created a miracle cure for all her deep-seated wounds; but she felt she had now removed the obstacle that was preventing 'time' from performing one of its natural duties. Gran had been wrong, as in so many things, there *is* something left after a loved-one dies – you only have to close your eyes and open your heart – to know that it's true.

As to James Fairbank, had her London friend been right? *If this chap you fancy is so eligible, how come he hasn't been snapped up before now?* Even Rick had said that *she* was the first female in years to share his table. James's embarrassment, at having to fend off a female he'd simply wanted as a friend (Lyn squirmed inwardly as she recalled opening the buttons of her shirt to reveal a little cleavage) had been what had spoilt the evening. This secretive, private-detective was obviously the one who held sway over James's affections; and by this time tomorrow, all, would be revealed.

10-15pm

James slipped his phone back into the pocket of his overcoat and turned into the wind towards home. He had been less than ten yards from Lyn's front door. He hated himself! Hated the cowardice that was threatening to deprive him of what he wanted more than anything else.

As Lyn's taxi had driven away from the restaurant, leaving James feeling bereft and inadequate, an inner voice – similar, in scathing tone, to Vincent Conway's – had taunted and scoffed at how, after being given the opportunity to 'fill his boots', the self-righteous idiot had let it slip through his fingers. The mocking continued until James, filled with a rush of determination, turned tail and followed in the wake of the taxi.

After dialling Lyn's number the cowardice had returned wearing a more subtle cloak. (How could she possibly trust me, after the disloyalty of allowing Vincent Conway to reside in such close proximity?) Again the voice inside his head taunted that life is too short not to have what you really want. And what was it that he wanted? Leaning against a nearby lamppost, James confronted his deepest desires.

A vision of Lyn, as she sat waiting for him in the restaurant, appeared before his closed eyes. Her hair was lustrous, tempting his fingers to play among the shining strands. Her eyes, alive with confidence and boldness, penetrated through an outer shielding that had been carefully set in place over the years and suddenly had been rendered useless. Her lips, smiling and sensual, inviting his to crush and taste the sweet promise of their delight; no words inferred it but he knew she felt a similar rising desire.

His fingers trembled and his loins stirred and stiffened as he played with the image. Slowly and expertly the remaining tiny buttons were unfastened on the shimmering silk blouse; revealing the fullness of her breasts and the soft, contoured valley where a suspended pearl nestled, warm and protected. This token of love, from an unknown admirer, was carefully removed; and with a trembling sigh James reached out for the woman he loved.

Charged with passion and determination, he retrieved his phone and pressed 'redial'. He would reveal everything about the last few days; but not before he had demonstrated how he felt. Five laborious rings and they were connected once again. "It's me; I've changed my mind about the nightcap; I'm standing on the wrong side of your front door."

Blind Truth

Is due for release in June 2012

One year on, and the chance to uncover the truth of Lyn Porter's parentage, compels her to travel to Australia.

Robbed in transit and castigated by her own flesh and blood leaves Lyn wondering whether the sacrifices made, have been worth it.

Meanwhile, back in the English-Riviera town of Torquay, corruption expands into marriages of convenience, kidnapping and attempted murder. Can a well-respected, long-established solicitor afford to get involved? James Fairbank doesn't really have a choice...

To place your order for BLIND TRUTH,
Email shorelinespublishing@hotmail.co.uk
ISBN No 978-0-9559710-3-7